PENGUIN C

THE GOSPEL SINGER

HARRY CREWS was born in 1935 at the end of a dirt road in Alma, Bacon County, Georgia, a rural community near the Okefenokee Swamp. His father, a tenant farmer, died before Harry was two years old. A mysterious childhood paralysis; a horrible scalding accident; his mother's second, turbulent marriage and divorce from a drunken uncle whom Crews had been led to believe was his natural father; and a move to Jacksonville, Florida, for his mother to find factory work were experiences that would feed his desire to imagine and, ultimately, to write. As a teen, Crews served a tour in the Marine Corps. On the GI Bill, Crews attended the University of Florida, where he earned a bachelor's degree in literature followed by a master's in education, with which he taught high-school and junior-college English. A protégé of Southern novelist Andrew Lytle, Crews published his first short story in the *Sewanee Review* in 1963. He published his first novel, *The Gospel Singer*, in 1968. Its publication earned Crews a new teaching job at the University of Florida and paved the way for the publication of seven more novels over the next eight years, including *Naked in Garden Hills* (1969); *Car* (1972); *The Hawk Is Dying* (1973), which was adapted into a film released in 2006; *The Gypsy's Curse* (1974); and the widely acclaimed *A Feast of Snakes* (1976). Crews's reputation as a bold and daring new voice in Southern writing grew during this time. In the 1970s, he wrote for popular magazines, including a monthly column for *Esquire* and essays for *Playboy*, and screenplays. In 1978, Crews's memoir of his youth, *A Childhood: The Biography of a Place*, was published to enduring acclaim. Two compilations of his nonfiction works, *Blood and Grits* and *Florida Frenzy*, were issued in 1979 and 1982, respectively. A decade of drug and alcohol abuse and creative lapses ended in 1987 with the publication of his ninth novel, *All We Need of Hell*. Crews retired from the classroom after teaching for thirty years at the University of Florida in Gainesville. Crews, who died in 2012 at age seventy-six, was a prominent writer in the literary genre known as Dirty South or Grit Lit, notable for its bizarre characters, grotesque violence, and satirical surrealism. His artistic forebears include William Faulkner, Flannery O'Connor, and Erskine Caldwell, but Crews remade Southern gothic in his own rough-hewn image in eighteen memorable novels, including *Karate Is a Thing of the Spirit* (1971), *The Knockout Artist* (1988), and *Body* (1990), dozens of riveting nonfiction pieces, and one of the finest memoirs in American literature. In 2002, the University of Georgia Libraries inducted Harry Crews into the Georgia Writers Hall of Fame.

KEVIN WILSON is the author of the novels *The Family Fang*, a *New York Times* bestseller adapted into an acclaimed film starring Nicole Kidman, *Perfect Little World*, and *Nothing to See Here*, as well as the story collections *Tunneling to the Center of the Earth*, winner of the Shirley Jackson Award, and *Baby, You're Gonna Be Mine*. He lives in Sewanee, Tennessee, with his wife and two sons, and teaches at the University of the South.

HARRY CREWS

The Gospel Singer

Foreword by
KEVIN WILSON

PENGUIN BOOKS

PENGUIN BOOKS
An imprint of Penguin Random House LLC
penguinrandomhouse.com

First published in the United States of America by William Morrow & Company, Inc., 1968
Published with a foreword by Kevin Wilson in Penguin Books 2022

LIBRARY OF CONGRESS CATALOGING-IN-PUBLICATION DATA
Names: Crews, Harry, 1935–2012, author. | Wilson, Kevin, 1978– writer of foreword.
Title: The gospel singer / Harry Crews ; foreword by Kevin Wilson.
Description: New York : Penguin Books, 2022.
Identifiers: LCCN 2021029225 (print) | LCCN 2021029226 (ebook) |
ISBN 9780143135098 (trade paperback) | ISBN 9780525506775 (ebook)
Subjects: LCGFT: Fiction.
Classification: LCC PS3553.R46 G6 2022 (print) | LCC PS3553.R46 (ebook) |
DDC 813/.54—dc23
LC record available at https://lccn.loc.gov/2021029225
LC ebook record available at https://lccn.loc.gov/2021029226

Printed in the United States of America

Set in Sabon LT Std

Contents

Foreword

"God's Greatest Gift to Man":
Harry Crews's The Gospel Singer

I was initially drawn to Harry Crews because he had a Mohawk and a tattoo of a skull, and I was twenty years old and had neither. I read Harry Crews because I wanted to figure out how, if you were a Southern writer, you didn't simply cover the same terrain that writers like Faulkner and Welty and O'Connor and McCullers had already exhausted. I wanted to know how you leaned in to what it meant to be Southern when you weren't even sure what that meant, exactly. And I came away from Harry Crews knowing, on some level, that I wouldn't ever write like him, could never open the wounds with the kind of ferocity that came only from knowing you'd survive it because you'd survived much worse. And I remain a fan of Harry Crews because I still don't know that I've read anyone quite like him.

My friend, the California writer Rufi Thorpe, wrote a brilliant novel called *The Knockout Queen*, and I emailed her to say how much I loved it. I mistakenly called it *The Knockout Artist*, the title of one of Crews's novels, and she instantly wrote back to ask if I knew of Crews and his work. She told me, "I feel like the thing about Harry Crews is that someone is supposed to give you, like, a used, crumbly paperback copy, and you read it and go: I didn't know you were allowed to write a book like that."

I found a crumbly paperback copy of *A Feast of Snakes* in the lounge of the English Department offices at Vanderbilt University when I was an undergraduate there. I read *The Knockout*

Artist and *The Gospel Singer* in rapid succession, and what I realized was, yes, I did not know you could write books like these.

My mentor at the University of Florida, where I received my MFA and where Harry Crews once taught, was Padgett Powell, and he spoke often of the dangers of lazy Southern writing, of creating what he termed "unmitigated pone." I had never been a Southern-by-the-grace-of-god writer, but I also knew how easy it was to lean on the stereotypes of the Deep South, the alternating nobility and savagery of rural life. And yet, if you look at Crews's first novel, *The Gospel Singer*, you have a traveling freak show, pigs allowed to roam the interior rooms of the family home, any number of broken country people with oversized heads and missing legs. You have the violence and Christ-hauntedness and freakishness. How does Crews keep this from becoming "unmitigated pone"?

In *The Gospel Singer*, he pushes so hard on the absurdity that the corn isn't baked, but rather turns into a mash, slightly poisonous, a fever dream. The Gospel Singer, a man possessing a beautiful voice and rumored to have the power to heal the sick, is a sex addict, who, when asked by his mother if he even likes to sing, replies, "Sometimes I do." The Freak Fair that is following the Gospel Singer from town to town is run by a man named Foot. He has a twenty-seven-inch-long foot. Not feet. Foot. He is, quite possibly, the sanest and most self-possessed character in the novel. If Flannery O'Connor, a fellow Georgia writer and obvious touchstone for Crews's work, has the Church of Christ Without Christ, Crews invents the Church of the Gospel Singer. The novel opens in a jail cell, where Willalee Bookatee Hull, an African American man and the preacher who serves the church, is being held for the rape and murder of the Gospel Singer's supposed betrothed, Mary-Bell Carter, who has been stabbed sixty-one times with an ice pick. The town itself, which awaits the return of the Gospel Singer in order to save its residents from their own tragedy, is named Enigma. It is, Crews tells us in the very first line of the novel, "a dead end."

But the chaos, the absurdity, the "mitigated pone," means

nothing without Crews's writing, sentences that seem both jagged and precise, so clear that you can't help but see things that you would prefer not to. Early in the novel, the Gospel Singer's brother, Gerd, remembers their Cousin Maze, dead from a mule's kick to the head, his wound "about as long and deep as a briar scratch on his neck at the hairline and a spot of blood no bigger than the end of a man's thumb blossoming out of his pale skin, but the back of his head was soft—like a balloon filled with jello."

In this chaotic and violent novel, Crews grapples with race and gender and religion and place, but he stretches them to the breaking point, until the crowd that has amassed in order to be saved by the Gospel Singer are whipped into such a frenzy, constantly edging closer and closer to the heart of the story, that you cannot help but be swallowed up by them. If you survive, it is pure chance, and there will be a scar to remind you.

The Gospel Singer's agent, Didymus, states that "suffering was God's greatest gift to man," and if this is true, and *The Gospel Singer* makes a convincing case in its favor, then Crews accepts this gift without hesitation. There are freaks, but they are not meant to be aberrations, not deviations from the order of the world. They are the physical embodiment of our shared existence, and if the Gospel Singer's fate is tied to that of Willalee Bookatee Hull at the end of the novel, Crews offers the flawed idea that "if evil set into motion a chain of events that caused an eventual good, larger than the original evil, then it ceased to be evil." The problem is the uncertainty of how long that chain of events will last. How much suffering and pain must be endured in the name of that original act of evil? Will we ever find that eventual good? Or does the evil act merely give birth to a new one, and the cycle continues, burying the past in the hopes that we can escape it? All Didymus can do when one of the family's dogs seeks to attack him, to "do an evil," is to reply, "You don't get me tonight!"

At the end of the novel, after all the violence and the shock at that violence, a reporter, Richard Hognut, sent to cover the Gospel Singer's performance in Enigma, notes that his audience would not have "expected him to solve anything. But they expected him to put it into some kind of context. And he did not even know how to begin talking about what had happened here." But Crews, somehow, does. While Hognut says, "To hell with the story! Let somebody else get it," you realize that Crews is right there, those brilliant detonations of language, that clear-eyed view into what makes us monstrous and human. It's a song, in a voice you've never heard, and it's calling you to come closer, toward your reckoning.

KEVIN WILSON

The Gospel Singer

CHAPTER 1

Enigma, Georgia, was a dead end. The courthouse had been built square in the middle of highway 229 where it stopped abruptly on the edge of Big Harrikin Swamp like a cut ribbon. From the window of the cell on the north side of the courthouse, Willalee Bookatee Hull could see the whole town. He swayed gently, shifting his weight from one foot to the other. Behind him on a wooden table a plate of peas was congealing in a gauze of pork fat. Two biscuits lay at the side of the plate. There was a slop bucket in one corner of the cell and above it at eye level a sheet of tablet paper on which someone had written in pencil the regulations of the Lebeau County jail.

Willalee Bookatee, in the breathless heat of the cell, swung before the brilliant square of windowlight like the pendulum of a clock. There was no sound except the steady drone of flies, stuck and sticking on the gummy edge of the plate behind him. The sun was in the west, dividing the street between shadow and light. At the far end of town where highway 229 burst free into the flat burning countryside, a mule was hitched in the sparse shade of a chinaberry tree. It was asleep under a wooden saddle and bloodfat flies swarmed languidly over it. On the sun side of the street, a 1948 Buick with a foxtail on the aerial and a *Go Navy* sticker in the rear window was parked in front of Marvin's Drugs, which was also the United States Post Office where a flag hung from an aluminum pole. The Buick was the only car in the street. It had not rained in two months.

Willalee Bookatee rocked on, half-dazed and lost in a kind of sleep, watching not the farmers or their hitched mules, but rather the tan canvas banner with red, white and blue lettering that stretched across the street. Anchored at one end to Harvey's Seed store and at the other end to Enigma Funeral Parlor, the banner read: WELCOME HOME GOSPEL SINGER! Even though Willalee Bookatee was a preacher of the Gospel, with huge pieces of Scripture memorized, he could not read, but he knew—just as every living soul in Enigma knew—the Gospel Singer was coming home. They had prepared for it, looked forward to it, prayed for it. An unabated hunger raged in the whole town for the sight and the sound and—God willing—the touch of the Gospel Singer, who had single-handedly focused the attention of the world on Enigma, Georgia. The Gospel Singer had given their lives purpose and meaning simply because they could say "I come from the town where the Gospel Singer was born," or "I known him when he weren't nothin but a boy."

Willalee had watched the Gospel Singer time after time on the Muntz television that he had bought in Albany, Georgia, and brought home on the back of a turpentine wagon and set up in his cabin. Now the Gospel Singer was coming home again! He would be here, he would, in this very Enigma! He was going to walk again in that fine tall blond body, a body so fine and tall and blond that it insulted the clothes that covered it, no matter how expensive and tailored the clothing was. And of course the clothing had become more and more expensive as the Gospel Singer had gone from the television studio in Albany to the one in Tallahassee to the one in Atlanta to the one in Memphis to the one, finally, in New York City.

When Willalee Bookatee turned on that Muntz television and the Gospel Singer's voice slipped out into his cabin, it was balm poured into a wound. Nothing mattered. The world dropped down a great big hole. Everything—whether it was a razor cut, or a tar-scalded eye, or a burning case of clap off a Tifton high-yellow whore—everything quit but that voice and it went in his head and down his flesh to where his soul slept. And he could stand whatever it was for another week.

The white folks talked of nothing else. In the fields chopping cotton or breaking corn or sitting on the bench in front of

Enigma Bank whittling tobacco plugs and spitting between their feet, the Gospel Singer was never far from them. Willalee Bookatee had once heard one of them say that the Gospel Singer carried enough clothes in the trunk of his car to put something on the back of every person in Enigma. Willalee Bookatee had seen the car, and it *was* big, but he knew that there couldn't be something in there for everybody in Enigma. And yet he *believed* it. Knowing had nothing to do with it. It was not impossible because he was the Gospel Singer, because everything turned to gold under his hand, the same as common air changed to angelmusic in his mouth. Yes sir! Albeeny, Tallerhassee, *At*-lanter, Memfis, Nu Yawk City. He had heard the white folks say the names so often they rang in his head like a bell. And he was glad to be able to sing them out—clicking over his tongue as a prayer wheel—just as everyone in the town was glad, because wherever the Gospel Singer had ultimately gone, he had started in Enigma, Georgia. Their Enigma. He had sprung from them and that was their pride. Out of their blanched flesh and hookwormed children and leached soil and poor-bone cattle—so starved that when they were murdered every winter at butchering time, their cut throats would not bleed a puddle larger than a lady's handkerchief—out of all the ills and evils of their world he had burst forth full as the sun and beautiful. Out of them, out of their kind, he had come, with nothing to foreshadow him or explain him. And every single soul felt, just as Willalee Bookatee felt, that someday in some mysterious and instantaneous way the Gospel Singer would save them from the tragedy that was Enigma.

He dropped his eyes from the banner and let his sight sift out through slitted lashes. Heat rose out of the earth distorting the town. Up and down the entire length of Enigma nailed onto posts and into the storefronts were red posters proclaiming FREAK FAIR ** CHILDREN UNDER FIVE ADMITTED FREE ** COME ONE COME ALL *** SEE THE MIDGET WITH THE LARGEST FOOT IN THE WORLD. The very night after the Gospel Singer's welcoming banner had been put up, the red posters had appeared. That was the day before they had put

Willalee Bookatee in jail and he got Uncle Judge, who was a
Nashville nigger and could read and write, to tell him what the
sign had said, and after he heard about the midget with the
foot, he made up his mind right then and there to spend a dime
or whatever amount of money it cost to see it. But as it turned
out, he did not even get to see where they were putting up the
fair tents. And the way it looked now, he never would see that
midget's foot.

Willalee Bookatee felt himself the center of a mystery. Nothing was the same as it had ever been, and nothing would ever
be the same again. He was a stranger to himself. He would
stare at his hands and shake his head. He would get on his
knees, and he, a preacher, could not pray. The nearest to prayer
he could come was to take a picture out of his back pocket and
carefully unfold it and there on his knees look upon it until the
agitation went out of his heart and he was calm. He had cut
the picture out of a magazine that Miss MaryBell Carter had
bought for him in Tifton. It was of the Gospel Singer, his beautiful white hands raised, his golden head dropped back and his
mouth open, singing. And so in the middle of the night with
the moon patterned by the barred window he would remain
for hours on his knees before the picture, not praying but calm
as prayer in a mindless wonder at what he had done. At times
he would whisper, "Murder? Me a murderer?" and the mystery would swell before him as bottomless as night.

From as far away as Willalee could see now, a pickup truck
was growing out of the black surface of highway 229. It caught
and held the arching sun in little bursts of light. He watched it
dreamily, indifferently glad for something new to look at because Enigma was only eight blocks long and during the three
days he had been in the courthouse cell, there had been nothing to do but look at it. The first two days were not so bad because everybody in Enigma had come by the courthouse to see
him, usually stopping by the funeral parlor first. A few people
had even driven all the way over from Tifton, where highway
229 turned off U.S. 41, to have a look at him. There had been
a steady stream of people between the parlor and the courthouse; and the sheriff, a fat man with one lung, had his wife

make up sandwiches and coffee to sell. It had caused a great noise in and around Enigma, almost—some were heard to say—threatening to confuse and delay the homecoming plans for the Gospel Singer. But business had fallen off as suddenly as it had begun. Enigma quickly adjusted itself to Willalee Bookatee Hull and the visitors had become fewer and fewer.

The pickup truck backfired into the street and hissed to a stop in front of the courthouse, not thirty feet from where Willalee stood. A tall, bloodless boy with chalky skin and hair the color of milk got down from the cab of the truck and stood squinting under the shade of his thin, paper-like hands. He looked up briefly at the sun, his jaw dropping suddenly showing tongue and teeth the color of mildew. Gnats swarmed at an open sore the color and size of a grape on his cheek. He looked up at Willalee, who looked away to the smoking horizon and gripped the solid warm bars more tightly. When Willalee looked back the boy was gone and before he could raise his eyes to the horizon again he heard the whiny voice of the Gospel Singer's brother, Gerd. The door opened behind him, but Willalee kept looking down the far line of highway 229 where it formed finally a daggerpoint that lay against the base of the sky.

"She's a sight, hey?"

"A mess, shore."

The voices rose behind him, with only a rough asthmatic wheeze to distinguish the sheriff's from Gerd's. The muted jangle of keys on the brass ring on the sheriff's belt punctuated the pauses as he caught his breath.

"Is he stay there lookin out the winder all the time?" asked Gerd.

"Most all the time."

"How come you reckon?"

"More'n likely lookin at the funeral parlor. Just thinkin about that white ass he got."

"That nigger got him some shore when he decided to git it."

Willalee listened and gripped the bars more tightly. The most frightening aspect of his crime was that everyone in Enigma had apparently forgotten his name. He had suddenly become "the" nigger or "that" nigger, but never Willalee Bookatee Hull.

He had grown up with Gerd, lied to him, worked for him or at least for his daddy, and stolen from him. Yet here Gerd was, just like everybody else, forgetting his name. And as for him standing there thinking about her white ass, he was not. He had never, so far as he knew, thought about Miss MaryBell's ass. Rather his eyes were riveted on the road out of which sooner or later the enormous black car carrying the Gospel Singer would rise. His only hope now was that the Gospel Singer would come before they hanged him.

"Coulda been worse. Coulda used a razor," the sheriff was saying.

"You right. A razor's messier'n a ice pick. But the ice pick's messy enough the way he used it. All them little purple holes," said Gerd.

"It didn't help her looks none."

"Did they ever settle for shore how many times he got her?"

"Sixty-one," said the sheriff. "Hiram wrote it on a pasteboard and put it in the winder. People coming to the funeral parlor kept on askin what the nigger done to her and Hiram got tired of sayin it so he wrote everythin the nigger done to her on a pasteboard and put it in the winder. You can read it yousef. Sixty-one."

"I'm goin back over there to look at that poor Christian girl," said Gerd. "I couldn't git no fitten look at her with all them people that's been over there."

"A virgin too," the sheriff shook his head sadly.

"The nigger struck a innocent shore when he struck Mary-Bell. If ittas one thing Enigmer knowed, ittas that."

"Do the Gospel Singer know?" asked the sheriff.

"Ma sent a telegram," said Gerd. "But you caint ever know when he's gone git what you send him. He's in one place yesterday and in another one the day before."

"It's gone be hard for him, coming home to that," said the sheriff.

"Well it happens."

"It shore does."

"The Lord works in mysterious ways," said Gerd. "Ittas a blessin he killed her, I guess. Now she don't have to suffer the rest of her days with everybody in Enigmer knowin she lost her flower to the nigger."

A match struck against the cell door. Willalee smelled the faint wisps of Prince Albert tobacco. His mouth watered. They had taken him out of his bed at three o'clock in the morning and brought him to jail without tobacco, and since no Enigma Negro had dared visit him, it was now three days since he had had a smoke. And to take his mind off the delicious cigarette, he tried once again to remember the ice pick and how he had come to have those incredibly bright splashes of blood over his clothes. He did have an ice pick. He kept it stuck into a two-by-four above the washtub that served as his refrigerator and held a ten-cent cake of ice wrapped in a croker sack. And that was where they found it. Stained with the same bright blood. And his right hand, when they dragged him naked and screaming from his bed, had been a solid glove of blood from wrist to finger tip. And she was there too, unstrung at the foot of his Muntz, her head turned off at a funny angle and something that was not a smile in her face and blood from her punctured neck vein framing her hair like a halo.

"Do you reckon the Gospel Singer'll git in today?" asked the sheriff.

"Yeah."

"Weren't he supposed to git in three days ago?"

"Yeah."

"Talk in Enigmer is he sent a wire," said the sheriff.

"Did. Cash brung it over from Tifton."

"What'd it say?"

"Said he weren't comin when he was suppose to come but he was comin," said Gerd.

"That Gospel Singer!"

"He's a sight."

"It ain't gone be easy on him," said the sheriff. "With Mary-Bell killed by the nigger and violated besides. The good Lord knows he's got his crosses like everbody. I never thought he had no real easy row to hoe bein a gospel singer. I know some folks did but I never did. All that runnin around and them other things he's got to do."

"I don't reckon it's a easy row," said Gerd. "It probably ain't the worst thing in the world neither."

"He ain't never forgot to take care of his own," said the sheriff. "Nobody can lay that at the Gospel Singer's door. How's them registered stock he sent in to you on the railroad? Must be near market size."

"They dead."

"Real sorry to hear that, Gerd. How come they die?"

"Just up and died. Pa said Enigmer killed 'em. Said a Poland-Chiney hog in Enigmer was a fish outen water. Said ain't never been no blooded stock raised in Enigmer."

There was a short gaspy laugh. "Your Pa ought to know better'n that. He raised the Gospel Singer. The Gospel Singer's a thirbred."

"He's a thirbred, all right. Ain't none of us never said he weren't."

"It's a shame he caint git home no oftener than he do. I didn't even git to see him when he was home before with all them people that follered him in. Seem like it gits longer and longer between visits."

"Next Sunday be seven month less a week he ain't been home," said Gerd. "We got letters though. He was off where he's needed, just singin his heart out."

"Gerd, I didn't mean that to speak agin him. They ain't no man fine as the Gospel Singer."

"He done a lot for us all right."

"He's a purely good soul, that's all."

Willalee wondered if he dared hope for the Gospel Singer to visit him. They had been friends years ago, when they both had been fifteen, the year the Gospel Singer's voice had suddenly changed from a cracked adolescent whine to a fantastic, powerful voice that had never found the limits of its range. The voice of course had separated them, and Willalee Bookatee had never been able to get close enough to speak to him since. The Gospel Singer had begun making appearances at various churches in the community, at evangelical revivals; then finally he had gone off to the television studio in Albany. And Willalee had gone to work dipping tar out of the stunted ring of pine flats surrounding Enigma. Every day, carrying the five-gallon lard bucket loaded with turpentine while his gummed clothes ate him alive, he would know in the cool of his mind that come Sunday he could lie up in his cabin and listen to the Gospel Singer on the radio or, after the Muntz came, watch him, standing tall, impossibly clean and handsome.

Willalee said a silent prayer to the Gospel Singer and hoped he heard it, because the Gospel Singer might be his salvation, his only salvation. He had an absolute and abiding faith that the Gospel Singer would know the details of his crime which he, himself, could not remember. They were going to hang him and Willalee Bookatee did not want to go to his God in a mystery. But the Gospel Singer could help him, the Gospel Singer could do anything. Albeeny, Tallerhassee, *At*-lanter, Memfis, Nu Yawk City. Wasn't he the only man born in Enigma ever to go out and beat the world?

"You seen the freak?" asked the sheriff.

"Freak?"

"The one with the foot."

"No."

"Know anybody has?"

"Somebody said they settin up out there on the edge of town. Ain't far from the Gospel Singer's tent."

"I'd go out there and check on what all they doin," said the sheriff. "If I weren't afraid to leave the nigger."

"I don't reckon it'd be no good idea to leave him," said Gerd.

"Some of the boys already been in to see about him," said the sheriff. "They might damn well end up by gitten him too."

Gerd was lighting another cigarette. Willalee Bookatee had heard the men talking earlier. They had been after the sheriff to let them have him ever since the night they brought him in. They were going to hang him. He knew that. With or without the trial, it didn't matter. He tried not to smell the cigarette.

"Gerd, do you think he'll come today?"

"Ma says she got a feelin in her like he will."

"How long he gone stay?" asked the sheriff. "He say?"

"Caint nobody tell," said Gerd.

"It's gone be good to have him back. Lift us up. Give us

somethin to look forward to." The gaspy laugh again. "Maybe
he'll bring the rain."

"Maybe."

"You goin already?"

"Thought I'd drop by the funeral parlor."

"Well, you come on back and see the nigger any time you
want. Cause he ain't gone be here forever. No sir."

CHAPTER 2

Gerd hated the sun. Something in him was not built for it. He never sweated; he festered. In the sun his skin drew tighter and tighter until it cracked like clear plastic. The cracks itched terribly and if he scratched them—which he couldn't help doing—they made fat puckered sores. Under his clothes, his skin was a scab, more or less pliable, but a scab still. Ordinarily he would not have been out in the heat. Ordinarily he would have been in the hammock made of croker sacks stretched under the cotton shed yelling to his younger brother Mirst to bring him a glass of iced tea and the purple medicine off the mantel to paint his sores with. But these were no ordinary times. On top of everything else that had happened in Enigma, the Gospel Singer was coming home. Maybe today. Gerd was *sure* today. So he had been out in the impossible heat all morning trying to make sure that he got a chance to see him before Mirst or Avel or his ma or pa did, and a chance to talk to him before he was surrounded by the multitude of Enigma, all six hundred of them.

Gerd stood in front of his truck debating with himself whether or not he ought to risk missing the Gospel Singer by taking enough time to go by the funeral parlor to see Mary-Bell. He had come in to town specifically to see her and Willalee Bookatee Hull—both of them because now that the nigger had not only killed her but raped her too, he could not think of one of them without thinking of the other. Yet it was getting late. His brother might roar into town any time.

He happened to look up and there was Willalee, dark and immobile as a shadow in the barred window. Gerd stood in the smoking dust and shook with anger. MaryBell! Gerd had lusted after her so hard it set his teeth on edge just to *think* about it. Now she was gone for sure and forever. That nigger! He couldn't be satisfied with just raping her, he had to kill her too. Put her so nobody could touch her. And after being raped by a nigger anybody probably could have got her. Gerd might even have had a chance at her! God!

Thinking about her wide, untouched skin, he left his truck parked by the courthouse and rushed through the street to Enigma Funeral Parlor, wooden and false-fronted, with a huge plate-glass window—the largest in Enigma—covered with yellow paper shades onto the bottom of which was sewn heavy yellow lace. In the lower right corner of the window was taped a piece of pasteboard, covered with slanting script done with a child's black crayon:

> Miss MaryBell Carter—icepick stabed
> by the nigger 61 time   raped 1 time
>   probly more

The door to the parlor was closed. Gerd opened it and stepped inside. It was dark, cooler than the street. A head of Christ—flowing brown hair, dead walnut-colored eyes—was nailed into the facing wall. Under the Christ, like a caption to a cartoon, was BUY BETTER FERTILIZER FROM HARVEY'S ENIGMA SEED in red letters. Under that was a two-year-old calendar.

At the back of the narrow room MaryBell was propped on a slight angle in a copper-hinged, white pine casket, on a catafalque made of boards across two carpenter's sawhorses and covered with an ancient strip of black velvet. Three ladies, one wearing a black bonnet, sat in ladder-backed chairs at the head of the coffin. They held wet, gray handkerchiefs. At their feet were two chrysanthemums, brown and dying, potted in Pure Oil cans. Overhead a single electric bulb burned.

A bluewinged fly circled down from the ceiling and lit on MaryBell's nose. The lady in the black bonnet without moving her head or even her eyes reached into the folds of her clothing and came out with a heartshaped, pasteboard fan with the face of Jesus in it and waved it on the heavy air. The blue-winged fly buzzed fatly back to the ceiling.

Gerd crept closer, his eyes starting in his head at the sight of MaryBell's cold, dead beauty. He had never seen her lying down until Hiram had opened her casket to the public view day before yesterday. Of course he had seen her on her back often enough in his dreams, but it was something else entirely to see her actually spread before him, seductive, beautiful—even if she was cold and three days dead with a lacy pattern of blue punctures running down the side of her neck and into the blouseful of breast Gerd had never seen. He touched his lips with his tongue and tried to imagine what her breasts would taste like but could not because he had never even seen a breast, let alone tasted one. He closed his eyes against the un-bearable beauty of her skin and vowed again for the uncount-able time that he would someday have a girl and see a breast and taste a nipple and make the mysterious covenant with an-other flesh.

"How you, Gerd?"

It was the lady in the black bonnet. One of the other ladies wrapped her nose with a gray handkerchief and blew.

"Better'n I was, Mizz Carter. Come by to pay my respects to your poor Christian daughter." Gerd spoke to the back of the black bonnet. It remained steady as carven stone. He moved closer to the coffin, his eyes drawn irresistibly down the little progression of wounds to MaryBell's swelling, stiffened bosom.

"Is he come?"

"Nome, he ain't come yet."

"She shan't be buried until he comes. MaryBell looked to seein the Gospel Singer. Poor thing couldn't talk of nothin else."

"I guess we all do," one of the other ladies said, her nose div-ing again for the handkerchief. "I guess she was just Enigmer's own. It ain't nobody Enigmer thought more of than MaryBell and the Gospel Singer."

A curtain parted just to the right of the fertilizer calendar and a small man appeared. He stood slightly out of focus. His right shoulder was higher than the other, which tilted his head, giving him a look of constant puzzled surprise. His eyes seemed to work independently, the left one periodically rolling off in some unique search of its own.

He went directly to the coffin. One eye looked down upon the powdered, composed face of MaryBell, and the other eye looked at Gerd. "A picture of life, ain't she?"

"She is, Hiram," said Gerd. "You done a real good job."

He leaned toward Gerd and spoke behind his hand. "Had a devil of a time with them ice pick holes."

"Know you did," said Gerd.

"Ain't nobody preshates the trouble I go through," said Hiram. "It ain't easy bein a undertaker without proper tools."

"Must be hell," said Gerd.

"Taken her to Tifton and they couldn't work her right in and I wound up haulin her all the way to Cordele. But they ain't nobody preshates that. Ain't nobody knows the trouble it is to bury the dead of Enigmer."

"I always said we was real lucky to have you," said Gerd.

Hiram gave a broken little smile and pinched the bridge of his nose between his thumb and forefinger. "Well, somebody's got to do it, somebody's got to put them in the ground."

In a sudden, lightning movement, the lady in the black bonnet smashed the bluewinged fly against the side of the coffin with her Jesus fan. "Blowflies git bad this time a year," she said softly.

"You don't have to worry about no blowflies, Mizz Carter. That's how come I taken her to Cordele."

Hiram's good eye beamed steadily upon Mrs. Carter while the other eye flicked busily between the coffin and Gerd. "She's embalmed against everythin."

"It ain't seemly to have flies buzzin her anyhow," said Mrs. Carter.

"That's true," said Hiram. "But since you went to all the trouble so you could keep her up for the Gospel Singer, you don't have to worry about no blowflies."

Gerd laid his hand on the edge of the coffin and with the end of his middle finger he could feel her arm—firm, only barely yielding, like inflated rubber. "She was too fine a Christian girl, and good too, to have the flies after her," he said.

"I don't want it for no girl of mine," said Mrs. Carter, scraping the ruined fly off the chin of Jesus with a square yellow finger nail.

Hiram leaned close to Gerd again and spoke behind his hand. "See, it ain't nobody that preshates the undertaker. It don't matter if you go to Tifton or Cordele or where you go for them."

"Gerd, you think the Gospel Singer'd sing *Farther Along* for my MaryBell?"

"Mizz Carter, I know the Gospel Singer'd be proud to sing at your daughter's funeral."

"That'd be nice too. But mostly I want him to sing it to her right here in the parlor. Just him and her in here together and him singin. Somethin in me feels like she'd hear it if he sung it to her with just the two of them together."

Gerd touched the inflated rubber arm again. It was cold through the cotton sleeve. And the cold only made the memory of her heat more intense, her great red mouth and yellow hair, standing barelegged and hot in the sun with swirls of dust rising just there under the heartstopping hem of her skirt. God! Gone, gone! And he had never touched her. Never even had the remotest chance of touching her.

"Do you think he'd do it? The two of them in the parlor and him singin?"

"Nobody can speak for sure for the Gospel Singer," said Gerd. "But he'll do what he can. If it's anythin you can count on, it's the Gospel Singer doin what he can."

"Oh, I know you caint speak for him," said Mrs. Carter. "And I guess everbody knows he'll do what he can."

"It's the one thing we all count on," said one of the other ladies.

There was a period of silence while they looked into the coffin. Gerd tried to pinch the flesh under the cotton sleeve between the ends of his fingers. Hiram's loose eye swept their faces. Another fat bluewinged fly buzzed into the silence and they all, without meaning to or even realizing it, raised their eyes from the coffin to watch it circling above them. The hand of the lady in the black bonnet stole into her clothes and emerged tense, ready to strike, with the Jesus fan.

Hiram watched first Mrs. Carter and then the fly and then both of them at once. A look of physical pain crossed his face as the hand, almost imperceptibly, drew back, poised. The fly continued the circling descent.

"Well!" shouted Hiram suddenly, waving his arms broadly over the coffin. "She's gone to a better place, I know."

The fly struggled back into the ceiling and lit upside down.

Mrs. Carter frowned at him. "I could've got him with the fan."

Gerd took his hand quickly out of the coffin. "Got who?"

"The fly."

"Is it another fly in here?" asked Hiram.

"He'll come down again," said one of the other ladies.

Hiram looked as though he wanted to spit. "Gerd," he said. "Can you step back here with me a minute? If you ladies will excuse us." He sidled away and disappeared through the curtain.

Gerd reluctantly drew his hand away from MaryBell and followed Hiram.

The back part of the parlor was only half the size of the part used for display. A coffin that Hiram was building sat on two horses against one wall. There were two finished coffins stacked one on top of the other directly in front of a long bench over which there hung a dim light covered with a metal shade. Along the facing edge of the bench were various sized earthen jars with flat wooden paddles sticking out of the tops of them. Hanging in the room like dead smoke was the mixed odor of lye soap and face powder.

And it was the smell of lye and cosmetics as much as it was the jars with wooden paddles sticking out of them that made Gerd remember the only other time he had been in Hiram's backroom. It was a long time ago—something over fifteen years—but Gerd remembered it as though it were yesterday. Gerd had been seven years old and his brother the Gospel Singer had been five (of course this was before the Gospel Singer *was* the Gospel Singer but after he had become the Gospel Singer everybody, even Gerd, remembered him as *always* having been one). Their Cousin Maze had been kicked in the head by his mule and he was lying dead, still dressed in his overalls and brogans, on Hiram's table. They had just brought him back from Tifton where the nearest doctor had an office and where Maze had stopped breathing the moment the doctor had pressed the silver neck of a stethoscope against his chest. Uncle Lorne—their daddy's brother—stood beside the table and behind Hiram who was smoking a tailor-made cigarette and undressing the corpse. Cousin Maze had a wound about as long and deep as a briar scratch on his neck at the hairline and a spot of blood no bigger than the end of a man's thumb blossoming out of his pale skin, but the back of his head was soft—like a balloon filled with jello.

"Don't that Mizz Carter beat all you've ever seen?" said Hiram.

"She's a sight," said Gerd, but he was not thinking of Mrs. Carter or even of MaryBell. Hiram was sitting now at an iron grille, rolltop desk. He turned on a gooseneck lamp. The light spilled over more of the earthen jars with wooden paddles sticking out of the tops of them. The jars were Hiram's true calling, and it was of the jars that Gerd had the sharpest and most vivid memory.

"She's gone set out there in my parlor and keep snappin them blowflies agin that coffin and I caint stand to stay out there and watch it."

"She oughten do that," said Gerd.

Cousin Maze was the first dead man either Gerd or his brother had ever seen. And though neither of them said it, they both had been stunned by how differently death appeared in the face of their Cousin Maze than it had the other times they had seen it—in the faces of various slaughtered and mutilated farm animals. Knock a cow in the head with an axe and when she hits the ground—before her throat is cut—she looks like a cow that has fallen broadside asleep. But even though Cousin Maze's face was unmarked, sleep was obviously not what was the matter with him.

"You do all in the world you can for them," said Hiram, lifting his palms in a gesture of despair. "Use ever craft and skill, and what do they do? What do they do?"

Maze's face was everywhere slightly concave. Mouth gaping and collapsing. Cheeks descending in the center like white, half-cooked dough. Eyes sunken, singing, through black sockets. Muscle, ligament and connective tissue flaccid.

"I'll tell you what they do," said Hiram. "They set out there and snap blowflies. Hell, I caint help it. I don't know any man that can."

"They ain't no man can," said Gerd.

They didn't know Uncle Lorne was crying until the corpse was undressed, white, incredibly still. He made no sound but they saw the tears break in the stubble of iron-gray beard.

"I'd sooner do this with you outside, Lorne," Hiram said, bringing a metal basin and two cakes of lye soap to the table. "This ain't nothin for you to be watchin."

But Uncle Lorne hadn't answered, had just stood there with the tears making stains on the bench where his dead son lay. And their daddy, his heart wrung too but unable to cry for Cousin Maze who was like a son to him, stayed also. Gerd and the Gospel Singer backed against a wall and kept their mouths shut around their hearts and watched Cousin Maze's face which had been strong and full and red and which they did not even recognize now. It was as though another's face had been grafted onto Cousin Maze's body, the body strangely unaffected by death—a relaxed, heavy-muscled sleep. Gerd almost expected it to breathe. But no one would ever expect that face to breathe again.

"You gone ask the Gospel Singer to come in my parlor and sing *Farther Along* to MaryBell?" asked Hiram. He picked up one of the small wooden paddles out of an earthen jar. It had a light powder on the end of it. He moved it in his fingers. Gerd watched it as if he expected Hiram suddenly to turn it into a snake.

"Mizz Carter wants me to," said Gerd. "I guess I'll ask."

"Caint see it's gone help, her bein dead and all," said Hiram. "It's enough livin needs it, without wastin it on the dead."

"The Gospel Singer likes to do what he can," said Gerd.

"That's what I'm gettin at," said Hiram. "It's only so much he can do, he ought to do it on the livin."

It wasn't until Hiram had the corpse washed and dried and dressed, with its hair combed, that he started on the face. That awful, felled face.

And he had done it all with the little wooden paddles, handling them as delicately and deftly as a woman handling a needle and thread. He never touched Cousin Maze's face with his fingers, but only with the slender pieces of wood. Open lips and insert pads of cotton. The hollow cheeks grow. Out of an earthen jar on the end of the woodstem a mound of fine white powder as big as a dime. From this a solid white mask. Blend into that another measure of powder the size of a pea and the color of flesh.

Gerd pressed his back against the wall and felt the breath slowing in his throat as he watched Hiram taking the death out of Cousin Maze's face. Everywhere Hiram touched with the wooden paddles, life bloomed out of the flesh. The dark circles sank; the sunken eyes rose. Hiram was bringing him back from death and Gerd would not have been surprised to have seen him bend and suddenly breathe life back into him.

"Now you take my little girl, Anne," said Hiram, flipping the wooden spoon back into the earthen jar on the rolltop desk. "She ain't never even seen the Gospel Singer."

That brought Gerd's head snapping back from Hiram's empty workbench where he had been watching Cousin Maze's ghost. Hiram's little girl Anne had never seen anybody. She was blind, born that way.

"No, she ain't," Gerd said, not because he thought it was something that needed saying, but because Hiram, strangely, looked as though he wanted him to say it.

"And the Gospel Singer could do more for that little girl," said Hiram, "than he could singin *Farther Along* to Mary-Bell."

"More for her?"

"By lettin her see him," said Hiram.

"*See* him?"

"Why just by gettin down there on his hands and knees and lettin her run her hands over him, by lettin her touch him, the Gospel Singer can do more for Anne than anybody in this world. She's felt faces before, but they ain't but one person in Enigmer—or anywheres—that looks fine as the Gospel Singer."

"God's own truth," agreed Gerd.

Beautiful. Yes, beautiful. Every memory of the Gospel Singer was of beauty. The golden hair, the strong but fragile face, the blue-fired rather close-set eyes, the finely-formed bone and ligament—all of it had come instantly, magnificently at birth. Gerd had heard it said that the Gospel Singer had been beautiful even before his mother's womb had been cleaned from him.

And his brother's beauty—not effeminate but hard man-beauty—had set him apart from other men. After Cousin Maze's funeral, Gerd had confided to the Gospel Singer how scared he had been when he saw Hiram working on Cousin Maze, bringing him back from the dead. The Gospel Singer, dressed in black short pants, his golden legs straddling, said it didn't scare *him* a damn bit. (Before his voice had fallen upon him, the Gospel Singer had been bad to curse.) Hiram (he said) couldn't bring anybody back from the dead. Because Hiram was ugly. Hiram gimped. But *he* could raise the dead. *He* could do anything. His eyes had flared and his cheeks had burned and Gerd, from that day on, had never again doubted him in anything. He had not even been surprised at the conversion of his brother's voice ten years later. It seemed to him a natural thing that his brother should have a voice that no one had ever heard.

"But you know how everbody in Enigmer'll be after him," said Hiram, standing up from the desk.

"He caint hardly git a minute's rest," Gerd said.

"With everbody wantin him to sing songs to dead girls and such, he got no time for his real business."

"Ain't it the truth."

"So if you'd ask him for me when you see him. Just say she's blind and she wants to see him."

"Why shore, Hiram. I'll ask him for you."

"It's a lot to ask, Gerd. Cause he gone be pushed for time. With everbody after him it ain't no tellin how long he'll stay. Do you promise?"

Hiram took Gerd's arm. The flesh-colored powder came off Hiram's fingers onto his skin. Gerd drew his arm away.

"I've got to be gitten back out to the place, Hiram. I only come to town to git a few things and I got what I come after." He was backing toward the curtain.

"Don't hurry off, Gerd."

"I got to go."

"Set and talk a while. It gets dreadful back here without I got somebody to do. Undertakers git lonesome too."

"You could go back out front with Mizz Carter."

"She's gone keep snappin them blowflies, and I ruther stay back here being lonesome than go out there and watch her make light of my parlor."

"I got to go. Pa said not to keep the truck in town." Gerd was already pushing through the curtain.

"Promise, Gerd!" And then when he did not say anything: "Do you promise?"

Gerd never answered him nor did he answer Mrs. Carter when he went through the display room because she too was asking whether or not he was going to be sure and try to intercede with the Gospel Singer for her. How he hated them for always being after him to talk to the Gospel Singer for them. The whole town. Everyone wanted something, and they all thought that Gerd could get it out of the Gospel Singer for them. But of course he couldn't. The Gospel Singer listened to each appeal and made up his own mind. Being his brother didn't help at all. And even if it had helped, Gerd had his own case to plead. He had lied to Hiram about having to go back to the place with his daddy's truck. His daddy'd most likely be in bed yet or if he wasn't in bed he probably hadn't been outside to miss the truck and would think Gerd was under the cotton shed in the hammock. But he sure as hell wasn't and he wasn't going to be, not this day. He was going to drive back out to the edge of town where the dirt road turned off 229 and led eventually to their place half in the middle of Big Harrikin Swamp. And he'd sit there the rest of the afternoon with the truck backed into a sapling thicket and watch the road for his brother's car—the big, black, chromeshiny Cadillac that, on his brother's infrequent visits, growled through Enigma and the surrounding countryside like some antique and vicious animal.

Gerd did not stop to look at Willalee Bookatee, who still swayed in solid shadow in the courthouse window. He was preoccupied now with Willalee Bookatee's victim. MaryBell! The name rolled in his mouth like sweet butter. And Gerd, thinking of her as he climbed into the doorless, banging truck and headed out of town, ignored the rising, incredibly dry heat, and the blinding sun and his own stinging, rupturing skin.

MaryBell crossed and recrossed his glazed dusty eyes. Slowly she rose out of the place where he kept her, into the place where his dreams were made. Even though dead, she came obediently, at his command and pleasure, the same way she had for countless hours as he gently rocked in the croker cocoon under the cotton shed. She loved him and kissed his leprous back and chest and stomach and————God of us all! He bloomed, was changed, was made beautiful as only the Gospel Singer was beautiful, and she couldn't get enough of him. No longer leprous, he was loved. He saw them married and the Gospel Singer singing at their wedding and that night *MaryBell-MaryBellMaryBell* taking him and holding him in her wide wet saddle and her breast lancing his mouth, the nipple hard as rubber against his rotted gums, the soursweet nipple taste spreading. . . .

Just where 229 made a wide slow turn toward the east, Gerd jerked the wheel, narrowly missing a hog standing in the middle of the road on its spavined, starved legs, and crashed into a ditch and down that, finally stopping against a concrete culvert. The vision shattered, MaryBell's saddle decomposing into fragments of thigh and stomach and yards of clabber-colored skin. Dust ballooned out of the floorboard and hung in the airless space before his face.

His thumb was in his mouth. It tasted of his dreams of breast. For an instant he was lost, unable to think where he was going and then he did and saw that he had passed the dirt road and the sapling thicket where he had meant to stop. From the attitude of the truck, inclined as it was in the ditch and jammed against the culvert, he knew it was hopelessly stuck. He was getting out of the cab, one long, unjointing leg already touching the ground, when for perhaps the hundredth time the terrible and absolute finality of MaryBell's death flooded him. Gone! Goddam the world! Never touched, gone! He sank to the rusty running board. His thumb was still in his mouth. A sob choked him. He groaned and squinted down the trembling highway. It was out of that black and fiery direction the Gospel Singer would come.

Gerd sat on the side of the ditch under a pine tree and held his head. Now that MaryBell was dead there was no reason at all for staying in Enigma. At least when she was alive he could catch sight of her from time to time, barelegged in the sun, her body bursting in flesh, breathing in and out under those breasts that started down from her collarbone and up from her navel and never seemed to stop in either direction. But as soon as he heard that she had been killed he knew once and for all that he had to convince his brother the Gospel Singer to take him away with him.

The idea of leaving Enigma had been in the back of Gerd's head for a long time. He didn't know when it had first occurred to him and for a long time he wouldn't even let himself think it, much less say it. After all, wasn't it impossible? He was Enigma-born, Enigma-raised, and what did he have to redeem him from his birth? He didn't know anybody except his brother who had ever beaten Enigma, but of course the Gospel Singer had his voice and his beauty. His brother was an accident. Everybody knew it; everybody accepted it. And at the same time nobody expected such an accident to happen to him. They didn't even hope for it. It was clearly too impossible. The odds were too great.

But the Gospel Singer *was* his brother. If he could get to him before his father and Mirst and the rest of the people of

Enigma surrounded him—yelping for attention—if Gerd could just get him in a quiet moment, he was sure he could get the Gospel Singer to let him get into that great black animal Cadillac car and leave Enigma forever.

Leave Enigma! Escape! Escape the heat, the drought, and his own bruised, unlovely skin. Get to a place where men didn't sweat, to a place where the streets were cool as wind and happy as rain, where the streams lay on the honeyed land like milk. He'd get himself a guitar and sit in the shade of a golden building where money rang and children laughed. He knew there were such places; he had seen them in the Tifton moving picture theater where he went to worship everytime his skin was well enough. If his skin allowed it, he would sit all afternoon and evening in the popcorn and urine dankness of the Palace and reverently watch the pale, sweet ghosts move through Hollywood heaven where Rock Hudson and Doris Day, sweatless, bloodless, hurtless, sat on either hand of God.

Gerd wanted a Doris Day of his own. MaryBell would have done better than any Doris Day he could have ever found, but now she was dead. There must be others in the world though. Somewhere there was one for him. But the only way he could get her was through his brother the Gospel Singer. Because, first, the Gospel Singer would have to make Gerd into a Rock Hudson. He would have to take Gerd away from Enigma and heal his skin and fatten him up and touch up his teeth. Maybe even reshape his whole face. He was putty in the Gospel Singer's hands. Anything to be a Rock Hudson. Because only Rock Hudsons got Doris Days.

He looked out of his webbed fingers. Heat sucked at the earth. His eyes contracted like marbles on a hearthstone; his whole body seemed one huge unlanced boil. But he'd wait right here the rest of the day for the Gospel Singer and into the night if necessary. After all it was from that sun, furiously burning over Big Harrikin Swamp, that the Gospel Singer was going to save him. He looked back into the web of his hands and tried to imagine himself in the hammock under the cotton shed with MaryBell, but he could not. His skin was alive with the sun.

He shifted his weight to hunker deeper into the pine shade and as he did, he looked square into the eyes of something that, in the same instant, made him scream and corked the scream in his throat. The something was sitting on a stump not twenty feet in front of him. It had arms that looked like legs and legs that looked like arms and a short square head jammed so deeply into its body that half its face was hidden behind collarbones.

"Hot'n hell, ain't it," said the Thing.

Gerd slowly crossed his fingers and then his legs and then, momentarily, even his eyes. He wanted to pray because he knew that what he was looking at had to be the Devil or one of the Devil's henchmen which was just as bad. He opened his mouth but all he could say was, "God, God!"

"You goddam right," said the Thing. "Ain't it the truth. This weather ain't fit'n for freaks." It reached inside what looked like it might be clothing or maybe it was inside its own flesh and came out with a toothpick. The pink underlip rolled down like the lid to a sardine can exposing one immense tooth on the bottom jaw. The lips bunched and the jaw worked like a rabbit eating a carrot. "What you doing out here?"

"Just settin," Gerd said.

"What's you name?" asked the Thing.

"Name Garvin, but they call me Gerd," he said, transfixed, not daring to ask what the Thing was called.

"It's a bad day to be settin in a ditch, Gerd," said the Thing. It tilted its shoebox head. "You ever seen a Freak Fair?"

Gerd slowly uncrossed his legs. "Is that what you are?"

"Well, I'm not the whole fair, if that's what you mean." Its lip flipped up, hiding its tooth and tilting its mouth sadly. "Honestly and to tell the truth, I'm not even a very good freak. That's why I'm down here settin in this ditch with you. Foot— that's the boss—Foot sent me down here to keep a eye out while the rest of the tents and booths and things git set up. But if I found a mark . . . a customer . . . to bring back, Foot wouldn't mind."

Gerd uncrossed his fingers and blinked. He even scooted across the ground so he could be a little closer to the stump where the Thing sat. "Sure," he said. "I know about you. Ev-erbody in Enigmer's talkin about the fair. I ain't never seen a freak before. Neither has nobody in Enigmer. They ain't never been none in Enigmer before. We're all comin to see it though. Right now most everbody's workin on the Gospel Singer Cel-ebration. You see, we're waitin on the Gospel Singer."

"Ain't everbody waitin on him?" asked the Thing. It wiped its sweaty forehead against its collarbones. "Hoooooooeeeee. I been out here in this ditch two days in a row. Burnin up. I hope he comes today, because if he don't I'll be right back in this ditch tomorrow."

"How come you waitin for him?"

"Mainly because Foot says I got to. We have to know when he gits in so we can be set for the flood that always follers. The Gospel Singer draws a good crowd."

"He's my brother," said Gerd.

"Sure," said the Thing. "He's my brother, too. And I know Foot thinks the Gospel Singer's *his* brother. Foot weren't doing a flip till he started follerin the Gospel Singer around, makin use of them crowds he draws. Now Foot's laying up in a trailer with a REA wire hooked to it, air-conditioned, with that red-headed whore he bought in Alpine, Texas, where we made such a killin at the All Texas Christian Church Alliance for Modern Christ where the Gospel Singer sung. Foot's in there with a normal woman and me settin out here in a ditch." It was not looking at Gerd now but staring off down the naked black vein of highway 229. It shook its head slowly and its voice lowered. "But it's only right I guess. I'm not the freak he is. I'm not the shortest or the tallest or the ugliest or the dis-gustingnest or the anythingnest—but that Foot—Foot's got the biggest foot in the world."

"But he *is* my brother," whined Gerd. "He really to God is my own brother." He had run into this before, people not be-lieving the Gospel Singer was his brother and it made him sick to his heart. The most wonderful, the most important single thing in his life, and nobody would believe it.

"Now listen, Gerd, you ever seen a freak fair? You got a quarter stuck down in them overalls of yours? You wanta see a man with a arm growin out of his back? Do you? Now come on, git that old rusty quarter outen them overalls and let's git up from this ditch and go see."

"I caint, I'm waitin for the Gospel Singer," said Gerd, and then under his breath: "And he is too my brother."

"If you got a dollar, you can see Foot," said the Thing. "He won't come out a that trailer for less than a dollar, a dollar a head cause he got the biggest foot in the world. Some freaks got all the luck."

"I caint go now."

"Not even to see a foot's half as long as you are? Toes big as a baby's head. Not even to see that?"

"Nobody's got a foot that big," said Gerd, showing his discolored tongue between his teeth.

"Git you dollar and make me prove it," said the Thing. It came off the stump, not with its legs walking, but in a flowing, squirming movement like a huge caterpillar. It flowed right up to Gerd, who was still sitting on the ground. "Come on. Let's git out a this ditch. For a quarter I'll show you a man with two eyes in the same socket and nothin but a hole in the other one."

Being this close to the Thing made Gerd nervous. There was a little nodule of flesh growing out of the Thing's neck like a horn, and suddenly Gerd was assailed again by the conviction that he was looking into the brimstone eyes of the Devil. He smelled sulphur. "Now I preshate it," he said. "Don't think I don't. An I'm comin out there to see all you freaks. I really am, but I got to be here when the Gospel Singer comes."

The Thing's eyes had shifted focus to the side of Gerd's face. It was staring intently, leaning in its solid, shapeless body. "What in God's word happened in you cheek?"

"I got a condition. I crack."

"That's a fine sore," said the Thing, nodding its head from the navel up.

"It ain't nothin," said Gerd. "You ought to see the ones on my back."

"On you back?" The Thing smacked its rabbit's mouth and scratched the end of its nose with its immense jaw tooth.

"I got'm all over," Gerd said.

"Really! Would you let me see?"

Gerd never liked to pass up a chance to show his crippled skin. He flipped up the metal hasps of his galluses and unbuttoned his shirt.

The Thing whistled out of the side of its mouth. "That's somethin! That's a real sight. Money in the bank! You ever thought of bein a freak?"

Gerd slipped his shirt closed and hasped his overalls. "My brother's the Gospel Singer. I don't reckon I'd be travelin in no freak show."

"Yeah, yeah," said the Thing. "But I'm talkin about hard money. Foot'll turn ever one of them sores into dollars. Don't you want to git out of this town and be somebody?"

"I already am somebody. I'm his brother and the Gospel Singer's gone take me away with him."

"I hear you talkin, but Foot'll do more than talk. Say—" it leaned closer "—do them sores scab over and run purple juice like that by theirselves?"

"That purple stuff's medicine. You can buy it in Tifton."

"Well, that don't matter. You can tell the customers you got purple blood. Customers'll believe anythin at a freak fair. We can git a few scales too and paste'm around on you."

"You ain't puttin nothin on me cause I ain't goin nowheres."

The Thing's square head tilted back like a weight, and it appealed to Heaven with its leglike arms. "You ain't listenin to a thing I'm sayin. Don't you *want* somethin out of this world, somethin more'n just being 4-F for the army? If nothin else, think of me. Foot'll give me a bonus for bringin in a new attraction. He's always on the lookout for freaks. He's a real great guy, real great. What other midget you know that's layin up in a air-condition trailer with a redheaded woman and a Cadillac to pull it? He's done ever bit of it with his foot. He can do the same thing for you."

"The Gospel Singer's got a Cadillac car," Gerd said.

"Right," said the Thing. "He's gone keep it too. Listen, I ain't no different from you. Except Foot found me in a ditch in East Tennessee. I was so sad I'd forgot how to cry. My folks couldn't stand to look at me. Kept me in the corncrib. Had me so I couldn't bear myself. Foot took me and give me a place. It might not be much but I make my own way. And I love him for it . . . well, maybe not love, but his word's law for me. I follow him like Peter followed Jesus."

Gerd stared at the Thing. "He do all that? Take you out of East Tennessee and everthin?"

"Sure did," said the Thing. "He'll take you too."

Gerd stretched his neck to look off down the empty highway which, now that the sun was striking the tops of the pine trees, seemed to undulate in the rising heat.

"Wherebouts is Foot got his trailer?" Gerd asked.

"We set up over just beyond them saplings. It won't take us but a minute to step over there and see Foot." The Thing slithered off two or three yards in that direction. It looked back and smiled, its tooth shining in the lancing sun. "Come on. *Come on!*"

"I might miss him, he might come while I'm gone."

The Thing appealed to Heaven again. "God amighty, don't you see what I'm tryin to give you, I'm from East Tennessee and I ain't normal but I been all over this country on ships and airplanes and trains. Foot took me and he might take you."

Gerd got suddenly to his knees. A heavy shadow rose under the pale skin of his taut face. "Dammit to hell, you don't know who I am. He's built a brick home for me and all my family. We got a brand new truck an blooded stock that died. You don't know who I am an I ain't goin with you." Gerd sank back onto his thin beveled buttocks like a stake being driven into the ground.

The Thing came part way back. When it spoke its voice was lower, as though inquiring after the health of a friend. "You crazy, Countryboy? You plumb busted in the head too? Cause it don't matter if you are. It just ups your chances with Foot. We got one-quarter, one-half, three-quarter and whole crazy people. You sound whole crazy, and they is the best kind."

Gerd was too weak from his day in the sun and from his outburst of anger to rise again to the Thing. But he felt in his heart that he wanted to get on his feet and kick it to death. It had no right not to believe in the Gospel Singer, but more than that it had no right not to believe that he was the Gospel Singer's brother. "I ain't no crazy man," he said, but his voice came in a whisper. "I ain't."

"Maybe you could Geek," the Thing said, stroking its baloney-shaped chin and looking meditatively upon Gerd. "You ever seen a Geek? You know what one is? Why, a Geek's just a ordinary man without no special talent. He ain't got a thing to show. All he has to be is ready to follow Foot and do like he says. It don't matter what his reasons for followin are. Reasons don't count. The Geek that Foot's got now is a certain kind of crazy, craves whiskey like a baby craves candy. So when Foot has two or three hunderd customers lined around lookin on—sometimes more than three hunderd cause a Geek draws people like shit draws flies—he don't stop to think or nothin cause he knows Foot'll be waitin after the show with a bottle of that whiskey."

"What do he do?" The question came out of Gerd like the last breath of life.

"A Geek can eat a live chicken in three minutes, feathers and all. Peel a snake like a banana and eat it before you can say boo."

Gerd wilted in himself and was shocked beyond breathing. He regretted ever having talked to the Thing. He regretted not getting up and taking off at a dead run when he first saw it sitting on the stump. "*You* crazy," Gerd said. "It's you that's the crazy . . . crazy . . . thing."

"Foot says I might be a one-quarter crazy," said the Thing sadly. "But one-quarter crazies are too common in the world. It don't help a bit to be one." The square, flat head sank like a weight until even the ears were no longer visible. It was shrugging. "Some of us got no luck at all. I could go a lot futher if I was a whole crazy." It looked up at the fire cast into the sky by the setting sun. "Well, you caint have everthin. But listen," it said, coming back suddenly from its muttering. "You comin with me to see Foot? Cause you can see the Gospel Singer ain't comin tonight. It's gone be black dark in a minute. You wouldn't be able to see if it's him anyway. Come see Foot. You comin? No, I can see you're not. You gone set right here in this ditch and wait for him that don't know you're alive and don't care anyway." It shook his head from the navel up. "They ain't no use tryin to help some people. No use at all. But I tell you what I'll do for you anyhow. I'll tell Foot about you. I'll tell him how you eat up with the purple cracks and how you might be a half-crazy on account a the way you go on about the Gospel Singer. I know he'll want to talk to you. If you lucky he might make you a Geek. He might take you out of Enigmer."

It had already slithered several yards before Gerd could find his voice. "Don't tell Foot. Please! Please don't tell him about me!"

The Thing looked back and its enormous tooth was a yellow flower growing in the dark mound of jaw. "Yeah, you at least a half and maybe a whole crazy. You got to be to talk like that." The flower blossomed yet again and the Thing flowed out of the ditch and into the shadowed saplings.

Gerd sat stunned, staring at the spot where it had disappeared. He wanted to leave Enigma, wanted badly to leave it, but not badly enough to leave it in the middle of a staring crowd where he had to eat snakes. And he felt in his heart that Foot would never be satisfied now to leave Enigma until he had made Gerd into one of his Geeks. His only chance was for the Gospel Singer to save him.

He jerked around and stared off down the highway, still empty, beginning to merge now with the darkening countryside. Twin streaks of light impaled the sky in the west. There was no wind. Gerd stood on the sloping bank of the ditch and listened to his own breathing.

And then he heard it, a sound far off and mourning. He felt the skin contract over his heart. What he heard was the high insistent whine of the Cadillac car. The Gospel Singer was coming home! Gerd stood transfixed in the weeded ditch as he watched the heavy, monstrous blur gathering where the road ran into the sky.

A black chariot swinging from Heaven!

He could almost hear the voice, his brother's voice, thundering in the whine of the Cadillac: *Swing down, sweet chariot, stop and let me ride!*

Great Godamighty!

And on it came, running without its lights and seemingly not even touching the road, racing on, more powerful and faster than Gerd remembered it. It began to take definite lines, the sweeping brow of the hood, the great, shiny breastbumper. And now that it was actually upon him, Gerd could scarcely believe it. He was here again. It had all come true.

Then in an instant he realized that the car was about to blast past and leave him standing alone in the darkness.

Gerd launched himself onto the road, screaming his brother's name, his arms spread and frantically flapping.

Then he realized that the car would not, could not stop. The chrome breasts exploded in his eyes; he screamed and turned at the last minute, trying desperately to escape the black, zooming belly of the Cadillac.

CHAPTER 3

The Cadillac was vast, domed, vaulted and trussed, specially built by Detroit to the Gospel Singer's own specifications, but costing as much as Detroit cared to make it cost, expense being no consideration with the Gospel Singer because he consistently made more money during any given year than he was able to spend. The interior was deep savage red: the seats and headliner formed in heavy leather; the floor padded in spongy carpet. A pale mauve light—indirect, as though emanating from the passengers themselves—lit up the Gospel Singer in the back seat where he lolled, long-jointed and beautiful under his incredible head of yellow girl's hair, and lit up Didymus— manager, chauffeur and confessor to the Gospel Singer— where he sat, narrow-faced and nicotine-stained, rigid in his dark blue businessman's suit. He turned to look over his shoulder at the Gospel Singer, his mouth like the blade of a hatchet. He wore a clerical collar.

"You imperil your immortal soul with such talk!" Didymus cried.

The Gospel Singer was chuckling, and it poured from his throat, resonant, vibrant, with the sound of a precision-tooled and heavily oiled machine. The dusking countryside swept soundlessly by, muted under the soft hum of the air conditioner. In the west, the sun had left twin pillars of light standing in the sky.

The Gospel Singer stared at the back of Didymus' thin gray neck. His voice when he spoke was quietly good-natured as though he were teasing a child. "Well, if God didn't have a sense of humor, why would he have made women bleed? Set

every man to hungering for it, hoping for it, dreaming of it in
the day and praying for it in the night, and then making it . . ."
He broke up in laughter. "Of all the jokes He pulled in the
world, that's the best one."

Didymus, his eyes shot with blood, turned to glare over his
shoulder at the Gospel Singer. As he did a soft thump trembled
through the speeding car.

"And for Christ's sake," the Gospel Singer said. "Turn on
the lights before you kill us all in a Lebeau County road hole."
And then as an afterthought—"You might look where you're
going too."

"Look after the direction of your soul, and the world will
look after itself!" thundered Didymus. "Look to the moment
of your death!"

"Don't start that, Didymus." Suddenly the Gospel Singer
was not laughing.

"You must never forget who you are," said Didymus.

"I know who I am," he said. "I sing gospel anywhere
anybody'll pay me to sing. I've made a hell of a lot of money
and I'm going to make a hell of a lot more."

"You fight it," Didymus said. "But it's in the nature of the
gift to fight it."

"My gift is singing songs, gospel songs, and I've never
fought it."

"I mean the other gift," said Didymus.

"You mean women," said the Gospel Singer, pushing a
laugh out of his throat.

"No," Didymus said. "You know. I mean . . ."

"I forbid you to say it, Didymus."

"All right then, keep me quiet," said Didymus. "But you
can't bury what I know, and what you know, in silence, nor in
the earth, nor in your heart. I . . ."

"I said silence!"

"All right."

And there was, for a moment, silence, except for the rushing
whir of various motors churning, metal over lubricated metal,
throughout the car.

"But you have penance, remember, to do for that crack

about God," said Didymus. His white lips tasted each other
briefly.

"Yes."

"Ten *Rock of Ages Hide Thou Me*'s!"

"Yes!"

"Make that fifteen. You are not contrite."

"I swear if you don't hush, I'm going to take you back out to
Tifton and make you stay there the whole time I sing the revival."

The Cadillac shot past the drying chinaberry trees and
slowed into Enigma between the solid faces of the darkened
stores. A single light burned behind the glass of Enigma Funeral Parlor. The black courthouse sat directly in front of them
at the end of town.

"Is *this* it?" asked Didymus, stopping the car in front of
Enigma Seed. "Is *this* the place where you were born?"

"Not here," the Gospel Singer said, his voice hushed, subdued. "Our place is back in Big Harrikin Swamp."

"Then why'd we come in here? We can see the *town* tomorrow or the next day or never. Let's get to your place. Come on
now let's go. I've been at this wheel since Roanoke, Virginia.
I'm tired. Besides," he cut his eyes slyly back at the Gospel
Singer, "you've got penance."

"I want to look at it for a minute."

Didymus left the motor running to keep up the air conditioning, and they got out and stood by the car. A full moon
was raining out of Big Harrikin Swamp like the sun.

Didymus put his hand to his throat. "I can hardly breathe. I
had no idea it could be this hot. It can't be this hot."

"Somebody's dead," said the Gospel Singer.

"What! What's that?" Didymus jerked about and looked behind him.

"Hiram's window is lit. Somebody's up with the dead."

"We're all up with the dead!" Didymus cried. "Every man
is . . ." He stopped short. "Who is Hiram?" He looked in the
direction the Gospel Singer pointed.

"That where the light is is the funeral parlor," the Gospel
Singer said. "Hiram's the undertaker."

"And somebody's sitting with whoever is in there dead?"

"Yes."

"Why?" asked Didymus.

"Why? Because they're dead."

"They don't do that in California," said Didymus.

"Well, they do here. Funny too," said the Gospel Singer. "They usually take the dead home and put them in the living room and sit with them there. Don't put many in the funeral parlor like that and leave them overnight. Never seen but one or two done that way. Maybe it's a stranger to Enigma that's in there dead."

Didymus quit jumping about and leaned against the fender of the Cadillac. He took a thin book out of his inside coat pocket and wrote in it briefly. "God, sit with the dead in the living room! Good, good." He put the book back in his coat. "Let's go," he said. "Let's get out of this heat."

"It'll be hotter than this in the swamp. Be still, I want to stand here a minute."

"What you looking at? Has it changed?"

"Nothing's been built in Enigma since I was born," said the Gospel Singer. "Nothing ever changes here. Except maybe my banner up there. They've got that now and that's new."

Didymus straightened off the fender. "They've got something else, too. Foot's here. There's his sign!"

The Gospel Singer spun around and looked in the direction of Didymus' pointing finger. The Freak Fair poster was across the street from them, directly under the welcoming banner. It had lost a tack and hung dog-eared at one corner.

The Gospel Singer made a sound like weeping and dived into the back of the Cadillac.

Didymus got slowly back into the car and released the brake. "There's no reason to act like that about Foot," he said.

"Turn around," said the Gospel Singer. "Drive me out of here." He was hunkered down in the back seat, looking very small with his face turned from the window.

Didymus turned the car around in the street, backing once to do it, and then drove slowly out highway 229. As they passed Enigma Bank, three men rose like ghosts from the shadowed

benches, and a shout, nearly a scream, cut over the night. "I
TOLD YOU ITTAS HIM! THE GOSPEL SINGER'S BACK!"
Neither Didymus nor the Gospel Singer looked toward the
men. Didymus stabbed the accelerator gently and the car leapt
forward.

"There's a road about a quarter of a mile up here," said the
Gospel Singer. "It's dirt. Turn on it."

"It's silly for a man like you to be afraid of a man like Foot,"
said Didymus. He looked straight ahead and spoke softly.

"Who said I was afraid?" asked the Gospel Singer, rising to
sit straighter. "Who ever said that? Did I tell you I was afraid
of Foot?"

"No."

"You mighty right I didn't. I'm not afraid of him, but he's
got no right following me. How would *any* man like it if he
knew something like that was on his trail? I'm going to see
him too, have it out once and for all. I didn't get to be the best
Gospel Singer in the country to be followed by a goddam
freak."

"How about now?" said Didymus. "I wouldn't mind going
through the fair again. No doubt he's already set up somewhere close by."

"No," said the Gospel Singer. His voice lowered, he wilted
on the seat. "But he's going to keep pushing until I have it out
with him. But I'm too tired now, I'm exhausted."

The Cadillac slowed and stopped in the highway. "Is this
where I turn?" asked Didymus. And then after the headlights
had swept full upon it, "Is *that* a road?"

"That's it and you drive slow, too. It's not used to Cadillacs."

Gallberry bushes and scrub saplings scraped the sides of the
car. Didymus wrestled the wheel through the ruts, slowing the
car until it was barely moving.

In the back seat the Gospel Singer sighed heavily and pressed
his forehead against the cold window glass. It felt as though an
iron clamp were being turned down about his skull. His eyes
burned. He closed them and tried to relax. His neck was stiff
and he could hear the whirring of his heart. He had been all
over America, up and down broad highways, over dusty roads,

fording creeks, crossing multi-spanned bridges, and of all the places he could think of to be, he liked Enigma the least. He had told himself on his last trip that it would be years before he came home again. More than once he had even said that he would never return. Yet hardly seven months had passed and here he was.

He didn't like to think of why he returned again and again to Enigma, more or less on the half-year mark. At one time he had tried to tell himself it was because of his family—his mother, his two brothers Mirst and Gerd, his sister Avel, and his father. He got the most pitiful letters from them. Separately they wrote him and jointly. Great bundles of letters tied in purple string that Didymus insisted upon keeping for God knows what reason. The letters poured in upon him wherever he was, begging him to come home, insisting, almost demanding, that he come back to Enigma and be with his own kind. But they were not his own kind, and had not been since he had found the gospel singing voice and probably were not even before that. Probably they had not been his own kind since he had been marked at birth with a kind of beauty that none of them had ever seen before. And the time had come when he couldn't even answer the letters himself because as the months went by it became harder and harder to lie to them, to tell them he *missed* them, to tell them he *wished* he was back home in Enigma, when in point of fact his every inclination was to bury Enigma, to deny that it had ever existed or that he was ever part of it. So he had had Mr. Keene, and after Mr. Keene had disappeared, Didymus, write the letters back making excuses about why he couldn't come home, about how he was out in the world singing his heart out, about how he was sharing himself and his gift because that was his mission, his cross. And with the letters he had sent money, white envelopes stuffed with green dollars. That helped some. They could understand money. But money eventually wore out and they wanted *him. HIM!* their letters shouted.

But finally, it was not for them that he returned. He had woke up ten days ago in a motel in Washington, D.C., and before his mind had cleared enough for him to be sure which city they were in, he knew he must go home again. He had dreamed of MaryBell and it was time. He looked over at Didymus, who never seemed to sleep and was sitting then by the window writing furiously in his book, and said, "I'm going home."

Erratic, trembling Didymus had jerked up from what he was doing and exclaimed, pointing a brown and bony finger, "You can't go home! Nobody can go home! Because the world is not our home and . . ." He stopped. His face calmed. His eyes seemed to draw together and focus. "Home?" he said wonderingly. "Home? The Gospel Singer is going home to Enigma?" Ever since Didymus had become his manager, he had been desperate to visit the place where the Gospel Singer was born.

"Yes," said the Gospel Singer.

"Enigma," said Didymus. "Such a marvelous, beautiful word." And he had turned to his book again and written more quickly.

So here he was on the dim road leading into Big Harrikin Swamp to the hog farm and the family he had been born to. And as surely as he had left the farm, he had left the family: the parents, the sister, the brothers. He had been separated from them in every way but love. Not only did he not resemble his family, but more strangely still, when he was away from Enigma he did not even *sound* like them. It was not just the quality and power of his voice either. It went much deeper than that. The Gospel Singer did not sound like anybody. He was an unconscious and absolute mimic. He automatically took the speech patterns—choice of word, inflection—of whomever he was with. In a kind of verbal osmosis, it soaked into him and became a part of his being. In Kansas City he was nasal; in Brooklyn he whined; in New England he was crisp; in Texas he mumbled.

Now he was taking the unknown tongues and the beauty and the voice back into Enigma where the people would stand nervously about, secretly touching him, whispering impossible requests in his ears, always there at his back like hungry dogs

over red meat. He would be forced to stand in their midst, im-
potent, castrated by his inability to relieve their suffering. All
he could do was bleed for them, bleed for their ignorance and
the condition of their world.

But while he bled for them, that did not mean he wanted to
share it with them. What good would it serve for him to be
mired in their condition with them? Particularly when it was
possible for him to escape. But while it was obvious to him, it
was not at all obvious to the people of Enigma. And especially
was it not obvious to MaryBell Carter. She was the particular
example of the general tendency to drown him in Enigma.

She was also the reason he had come back. This time and
everytime. It was for her: to see her, to hear her. She was his
touchstone. He felt sometimes that it was only by her that he
knew himself real. When the converts started falling before
him like wheat before a scythe, when the whole world started
turning on his word, he needed MaryBell.

He sighed. She was not, however, without her problems.
And it was true that sometimes for several days running his
every waking effort was to keep *from* thinking of her, to keep
from seeing her in the dark of his mind waiting for him to return. The fact that she obtruded upon his thoughts now was
enough to make him withdraw his head from the window and
slowly, trying to appear casual even to himself, lift his hand
and lock the back doors.

Didymus was alternately groaning and whistling in the front
seat.

"What *is* the matter, Didymus?" asked the Gospel Singer
shortly, angry at himself for being silly enough to be afraid
that MaryBell would suddenly jerk open the door of the slowly
moving car and vault in upon him and knowing at the same
time that it was not silly and fully expecting at any moment to
see her, stretched and desperate, flying at him over the back
seat.

"This country is wild," Didymus was saying. His head
bobbed blackly in the glow of the dash lights. The car was
nearly stopped, rocking and swaying, scraping, bellying over
the road. "I don't believe it, it's beautiful, too good."

"Watch the road," said the Gospel Singer, although Didymus was staring straight ahead. "Watch where you're going."

"He came out of the swamp and he sang of God," said Didymus.

Didymus was fond of using the third-person pronoun for the Gospel Singer. In the past it had been amusing to the Gospel Singer. At the moment he found it annoying. Didymus groaned and whistled and sighed and tried to keep his eyes on the road and off the moonstriped, shadowing countryside. While in the back seat, the Gospel Singer, in an effort to take his mind off MaryBell, dwelled upon Foot. The specter at his back. The phantom that for some reason had fastened upon him. It had been almost five months ago when the Gospel Singer had first noticed that Foot was following him. He remembered it distinctly because it had been the week after Mr. Keene had disappeared and Didymus had taken over his affairs. The poster had been nailed on the very building where the Gospel Singer had his dressing room, right across the street from the Open Air Evangelistic Revival for Christ where he was appearing in Houston, Texas. He saw it and commented upon it as he was leaving after the performance.

"A freak fair?" he said to Didymus.

"Affliction is the fruit of sin and sin is the fact of man!" wailed Didymus, rolling his eyes and whirling to stare bloodshot before he had even known what the Gospel Singer was talking about. Then he too saw the poster. He calmed, stopped, and looked a long moment. "Well, now," he said. "I've never seen one, but it'd be a lesson to us all. We must go and see."

"Not me," said the Gospel Singer. "I'll not go to such a thing."

As it turned out, Didymus didn't go either, at least not right away. It was not until three engagements later when they were playing Tulsa, Oklahoma, that they saw the poster again and knew that Foot was indeed following them.

"But why would he follow me?" asked the Gospel Singer. "This is a free country, and I've got a right not to be followed."

"We must go and see him ourselves," said Didymus.

"No," said the Gospel Singer.

"Why?"

"Who wants to see a goddam freak?"

"That's no answer," said Didymus. "And don't use the Lord's name in vain."

"Because . . . because I can't help them."

Didymus smiled. "Why, they know that. Surely they know that."

"At least I can *not* stare at them," said the Gospel Singer.

"But that's what they're there for. What do you think freaks are for? That's why they're in this world."

"I'll not go to such a thing," said the Gospel Singer.

"Then I'll go," said Didymus.

And that night Didymus had gone to the freak fair while the Gospel Singer lay in his cold skin on the hotel bed and waited, a curious anxiety running in his blood. What might a freak fair be like? No doubt it was a kind of concentrated Enigma, the very kind of thing he had run half around the world to escape. He lay on the bed and dreamed of freaks, caterwauling, lined in cages.

And as he lay there dreaming of things he had never seen, his superstition of God opened in him like an old wound. Could it be that Foot was the terror God had sent to hound him through the land? He was by turns contemptuous and terror-stricken. What had God to do with him? Who was he, the Gospel Singer, anyway, for God to be concerned with? A poor pig farmer's son lucky enough to make a name for himself singing gospels, that was all. And yet . . .

He leapt from the bed and did three *Wings of a Doves*, and when that didn't help he got on the phone—deciding to go both theological directions at once—and called the Evangelical Choir Leader, who had flesh softer than sin and who turned out to be a virgin besides, to his room, but she didn't help either, and when she left he settled again on the bed, his skin still ice, because her mouth had been red like the poster and he had stared into it knowing that he'd have now, on top of everything else, to tell Didymus about *her*.

Didymus had returned in a religious frenzy, Moses come back from the mountain with fire in his hands.

"They are God's *WRATH!*" he screamed, bursting through the door, arms and legs outstretched, crucified in his own angular delirium.

And the Gospel Singer, knowing already who and what he meant, lay spread-eagled in his white silk drawers and said nothing.

"You must come and see," cried Didymus. "All the perversions of the flesh are there, every form and kind of wrecked body. They are signposts for humanity! You'll never see as clearly as you will looking into the face of the man that has no eyes, not even holes for eyes, nothing, solid from the nose up!"

Then, to the Gospel Singer's horror, Didymus launched upon the catalogue of afflictions which he had seen at the freak fair.

"Keep it to yourself, whatever you saw," said the Gospel Singer.

But Didymus would not stop. He used the Gospel Singer as a foil, as a ground out of which to build his frightening images of twisted flesh. He made the Gospel Singer stand before the dressing mirror which was attached to the back of the bathroom door, and as he spoke of legless wonders he would point to the Gospel Singer's own finely shaped and tautly muscled legs to drive his point home.

Didymus had saved Foot for the last. Foot was the mastermind, the freak responsible for organizing all the other freaks. Didymus had seen him—even, it turned out—talked to him.

"He is the greatest freak of them all," said Didymus. "He's specialized. His affliction has focus, all in his foot."

"His foot?"

"Whence the name," said Didymus. "*Foot!* The biggest foot in the world. Surely one of God's chosen creatures!"

And since that time, Foot had been steadily on the Gospel Singer's trail. In every town, at every meeting in God's house, at every open-air, overflowing tent revival where the Gospel Singer opened his throat and let out the sacred hymns, everywhere he went, he now saw the sign of Foot. There was not any telling how long he had been back there before the Gospel Singer noticed him either. Probably years. Maybe his whole life.

"This road's getting worse," said Didymus, leaning forward to squint through the windshield.

"You're almost there," said the Gospel Singer. "It's not much farther."

"Were you really born back here?"

"Yes."

The Cadillac suddenly growled and burst free of the rutted track and into a clearing, flat, sandy, where a brick house sat in the moonlight. Palmetto and dog fennel grew right up to the front porch. Several outbuildings were collapsing to the left and right of the house.

"What in the world is that noise?" asked Didymus.

"Hogs," said the Gospel Singer.

"Then I won't ask you what the stink is."

"I told you what it was like before we ever started."

"I guess I never believed you," said Didymus.

The house was large with a wide, roofed porch and columns of round marble and high, arched windows with lead dividers separating the panes of glass. The windows in front were lit with faint yellow light.

"Hog farming must be profitable," said Didymus. "That's a real house."

"I built it," said the Gospel Singer. "Cost seventy thousand to put it up and furnish it and they've already ruined it, but I don't grudge them a penny of it."

"The Gospel Singer built them a home like they had never seen," said Didymus.

"They can tear it down around their ears as long as I don't have to be in it with them."

Didymus turned off the car but left the lights on. He opened the door. Several dogs barked. They came out of the shadows, wide-headed, thin-loined mastiffs with yellow eyes. Didymus closed the door. "Mean-looking dogs," he said.

"We better wait for somebody to call them off," the Gospel Singer said.

The front door opened and a dark knot of people bunched there behind a thin, tall man carrying a kerosene lamp in his right hand raised level with his face.

"You dogs," said the man.

The dogs quieted and sank back into the shadow of the house.

"It's a Cadillac!"

"It's him!"

"HIM!"

A form separated itself from the group in the door and swept across the porch. It was wide and solid like a section of the wall springing away from the house itself. A woman, long braided hair knotted on her neck like a club, heavy skirts flapping, vaulted across the yard. Soundlessly, her face twisted in wet grieving laughter. "My son! My baby come home!" The Gospel Singer was half out of the car when she caught his slender body and hauled it into her, wrapping it in her massive arms and rocking while she crooned steadily, making a sound like laughter now even though the tears still fell into the Gospel Singer's golden hair where he was crushed against her. His voice muffled on her shoulder, he tried to comfort her, telling her it was all right, that he was home now. Didymus hooked one elbow on the fender of the car and leaned there looking anxiously at the end of his shoes where he drew pictures he could not see in the dark sand. The man with the lamp came forward slowly until he was standing next to Didymus, but he was looking at the Gospel Singer. The boy came down the steps and stopped in the yard. He was dressed entirely in black with long, wet-looking hair that fell about his ears and across his flat forehead. His clothes were so tight that his shirt looked as though it were breathing for him, pulling his thin chest up and then pushing it down again. He had a guitar strung about his neck on a red strap. A girl stood on the porch at the top of the steps. She was very large with pale skin and a beautifully formed mouth. She was barefoot.

The Gospel Singer pushed out of the woman's bosom. "Ma, this is my new manager. His name is Didymus."

"Glad to make your acquaintance," she said, but she never stopped looking at the Gospel Singer. "Son, I've been waitin it seems like forever. We *all* been waitin." She turned on her heel. "Mirst, you come on up here and kiss your brother. What you hangin back there for? Avel, you too! Is that a way to welcome your brother home?"

Mirst came forward, a shy smile in his face, still glancing about, looking momentarily at the Gospel Singer before averting his eyes.

"Ain't he growed?" said his mother.

Mirst stopped in front of his brother and put out his hand hesitantly as if to touch him or take his hand but quickly drew it back instead and scratched himself. "I got a geetar," he said.

"I see you have," said the Gospel Singer. "That's a fine-looking instrument."

"I been practicin and . . ."

The man with the lamp stepped around Mirst and took the Gospel Singer by the shoulder and shook him gently. "Good to see you, boy."

"Pa, I thought I was gone git to come home two months ago, but it's just been first one thing and then another. And then when I did start home, why, I broke a axle in Virginia and I don't know what all else."

"Well, come on in," said his father. "It ain't no use to stand in the yard to talk."

The Gospel Singer stopped beside Avel who had never come off the porch. "You lookin real good, Avel. You made a woman since I was home last. How you been?"

"Fine and dandy." She did a half-curtsy, half-sliding step with her feet. "Mirst and me sing to his geetar. We singin all around and gitten real good at it."

"Hey," cried the Gospel Singer. "Wait a minute."

His father, who was already inside the house, came back to the door with the lamp. Mirst, who had been strumming his guitar, left off but kept his fingers carefully placed on the frets marking the chord.

"Where's Gerd?" asked the Gospel Singer. "How come he ain't here?"

"Gerd's been gone most all day," said Avel. "He ain't back."

"But there's the truck," said the Gospel Singer, pointing to the new GMC truck gleaming in the moonlight where it was parked in front of the house. The cab door was open on the far side and the tires were choked in weeds.

"He got the old truck," said his father, turning back into the house. "That GMC's got a litter of pups in the floorboard."

"A litter . . ."

Mirst struck his guitar a savage blow and then another one even though his fingers had slipped loose from the frets.

"That ain't how come he didn't drive it though," Avel said softly. "It's broke."

Avel went through the door and Mirst followed her trying desperately to make both his hands work at the same time on the guitar. The Gospel Singer was left staring at the truck. He was slowly shaking his head. Didymus stopped beside him.

"That truck cost you four thousand dollars and it's not two months old," said Didymus. "Broke? How broke?"

"You ain't seen a goddam thing yet," said the Gospel Singer.

"Don't use the Lord's name in vain," said Didymus. "You already got a penance to do for lying to your daddy about that broken axle in Virginia."

"What did you want me to tell him?" asked the Gospel Singer. "That I was getting laid and couldn't let it go?"

"I didn't expect you to lie."

"You didn't expect me to tell the truth either, did you?"

"Well, no," said Didymus.

Didymus followed him into the house. Mirst, waiting inside, struck two chords as they came through the door and looked up and smiled his quick shy smile.

"You gitten pretty good with that thing," said the Gospel Singer.

"A man can make a lot of money with one of these," said Mirst, taking hold of the neck of the guitar with both hands as though it were something live and he meant to strangle it.

In the living room, a kerosene lamp burned on the mantel shelf over a stone fireplace. A hound with a bone caught between its teeth slept in a deep sofa by the hearth. There was a carpet on the floor from wall to wall and a black trail led through it from the door where they were standing to the hallway that connected the living room to the bedrooms and which finally opened into the dining room and kitchen at the back of the house. The Gospel Singer patiently watched Mirst struggle with the guitar while Didymus looked about him at the ruined disorder of rich furnishings: the black trail in the carpet from which there floated the rancid smell of hog manure, a three-legged French Provincial chair, a stopped grandfather clock with a cracked face.

A hog wandered into the living room from the darkened hallway. The hair on its back was sparse and patches of red skin showed through. Its backbone was high and curved and ridged with bone. The eyes that stared up at Didymus were the color of dried rosin behind long, brittle-looking whiskers growing out of the side of its thin snout.

Didymus crossed himself. "God love us, and what is that!" he cried, retreating a step and pressing his back against the wall.

"Sick shoat," Mirst said over the tune that he could not quite find in the tangle of guitar strings.

"Screwwormy?" asked the Gospel Singer.

"Don't seem to be," said Mirst. "Pa don't know yet what ails it. You know, I don't think this A string is right. You think it might be sprung?"

"It might be," said the Gospel Singer, but then he took the guitar in his hands and touched the A string with his slender tapering thumb and the sound that came was not the sound Mirst had made because now it had become music.

"Shit, it ain't sprung," said Mirst, snatching it back and concentrating so hard as he slammed into a chorded version of *Sweetheart, What You Doing to Me?* that the veins leapt under the skin of his forehead.

There was a black knot behind the pig's ear that Didymus had been staring into because the black spot looked sometimes as though it were moving, and when the Gospel Singer's mother screamed down the hall for Mirst to quit bothering his brother with that damn guitar and let him come on and set down and eat some supper, the black knot exploded into a hovering swarm of flies over the pig's back.

"We better git on back there," said Mirst, leading the way

out of the living room into the hallway at the end of which
they could see the Gospel Singer's daddy sitting in a ladder-
back chair with the lamp on the edge of the table but with his
hand still wrapped around the glass base.

"Did you see that pig? Did you?" hissed Didymus.

"Hush, Didymus. This ain't Nu Yawk City."

Two places were set. There was a platter of meat and bread
and in a clear jar, syrup, with a dark ring of crusted sugar
around the pouring spout. The Gospel Singer's father got out a
sack of tobacco and a book of cigarette leaves. Avel and her
mother sat across from one another, both of them leaning on
their elbows. Mirst leaned against the wall and casually made
a noise with his guitar. The Gospel Singer was about to sit
down when he suddenly looked at Didymus and asked, "You
git them fuses?"

Didymus looked hurt. "Don't I always do what you ask me
to do?"

"Are they where you can git them easy?"

"In the pocket of the car," said Didymus.

"Would you bring them in before you set down?"

"He's a funny-lookin one," said his father after Didymus
had gone.

"He's a good man," said the Gospel Singer.

"What kind of a name is that he's got?" asked his mother.
"He ain't our kind of people, is he?"

"He's a monk," said the Gospel Singer. "That means he's
give up the world for God."

"Hell of a name for a man of God to have, Didymus Monk,"
said his father.

"Smokes a lot for a preacher," said Mirst. "Must burn up
five, six packs of them tailor-mades a day."

"He ain't a preacher," said the Gospel Singer, "and he does
smoke a lot, but then we ain't none of us perfect."

"What happened to Mr. Keene?" asked his mother. "He
was a nice man."

"He . . . he disappeared, Ma. One day he just wasn't there
and along come Didymus and he was a good man, and I
needed a manager so I hired him on."

"Funny," said his mother. "A man like that droppin out of sight. All that land and money. It ain't natural. Last month, we sold some shoats at the Tifton sale and I asked after him. He still ain't come home. Funny."

"A man caint trust nobody but his kin," said Mirst. "It some that say even kin ain't to be trusted."

Didymus came in with a small sack. He laid it on the table beside the Gospel Singer. Mirst looked at his mother and winked. She smiled at Avel who didn't see her because she was concentrating on what the Gospel Singer was doing with the sack. He ripped it open and took out six fuses.

"Set down," he said to Didymus. "Git some of that meat and syrup. I won't be but a minute."

Didymus sat down but he didn't eat. He too stared at the Gospel Singer as he lit another kerosene lamp and left through the kitchen door bearing the lamp in one hand and the fuses in the other.

"Ain't he something," said Mirst.

"Yes he is," said Didymus. Then, "Where is he going?"

"You'll see," said Mirst. "Won't he, Avel?"

"Sure will," she said.

Suddenly lights came on all over the house, in every room, even on the front porch. Bulbs blazed in the ceiling of the dining room. Mirst looked up. "He done it again." They were all chuckling except Didymus and he had snatched out his book and was writing rapidly with a short, bitten pencil.

Directly the Gospel Singer came back. The lamp in his hand was no longer burning. His father leaned forward, cupped his hand over the glass, and blew out the lamp in front of him.

"Well, Ma," said the Gospel Singer, settling himself at the table and spearing a slab of red ham with his fork, "what's been the news since I was home?"

"If you leave out what that nigger done, they ain't been much happen," said Mirst. "How would you like me and Avel to sing a little somethin for you?"

"Which nigger?"

His mother sat straighter on her chair. "Son! I wrote you all about it. Didn't you git the wire I sent, neither?" She had put her hand to her mouth. "We thought that'as how come you was comin home, to be at the funeral."

The Gospel Singer had stopped eating. "The funeral? Whose funeral?"

"MaryBell's," said his mother.

"The nigger got her," said Mirst. "Me and Avel's been tryin to git on the television in Albany. We even tried the same station you started on."

The Gospel Singer had paled. He was holding the edge of the table as if balancing on the chair. "MaryBell Carter?" he whispered.

"Did you know her?" asked Didymus.

"Did he know her?" asked his mother. "Why, him and her was just like that." She held up her crossed fingers.

"Yes," said Didymus. "If he knew her, that's the way they would have been."

"He raped her and killed her, son."

"With a ice pick," said Avel.

"Who done it?" asked the Gospel Singer.

"Willalee Bookatee Hull."

"I caint believe it. Not Willalee."

"If he didn't do it, they got the wrong nigger in Enigmer jail right this minute. It was him though. Used his ice pick and they found her at the foot of his bed with him asleep in it."

His father, who had not spoken, looked up. "Nigger's like a mule. Plow one twenty year, think he's the best mule in the world, bend down one day to unhitch a trace, kicks you head off your shoulders."

"Avel, you ready?" asked Mirst.

"I'm always ready." She stretched her beautiful mouth in a smile. She had bad teeth. "Ain't I *his* sister?"

"But I know Willalee," said the Gospel Singer.

"We all known him," said his father.

"This is just a little thing me and Avel heard on the radio bout a gal that lost her love at the high school dance," said Mirst, busily twisting the strings tighter on his guitar.

"You childern shut up," said his mother.

"Maybe I'll go see him," said the Gospel Singer.

"I'd stay away from that nigger," said his father.

Mirst loosened the strings again and stamped his foot three times. On the third beat he slapped the guitar and Avel leapt from her chair and they both screamed, and Mirst hunched as they rolled their eyes and wailed at the ceiling. They hipped their way around the table until they were standing right in front of the Gospel Singer who by now was slumped in his chair breathing shallowly but weakly smiling, encouraging them with his eyes. Avel's enormous body quivered and vibrated and her dark straight hair whipped across her neck. The black skin of Mirst's shirt spotted with sweat. Finally, they stood hushed, breathless before the Gospel Singer.

"Theym childern's got talent," said their father.

"They's a fortune waiting on the TeeVee," said Mirst. "If you'll git us on."

"We'll talk to Didymus," said the Gospel Singer. "He's the manager. Managers know about such things."

Their mother pushed them away from the Gospel Singer. She put her hands on his shoulder. "Not now though. Quit botherin him. Caint you see he's grievin? An he's bone-tired from the trip besides. Ain't you, son?"

"Didymus and me both's nearly done in. We been ridin since day before yesterday."

"Mr. Didymus, you ain't touched a thing on you plate," said Avel.

"I'm really not hungry," said Didymus.

"Didymus limits his bodily food," said the Gospel Singer.

"That's how come he's so puny," said the Gospel Singer's mother under her breath.

"How'd we sound to you, Mr. Didymus?" asked Mirst.

"You've got promise," said Didymus.

"Well, after all, I am *his* brother," said Mirst.

His father went to the window and looked out. "It ain't like Gerd to be gone this way," he said.

"How is Gerd been?" asked the Gospel Singer.

"Still having the trouble in his skin," said his mother.

Didymus ducked and crossed himself. "We all have trouble in our skins! It . . ."

"You, Didymus, hush!" said the Gospel Singer.

"Didn't you take him to that specialist I found out about in Atlanta? I wrote you about it and sent the money."

"They's a long ways between sendin the money and seein the doctor," said his father. "We done the best we could. We got to Atlanta all right, but we never did find where the doctor was at. It's a big place and it ain't no Enigmer, shore. Spent the day askin people and walkin up first one street and down the next. Hot sun, Gerd's skin crackin and itchin, him goin crazy, wound up in a movin pitcher show cause Gerd wouldn't have it no other way after he started goin crazy and seen that Doris Day and that Rock Hudson stuck up on the front like they do, you know."

"And you ain't been back?" asked the Gospel Singer.

"Hogs took the scours. Some died. Some still do."

"What's scours?" asked Didymus.

"They bowels loosen up," said Mirst. "Then they git like water and then they don't stop at all. Drip. When a inch a gut shows in they ass, they die."

"Mervin!" said his mother. "Watch that mouth of yours. You brother's here!" She rubbed the back of the Gospel Singer's neck.

"Ma, I think me and Didymus better go on to bed," he said. "It'll be a big day tomorrow."

"The revival tent is hauled out there on the edge of Enigmer all ready to be set up in the mornin," said Mirst. "Never seen such a one. They say it's the biggest one in the state of Georgia. That preacher's gone all out. Been here a week stayin over to Lambert Treewright's house. Boy, is he lookin to hold a meetin with you. He even asked me and Avel to be on the program. But we caint. We don't sing no songs about nothin but how lovin hurts so bad. Gospels? They's your department. He keeps askin though. We might wind up doin a little number yet."

"Set down and shut you mouth," said his mother. "Seems like you been talkin steady since they got here. Come on, son. I'll show Mr. Didymus where bouts to sleep."

The Gospel Singer and Didymus followed her out into the

hallway. She stopped by a door. "I'll see you in the mornin, son. You have a good rest, you hear?" Didymus started into the room. She caught his arm. "You sleep down here, Mr. Didymus." She pointed toward the end of the hall. Didymus looked at the Gospel Singer.

"We usually get a room together, Ma. We have things to talk about at night."

"Not tonight," she said firmly. "Whatever it is can wait. You need you rest."

"Won't be but a minute," said Didymus. "There's just a couple of things. . . ." He grabbed the Gospel Singer's arm and charged into the room and shut the door behind them before she could stop them. In the hall Mirst and Avel struck up another song and his father shouted above the noise that he hoped he had a good rest his first night back home in Enigmer.

The Gospel Singer sat on the edge of the bed and put his head in his hands. The bed was large and covered with a patchwork quilt in the design of a cloverleaf. The rug on the floor was stained the same color as the one in the living room. Two chamber pots, one half-full, stood at the foot of the bed. Didymus stopped over the pots.

"Chamber pots?" he said.

"Yes," said the Gospel Singer.

"There are bathrooms," said Didymus. "I saw one. In a house this size there must be more, several even."

"They're used to chamber pots," said the Gospel Singer.

"They've got hogs in this seventy-thousand-dollar house," said Didymus.

"Don't you think I can see? I tried to tell them. I even offered to . . ."

"About those fuses," said Didymus.

The Gospel Singer tried to smile. "That's crazy, ain't it? They just always had the lamps and I never could get Ma to throw them out so . . ."

"Do the fuses all burn out at once?"

The Gospel Singer was very still suddenly as though he had turned to something solid and fleshless. "The fuses are never in the box when I come home. I don't know who takes them out. I never asked. They . . ." He looked away. "They like to see me do it."

There was a loud banging at the door and the Gospel Singer's mother was yelling to him that he had to git his rest because tomorrow was the big day.

"About the girl?" said Didymus.

"Yes?"

"You didn't tell me about her?"

"I haven't told you a lot of things," flared the Gospel Singer. "She was just a girl, that's all, no different from any other."

"She's dead," said Didymus. "That makes her different. Besides, if she was like all the others, you would have told me about her."

There was a great commotion outside the door.

"Go to bed," said the Gospel Singer. "You'll have them all in here if you don't."

Didymus walked over and opened a door that led into a closet. It was empty except for one dark shoe and several coat hangers.

"You wouldn't forget your penance, would you?"

"No."

"It'll only double tomorrow if you do."

Didymus opened the door and Mirst and Avel tried to get past him into the room, Mirst clawing at the guitar with both hands and Avel making a motion with her body like a huge tortured bug. But their mother managed to get a hand on them and pull them back into the hall.

"You children stay outen his room!"

She slammed the door and the Gospel Singer was left staring at the closet door. He took off his clothes, placed them neatly on hangers, and put them in the closet. Then he got into the closet with them, naked, and closed the door. He knelt between his coat and trousers. He opened his mouth and let out his voice. An undulating snake of sound wound round him. But softly, gently.

Rock of Ages Hide Thou Me.

The thousands of faces that had been turned up to him under those words! Bland, ordinary faces made ecstatic by hope! The hopeless, hopeful faces feeding on words, but mostly feeding on him, the Gospel Singer, on the beauty of his face and the beauty of his voice.

A quiet horror filled him. Loathing. He smelled his sour skin. At these moments of penance how he hated his voice and his beauty. Not only had the voice displaced him, made him uncomfortable among his own blood kin, made the place of his birth strange and unreal, but it had brought him into the presence of God. More even than that. It had made him God's own living symbol in the land. He had not *tried* to be a Gospel Singer. The voice had simply come out of his mouth one day and he had used it. It was a gift that he had not asked for and that at first he had not known what to do with. It had even been amusing in the beginning to see people stop startled, amazed before his voice. But the gift had proved a curse. Because the simple, frightening truth was that a gospel song in his mouth could convert a man to God, or as in the case of MaryBell, the memory of whom burned him now like fire, it could destroy utterly.

He sang on.

CHAPTER 4

Didymus, violent murderous lover of God, knew that he had followed his master into the wilderness and he was ecstatic that it was so. His heart had been quietly cold ever since he turned the Cadillac into the dirt road off the highway. Didymus had seen the Gospel Singer burning blondly on the altars of revival churches from Boston to El Paso—his throat pulsing with the Word of God and sinners falling to their knees like axed cattle, eyes rolling, spewing their sins against the Holy Ghost—and he had known before the Gospel Singer had ever told him that he must have come from just such a land as Enigma.

Didymus lay with his mouth open, trying to find enough air in the hot humid room. Sweat ran on his body. His breath hung where he breathed it into the space above his face. The moonlight, bright nearly as the sun, seemed to steam where it fell through the window. He got off the bed and walked nervously up and down the room. He wore only his clerical collar. At irregular intervals he heard the spangled sound of Mirst on the guitar and the addled whine of Avel as though Mirst might have been beating her with the instrument. It was the only kind of brother the Gospel Singer could have had. Didymus thought him too good to be true. But then the Gospel Singer himself was too good to be true. He was the miracle for which Didymus had spent his life searching.

He rushed suddenly to the window and thrust his head out into the still night. He had not seen a whole screen in any window in the house and this one in the bedroom had none at all. He climbed into the open window and sat there naked, trembling in the hot yellow moon. He wanted to walk, to dash about over the land, around the outbuildings, through the stunted, swampy cypress, and see and touch all that his master had seen and touched. He swung his legs over the sill, thought better of it, and went back into the room to get his trousers. He was just about to lower himself to the ground when he saw the huge mastiff bitch watching him. She was the color of earth with a deep bony chest and amber eyes. Her body was raked with long dark scars where the hair did not grow. Her head was broad and flat and her ears stood forward as she watched him. She had not barked or even growled but sat by a leafless bush silently, her black tongue dripping black saliva. Facing him, her front legs spread, he could see quite plainly that she was a bitch and not a male and it pleased him to think that she would probably have killed him without ever making a sound if he had dropped to the ground in front of her—would have torn out his throat and the last thing he would have seen of this world would have been those enormous eyes looking into his, her mouth dripping his blood.

He shivered deliciously and sniffed the air. It was the odor of slop and mud and hogshit so layered by time that it seeped out of the ground and grass and weeds and trees and, it seemed, out of the very brick and mortar of the house. He strained in the silence suddenly made as Mirst and Avel left off in mid-verse on the song they could not quite sing. What he was listening for he knew very well he would not hear. The whole point of the Gospel Singer's penance was that the Gospel Singer had to listen to his hymn-singing voice *alone*.

Didymus lit another cigarette from the quarter-inch butt in his mouth and thought of the Gospel Singer kneeling in the closet quietly singing *Rock of Ages* again and again, the sweat like scented crystal standing on his forehead, the blond hair damply curling at his ears. He was kneeling this very moment using the gift God had given him and in the act of using it he was suffering most exquisitely. Didymus sucked his cigarette and contemplated this as he usually did while the Gospel Singer was doing penance.

"Suffering is God's greatest gift to man," he said, breathing the words out of his mouth.

It was his favorite statement and the cornerstone of his whole existence. He sometimes spent hours lying flat on his back, saying the words, his eyes fixed and staring but unfocused so that finally it seemed the place where he lay did not exist nor his body nor the world but only the words—*Suffering is God's greatest gift to man*. And he would lie there until the words wrapped him like a mother's flesh and he was transported into the womb of God.

He had known for a long time that suffering was the true path to holiness. He had learned it slowly but well during the first ten years of his life—the ten years that it had taken his father to beat his mother to death. It was in his tenth year that his mother had hemorrhaged after a beating and died calling to her God and blessing her husband who stood above her with a two-ply razor strap refusing to go for a doctor. That afternoon his father had run amuck with a knife on the dock in San Francisco, California, where he worked as a header and gutter of fish, and in his frenzy had fallen into the sea and drowned while the man he had been trying to kill with the knife cursed and tried to stab him with a gaffing hook.

Didymus went to an orphanage. He was not an attractive boy, small and dark, with an intensity about him that at first frightened the other boys and then angered them. He prayed as his mother had taught him, quietly absorbing the punishment of his fellows by day and piercing his skin with needles by night in an ecstasy of revulsion because he had been taught by his mother that it was only by denying the flesh and triumphing over it that he would finally be received into the kingdom of Heaven.

When he slept, his mother's spirit, from its place at the right hand of God, approved his self-mutilation and called him prophet.

In his seventeenth year he left the orphanage and entered a religious order for men as a novice in the state of Arkansas. It had all been arranged by the orphanage officials. They had not missed his devoutness, which they took to be a kind of insanity, so they shipped him where they thought he would best be cared for. Didymus had not resisted. Talking directly to his mother from her position at the right hand of God during the night, and recording their dialogues in his *Dream Book* during the day, he was at one with himself and said that it did not matter where he lived.

But of course he had been wrong. The order had been unbearable. There was too much food and too much rest and too much security: brown men walking between brown walls sighing brown sighs and sleeping too soundly in the night. Didymus sank lower and lower. In spite of himself, he gained weight. He stared at his fleshing body in horror.

He did not remember just how his attempted suicide had taken place. He only remembered becoming more and more depressed until finally they were carting him off to the Arkansas State Asylum for the Insane and it was only after they got him there that they told him what he had done. He was so thankful that he had not been able to accomplish the ultimate sin against God that he fasted in the asylum until they had to feed him through the vein in his right arm.

Didymus didn't really remember much about the asylum. It had in fact been rather like the order. With one exception. There was more talk. More talk than any man could bear. Every way he faced, there was somebody waiting there to ask him about his mother.

"How long has she been in Heaven?"

"And you've been talking with her for quite some time, you say?"

"Do you . . . ah . . . do you ever talk to God?"

"What does He say?"

"Do the three of you—God, your mom and you—ever get together for a chat?"

"What do you discuss?"

"The *world*?"

Countless numbers of white men in white clothes walking between white walls sighing white sighs and apparently never sleeping in the night. And all of them had an insatiable curios-

ity about his mother. So finally he did the obvious thing: He
pretended, in the way he knew the men in the white clothes
wanted him to pretend, and for the pretension they let him out
into the ward, then into the day room, and then out onto the
asylum grounds to take the sun where he took the director's
car instead and escaped.

Didymus sat with his legs drawn up in the window, watching the blackly smiling bitch and remembered his mother. She
was a saint. And *Didymus* was going to be a saint when it
came his time to die, but for the moment he was being kept
alive for something very, very special. His mother had told
him. She had told him everything since he had been ten. It had
been she who had sent him after the Gospel Singer.

He had been sleeping in the Holy Light Christian Mission in
Redwood City, California, dreaming among the drunks in the
heavy wine air, when she had appeared to him as she always
did, kneeling, her hemorrhaging mouth gushing smiles and
blood. Didymus slid obediently from his bed to the cold gritty
floor and began to pray. But it brought no release; she was still
there. The bleeding smile spread behind his tightly closed eyes
urging him on. An anxious disquiet and unhappiness filled
him. He got off his knees and rushed from the mission into the
street. It was not yet daylight. It had snowed heavily during
the night and snow was still falling. The snow caught in his
uncovered hair and eyebrows. His fingers turned blue and for
blocks he did not see a living soul.

He knew his mother had sent him for a sign. He was prepared to receive it. He walked warily on, looking to the right
and to the left, glancing now and again into the black void
above the city. He wondered vaguely whether or not he would
die of the cold for he wore only his blue businessman's suit of
thin summer cloth and the starched, warmthless clerical collar
bound about his neck. Could death be the sign? His own
death? He thought his mother might at last be sanctioning his
early departure from this world.

A truck careened around a corner and slammed to a stop in
front of him. A tarpaulin crackled in the cold air and bound
bundles of newspapers came flying out of the truckbed and

landed at his feet. The truck roared off down the street, its chained tires grinding over the freshly layered snow, and out of the shadows of a building to his right four boys muffled in caps and coats and winding scarves trotted across the white and broke the bundles, sorting and stuffing the papers into bags which they affixed to their shoulders.

"Want a paper, Mister?"

The boy that spoke to Didymus was completely covered about the face except for the mouth which issued forth from a specially prepared hole in his mask. The lips and tongue were red. Didymus took a paper for a dime. On the front page he discovered the sign. It was the Gospel Singer, a human interest story. There was a picture of him singing, sweating in the grand manner, before a congregation of sinners in Stillwater, Oklahoma. Reverend Bubba Plow, the famous evangelist, was in attendance. The Gospel Singer was a paid guest. But the Reverend Plow never got to speak. Bubba was a fifth wheel. And that was the human interest. Every soul present, man, woman and child, gave up to God before the Gospel Singer's fourth hymn. A mass, simultaneous conversion to the faith. It was a sign. Didymus fell to his knees in the snow and began to pray.

The bitch came closer, twisting with the snakelike movement peculiar to huge but emaciated dogs. It sat directly under him where Didymus had covered an area the size of a basketball with cigarette stubbs. Its amber eyes were wide, friendly. They never seemed to blink. Didymus had a compulsion to let himself through the window to the ground, to test his flesh in those dripping jaws. There was a time in his life when he would have done it, and even now he had to hold tightly to the window sill to keep himself from doing it. He could not afford the luxury of pain. His mother had sent him to control the Gospel Singer's soul. Penance was the only way. Which meant someone to assign penance. Someone whose mother sat on the right hand of God interpreting His Word for the world.

That was what Mr. Keene, the Gospel Singer's former business manager, had never understood. He could not understand

the necessity for penance, for the obligation to direct and control the Gospel Singer's soul, and therefore Mr. Keene could
not understand why he, Didymus, had to have Mr. Keene's job
as business manager to the Gospel Singer. The only thing to do
had been to kill him.

The Gospel Singer and Mr. Keene had been staying at the
Waldorf in New York City. Didymus had been on their trail
for months. He knew the Gospel Singer's terrible habit of in-
discriminate sexual intercourse. He also knew that the Gospel
Singer was entirely unrepentant for his sins against the female's holy temple. And, oh! how he did defile the temple! All
the while, with Mr. Keene looking the other way, ignoring it.
Didymus himself had never had a woman, his mother having
extracted a vow of perpetual chastity from him the first time
she had called him prophet in prayer. But he had trailed the
Gospel Singer, hiding in closets, under beds, and peeping
through transoms. Didymus had thought to blind himself the
first time he witnessed the bestial spectacle of the naked Gospel Singer performing with a girl of fifteen, directly after a revival meeting during which the girl had flung herself before
the Gospel Singer sobbing that she was saved and that her soul
was with God. And that was how Didymus had come to have
to kill Mr. Keene.

He had knocked softly on the door to the apartment after
first having made sure that the Gospel Singer had gone out.
Mr. Keene answered the door.

"I've come for the Gospel Singer," said Didymus.

"He ain't here," said Mr. Keene. "And who the hell are you
anyhow?"

"I'm his new business manager," said Didymus.

"Go away. We don't want any, whatever you're selling."

"You're not listening," said Didymus. "I said I was the Gospel Singer's new manager."

Mr. Keene watched him for a moment without speaking.
And then finally in the patient way one speaks to a child or a
madman, he said, "Do you want me to call the police? Is that
what you want? Do you want to spend tonight in jail?"

Didymus spoke back in the same patient voice. "Do you want to die? Is that what you want? Do you want to spend tonight in Heaven with my sainted mother?"

Mr. Keene's eyes grew big. His complexion mottled, then blanched. "Whaaaat!"

"If you don't give me the Gospel Singer, I'll chop you up and throw you in the river."

Mr. Keene leapt backward, the fat on his jowls trembling. The door slammed. Didymus heard the lock, followed by the night latch, and behind them both, Mr. Keene shouting Operator! Operator! over the banging telephone.

Didymus hurried away and returned later that night while the Gospel Singer was pleading the case for the Lord in Carnegie Hall, where Mr. Keene had booked him because as Mr. Keene said, You can save souls as well in Carnegie Hall as anywhere else and the pay is a hell of a sight better. When Didymus returned, he knocked on Mr. Keene's door again and called, "Telegram." But when the door opened, he delivered not a telegram but a blow to the head instead and carried Mr. Keene to the East River, where he tried to explain it all as he unwrapped the newspaper from the double-edged axe, *Suffering and pain is the legacy of the Lord*. Didymus had learned it as a boy, watched it in his mother's face as she died and had her confirm it every night of his dreaming life. It was right to kill Mr. Keene because it would allow Didymus to step in then and guide the Gospel Singer's soul and that was a greater good which balanced the divine scales. Besides, he was actually doing Mr. Keene a favor. Killing him insured that Mr. Keene would go to Heaven.

All victims went to Heaven. Didymus remembered clearly his intensive studies during the short while he was in the monastery, before they found him face down at the sign of his Savior quietly bleeding from cut wrists. He had especially liked the books on church history and lives of the martyrs. Did anyone doubt that every Roman lion ate a saint, that every death in the Coliseum set a soul on the streets of Heaven? And surely the lions were as much to be praised as the men and women willing to die for their beliefs because if not for the lions, what

chance for sainthood had that scum of Roman society? No
more chance than a Tifton, Georgia, tobacco farmer who had
booked God's man into Carnegie Hall. Didymus explained all
of this to Mr. Keene just before he split his head with the axe.
But, from the look on Mr. Keene's face, he never really understood it.

Certainly it was very clear to Didymus. The logic of it was
as indisputable as the ABC's, simply not the sort of thing one
argues about. He had it all from his mother. She showed him
how it was wrong to hate his father, whom he had in the pur-
plest way, until she began to talk to him in his dreams about
the mysterious ways of sainthood. Before that Didymus had
thought of leading an evil life—evil to no purpose—just so he
could go to hell and harass his father for the way he had treated
his mother and for ultimately killing her. *But he had come to
find out his father was in Heaven too!* He had awoke trembling from the revelation. His mother had carefully explained.

If evil gave the opportunity for good, it ceased to be evil; if
evil set into motion a chain of events that caused an eventual
good, larger than the original evil, then it ceased to be evil. He
had seen the logic of that at once. And from that logic he had
concluded that pain and suffering was God's greatest gift to
man. His mother, of course, had confirmed the reasoning. As
she pointed out, without suffering there can be no hope of
martyrdom. All of religious fervor should be a seeking of the
greatest discomfort, a lusting for the greatest danger to life
and limb. Go into strange lands where the people have never
heard of you and tell them things they do not want to hear and
cannot understand. If you are lucky they will kill you and eat
you. Oh! great good fortune to be stripped of flesh, cooked in
a pot, and flushed down some pagan's throat! Lucky man that
flops about being hit over the head with clubs, bashed with
bricks, and set upon by vicious dogs. That is the way to God,
righteousness and the moral life.

Didymus shivered and squirmed on his seat in the window.
The bitch grinned beneath him. The teeth rose darkly in the
black mouth. He could see the wet nostrils flare to catch his
scent. He got down and knelt on the floor, resting his elbows

on the window sill as on an altar. The sky had partially darkened.

"You want me, don't you, bitch?" he said. "Because you are teeth and I am meat." The bitch did not so much growl as it groaned. It sounded to him like the purest agony. "You want to do an evil, don't you, bitch? You're sitting there aching to take a life." His voice grew louder. "But it's not me this night. You don't get me tonight!" The dog laid back its ears and then its head. The dark mouth flashed as the clouds for a brief instant released the moon. A slow moan started in the bitch's throat and rose toward the disappearing moon. "Go on," Didymus cried. "Howl for my blood, bitch! You'll never have me tonight. You never will!" He had raised his eyes until he too was looking at the place where the moon was drowning in the sky. A long way off, thunder rolled.

CHAPTER 5

It had been an exhausting night for the Gospel Singer. It was not yet daylight. For some time he had heard thunder. He hoped that it would not rain, but the sky did not look promising. It was dark, boiling, with no star visible in it. He knew what the rain would do to Enigma. They would say he brought it. They would point to him and whisper. They would joke and laugh about it, but in their hearts they would be quietly and firmly convinced that he had made it rain. It would be just one more cross for him to stagger under until he could leave, escape from Enigma.

He moved on the bed, and the sheets adhered to his body. He felt as though he might gag on his own breathing. Everything around him—the room, the walls, the bed on which he lay—seemed unsubstantial and moving in the warm soupy air. He dreaded what faced him, and hated himself for coming here to face it. All of Enigma was out there waiting to stare at him, to touch him, and to suck consolation out of him. They would gather about his Cadillac as though it were a magical chariot that would carry them to Heaven.

And tonight there would be the revival meeting. A shiver ran in his blood and a fresh sweat popped on him. He pressed his hands over his eyes and writhed as if in pain. There would be the shouting and the clapping tonight, the hand-holding, hand-shaking, hand-about fellowshipping, the brothers and the sisters straining to give it all up to God and he, the Gospel Singer, straining to bring them there, to let them know *Him*, to be with *Him*. Oh joyful hallelujahing time! During the golden, useful, religious moment when God burst his blood and came out of his throat to establish *Himself* in the shining, sweating faces and in their hearts, the Gospel Singer found all things good and beautiful—even his voice.

Then the moment would be over and *they* would be there. Women. And women. Girls with scrubbed faces, innocent open-eyed open-hearted faces, with blond braided hair and black brushed hair and curly hair and straight hair framing their oval innocence as it stared up to him wonder-eyed telling of the mystical revealed experience of God that he had just brought them. Mothers with bodies that stood roundly and authoritatively, almost militantly, under the thin cotton prints, the great wide breasts pointing in opposite directions: a sea of female flesh, wet, violently heaving, smelling slightly of salt, surrounding him at the altar after the hymnsinging had ceased, the warm waves pressing in, eddying about him, a collective air coming off them smelling of breath and love.

Only the women came, never their men. The men, after a service, would bunch at the back of the church or tent and trickle out into the night where they would stand about smoking, glancing apprehensively now and again at the sky as though they expected the God of the Gospel Singer's hymns suddenly to reveal Himself.

But the women came and kept coming. Finally he would put out his hands that they might touch him and raise his face to the ceiling that he might escape drowning. But he had never been able to survive that sea and he felt the heavy presence of God as he sank under the first wave of flesh—not giving up but unable to save himself. His face would come down among the women, his eyes red, almost weeping, outraged as he was by the black villainous part of himself that would rise up even on the altar of a church. And the women, seeing the beautiful contorted face, the saddened inflamed eyes, mistook his lust for a religious ecstasy and a gentle, collective relaxing engulfed them as they yielded toward him, all their defenses down before God. And it was there, in that vulnerable moment, that he chose the woman he would have. He might take her in any number of places—back of the church, in her apartment, in a hotel, even in the back seat of the Cadillac with Didymus roaring down the highway at one hundred twenty miles per hour shouting over his shoulder that God did not love fornicators.

The Gospel Singer rolled onto his stomach and looked out the window. A tree of lightning stood briefly in the sky. He hid his face in the sweating corner of his arm. Soon the long, insufferably hot day in Enigma would begin and he had to walk through it exhausted. His flesh cleaved to his bones like a weight.

It had been a terrible night, starting while he was in the closet on his last *Rock of Ages*. A sound, long and drawn like singing, came to him from outside. It was distracting because from a distance it seemed just about the volume and pitch of his own voice. Without stopping to listen, he decided that it was one of the dogs howling. He clenched his fists and tried to concentrate, determined to get through the hymn, determined not to miss a word, but the longer the dog followed him up and down, rising in pitch and dropping, the more it seemed that he, himself, was howling instead of singing. Finally he could not hear the words and no matter how hard he tried he could not convince himself that he was really singing.

When the dog quit, he quit, not sure whether he had completed his penance or not. His knees were numb to the thigh. His back ached and his mouth tasted of grit. He struggled out of the closet to his bed where he fell face down in the covers. The dog had ruined it for him. He was not relaxed at all. The hymn and the voice—the sweet flowing curse of his life— usually revolted him in the final minutes before the penance was over. Being shut up with the sound of his voice was like being chastised with a switch. If all went well, he was purged, relieved of the responsibility of his actions. But the dog had ruined it, and consequently he could not sleep. He had come to depend upon Didymus' penance like a drug. That was the main reason he had never missed Mr. Keene. Didymus knew how to let a man sleep.

MaryBell. She moved in his mind like a shadow. He was glad she was dead. No, *glad* was the wrong word; he was relieved she was dead. But was not that much the same as being

glad she was dead? He knew it was and he thought about getting up to sing another *Rock of Ages*, but he felt he did not
have the strength to drag himself back into the closet, much
less sing. He made himself breathe slowly in and out. Regularly. In and out. He must sleep if he were to forget tomorrow
and at the same time strengthen himself for it. The dog was
howling again. He thought he heard someone shouting. It was
probably his father giving the dog hell for waking him up.

Gradually in his swimming, sleep-ridden mind, the howling
subsided and he was deeply asleep—and aware in the same instant that he was waking up. There was someone beside his
bed. The moon was gone from the room and he could only
vaguely discern a form beside him in the darkness. Whoever it
was knelt by the bed. A warm smooth hand covered his.

"Is my baby asleep?" It was his mother.

"What is it, Ma?" He struggled to make his eyes focus, to
come fully awake, but he swam dizzily on the surface of sleep,
feeling in a kind of panic that something was wrong, and at
the same time unable to make any response.

"I come in to talk to my baby."

"I . . . let me . . ." He made a gesture to rise, not really feeling he'd be able to do it or even that he wanted to, but she
moved her hand and pushed him down, half-cradling his head
in her arm. He could smell her hair and her great warm body
and he remembered the time, as though it were yesterday or
maybe right now, when he sat in her lap, the time when he was
not the Gospel Singer, but only a small boy who sat in her lap
and was glad to do it because there he was safe and loved.
"Hush," she was saying. "You hush now." Her breathing became his breathing and then she was talking again. "Come
home, son. Come back home and be my baby again. Give up
the gospels."

He turned his head in her arms. In the dark her eyes were
black holes that blinked. Had he heard her right? Could she,
who had always so loved his singing, be asking him to stop?

"I don't want you to never go away again," she said. "You
got to quit singin."

"Quit singin, Ma?" he said. "You don't want me to do that."

"I got a bad feelin about it. Everthin is getting too big and complicated. They all want too much."

"What is it *you* want?" he asked.

"Evertime you go away it gits a little longer before you come home again."

"Ma, I know that. But don't think I don't miss you—all of you. The United States is a big place though, and I'm a singer—a worker in the vineyard as the song says, and the vineyard, well it's so big I caint hardly git through it."

"I know what the song says. I ain't talkin about the vine-yard either. I'm talkin about Enigmer and you. I want you to come back to Enigmer and forget all that and be with *us*. We need you. Your daddy needs you. That money you send don't help none. Not in a real way, it don't. Your daddy's here on this pig farm with Gerd and Mirst. You think about that: one of them playin a guitar all the time and the other lyin in a hammock healin."

"But you could hire somebody," said the Gospel Singer. "I sent you enough money to . . ."

"No-count workers in Enigmer. Don't want nobody. Your daddy wants what's his."

"You know I want him to have . . ."

"We got some rights. It taken just as much pain to bring you into the world as ever it did Mirst or Gerd or Avel or the little one that died."

"You hurt me, Ma. Didn't I build this house and send you money for a truck? That counts for something."

She touched his forehead with her flat warm palm. "They ain't none of it *you*. We don't need no new truck in Enigmer. They ain't nobody else got one. I think them boys broke it apurpose to keep from havin to ride in it. And your daddy is the first I ever did hear tell of to bring hogs in the house. I still ain't sure how come he done it, and he don't know either. But he likes to bring folks from town out to see the pigs where they are in the back room and when they say somethin about they bein pigs in a beautiful house like this he says we weren't usin the room nohow which is the truth shore, but it's a spittin poor reason to put pigs in it too."

The Gospel Singer partially turned his face from her. "I done the best I could."

"I know you have, son."

"It don't seem right not to sing gospels if you a gospel singer."

"I know it don't," she said.

"Singin come early to me," he said. "I know a sight more about it than I do pig farmin."

"I think on that more than some," she said. "I got a feelin in me that turns me cold as ice. They got to be something wrong. You never known your Uncle Felix Ballard, but he had a voice so pure and sweet that the birds come to listen. When he started singin it was like some sweet-smellin thing opened in your heart. Women cried and men shook hands with blood enemies."

"They say I got his voice," said the Gospel Singer. "Say even that we favor some."

"Except his hair was black as a crow and full of Rose Pomade. But they was somethin else too. Your Uncle Felix would sing his heart out all night long, and you know what he'd git? A sack of peas or some chickens or maybe fifty cent to buy him some of that Rose Pomade when he went to Tifton. He'd come ridin his mule home with two chickens tied foot to foot and slung on the knob of his saddle, still singin. You could hear him up the Harrikin half a mile."

"Folks told me about him all my life," said the Gospel Singer. "Said I was just like him."

"Then, son, how come they pay you so much money? I never said nothin about it but right from the first I misdoubted all that money. And it's worse now than it ever was. They just keep bein more and more money."

"Ma, that's the way they do it. You caint expect a TeeVee studio to pay me off in a sack of peas and a couple of chickens."

"You dast make fun of me? That ain't what I'm talkin about. How come they so much money? How come even when you ain't on the TeeVee, they is still so much money? What is it they payin for?"

"They payin me for what I do," he said. "I sing gospel."

"I misdoubt it," she said. "You singin nothin but hymns and the bank pressident hisself come from Tifton with a check for four thousand dollars."

"You said you needed a truck. I got money in the Tifton Bank so I wrote them to bring you a check. They don't give trucks away you know. You have to pay."

"I didn't raise you to talk to your ma like that." She rose heavily to her feet. "And I still don't know what they payin you for. All I know is I feel like no good can come out of it." He followed her sound to the door. There it stopped. The door did not open. He waited.

"It ain't no way to tell you," she finally said. "But I want to anyway, how sorry I am bout MaryBell."

The Gospel Singer kept very still. Even the mention of her name struck a note of fear in him, a fear that was, he told himself, groundless. She was dead, and death, after all, was the end. He was through with all that.

"I'm sorry you didn't git the wire and had to come home and find out like this," she said.

He made a strangled noise in his throat.

"I know, I know, son. Me'n Mizz Carter's talked about it more'n some. The double tragedy, you and MaryBell. And you havin to find it out by just ridin into it this way."

"It's all right, Ma." He wanted her to leave.

"She wants you to sing over MaryBell, son. You ought to git by there tomorrow too. I guess they'll bare the poor thing Sunday."

The Gospel Singer opened his eyes. "She wants me to sing over her *before* the funeral?"

"At the funeral parlor," she said.

He propped himself out of the bed on his elbow. "How come she's in the funeral parlor? How come MaryBell ain't home?"

"Mizz Carter thought it was the fitten place for her. Had the poor thing embalmed and everthin so they could keep her out until you got here. Everbody in Enigmer said the funeral parlor was the place for her, to honor the poor thing, don't you know. After all, she was *your* girl. Being in the funeral parlor that way everbody could go by and pay last respects to the only girl you ever had."

The Gospel Singer fell back into the bed.

"I wish they was somethin I could do," she said. "But they ain't. I guess I'll go on to bed."

"Yes, Ma. All right."

The door opened but then closed too quickly. The Gospel Singer looked out of the covers but he could not see her standing against the dark wall. There was a long drawn moment in which he heard her breathing.

"Son," she said. "They's somethin I got to ask you. It's been on my mind until I've got to know."

He did not ask her what it was, because he was afraid it was about MaryBell.

"Son, can you heal?"

"What! Can I what?"

"Heal. Can you make a man whole?"

"No," he said.

"They say you can."

"I know what they say. It ain't true."

"A man come to Enigmer not long ago," said his mother. "Said he heard you in Atlanta. Said he heard God in your voice."

"He heard me sing. He didn't hear God."

"They say they hear God in your voice."

"Yes, I know. I know that."

"I read about the meetin you had in Cincinnati," she said. "I read it in the *Tifton Banner*. Everybody in Enigmer read it. It said a man got out of a wheelchair; it said a blind man took the pulpit and read from the *Bible*."

The Gospel Singer was not sure now whether it was her breathing or his own that he heard.

"Did that happen, son?"

"I don't know anything about it," said the Gospel Singer. "I didn't have anything to do with it. I was singin and when I finished, it happened. But it wasn't me. They hired me, I sung gospel. They paid me, I left."

"It scares me," said his mother. "It ought to make me happy

but it scares me. You reckon that's how come they give you so much money?"

"All I know is I'm a singer and that's all I am."

"Do you like to sing?"

"Sometimes I do."

"I caint remember ever hearin you sing when you out by yourself or just walkin around the house. Not even hummin. Uncle Felix Ballard use to git up singin ever mornin, and most any time you seen him, he'd be goin after a little snatch of song."

The door opened and closed and she was gone.

And me, he thought, any time you see me I'm going after a little snatch, period. Was that the difference between him and Uncle Felix? He knew it was not. When he was younger, just beginning to get his voice, he had heard some of the sly stories told on Uncle Felix. A man did not load his hair down with Rose Pomade for nothing. No, the difference between him and Felix Ballard lay in what the Gospel Singer had *never* heard about him. The Gospel Singer had never heard of his Uncle Felix making a convert. And apparently as he had grown older and stopped wearing Rose Pomade in his hair, he had really tried, too. Uncle Felix had even taken to preaching a little bit. And at the end of the sermon he would sing *Sinners Come Home*. But none had come.

But they had come for the Gospel Singer and kept coming. It seemed a fact of the world that the Gospel Singer could save a soul. No matter how hard he argued against it, sinners at every turn accepted God on the strength of his voice. All his troubles, he told himself, stemmed from that. Because it was true, people began insisting he was something he was not; because it was true, people began insisting that he could do other things he could not. He was not willing to give up singing gospels because singing was what had allowed him to escape Enigma and live as he pleased. But neither was he willing to stop living as he pleased just because the songs he sang, in some mysterious way he had never understood, saved souls.

He had made his first convert when he was twenty years old. He had not been trying to do it; it had just happened. He had

already sung on the television in Albany, Georgia, and been
one of the main attractions at several of the all-night sings in
Tallahassee, Florida. He had found the full range of his voice
and had been told by one of the older gospel singers at a camp
meeting that he showed real promise as an actor. It was on a
lovely Sunday evening in the spring of the year that it happened.

He was leaving early the next day for his first trip to Atlanta
with Mr. Keene who had taken a special interest in him and
consented to become his manager for forty percent of the prof-
its, and the Gospel Singer was very excited because he had
never taken a train trip before. Perhaps it was the thought of
the train ride or the fact that he had just bought a new suit (his
third, being as his father told him, more suits than any man in
Enigma would normally own during the course of his entire
life) or it might just have been the prospect of getting out of
Enigma again which, there can be no denying, sweetened his
life and cheered his soul, but whatever it was when he rose in
Big Harrikin Swamp First Primitive that evening he let a
unique thing into the church. It was not the voice alone, nor its
range or its volume or its grace. Rather, it was *all* of him: his
body, his enthusiasm and his voice acting together to give a
single unified impression that seemed to touch all the senses at
once. They in the church felt him not only in their eyes and
ears but they thought they could feel him in their fingers too,
on their hands and arms, warmth, as though from an open
fire. And there was a sweetness on the tongue, permeating
their mouths and throats, rather like the smell of honeysuckle
which is never only smell but also taste.

He sang only one song: *This World Is Not My Home.*

When he finished there was a stillness in the church, an ab-
sence of breathing. And into the silence there gradually came a
sound, softly at first like someone trying to cough quietly, then
louder and it was weeping. No one wanted to look, embarrassed as they were because they already knew that it was God
come into a heart right there in their Enigma Church, but they
all did look sooner or later, out of the corners of their eyes or
from under bonnets, and she was sitting on the end of a bench

next to an aisle, her head inclined, her pale skin flushed, her magnificent, virginal seventeen-year-old body pulsing as she sobbed, making every man in the church aware of the inadequacy of his soul the moment he looked at her, causing every man to sin instantaneously by lusting after the flesh of the convert while he sat in God's House watching the miracle of salvation.

MaryBell Carter rose from her seat and stepped into the aisle. She stood still and looked down the length of the church where the Gospel Singer had not moved since the hymn ended. He had seen saved people before. He knew the signs. And there was no doubt about it; she was saved. Her eyes shined. A beatific light flooded her face. Her mouth unpainted but red and wet as crushed cherries, hung slightly open. He could see her tongue moving now and again behind, over, her lips as though she were trying to say something but could not because what she knew was beyond words. He stood stock still, astonished that she had risen from the congregation saved and born again before the preacher had given the first line of the sermon. He watched her as she began to move toward him. And she was half to him before the full weight of what had happened fell upon him.

He had saved her! He shrank before the realization. He even staggered a step backward, putting out his hand, afraid he would fall. He couldn't possibly have saved her! He hadn't wanted to save her! Yet here she came toward him with a light in her face that he had clearly given her. And he simply could not believe it because while he had been singing he hadn't been listening to the words or thinking about the church or the congregation, and certainly he had not been dwelling on God or the prospect of saving anybody's soul. He had sung the hymn enough times that all he had to do was open his mouth and get it started and it took care of itself. He had in fact been thinking about a steak—red, thick as his wrist—and a pan of biscuits. Good steak could not be bought in Enigma and Mr. Keene had promised him the best bed in the best hotel in Atlanta and a steak besides if he would go up to Atlanta and audition for a television studio.

He could do nothing but watch her come toward him. Somebody in the church quietly said Amen. Someone else said it louder. And she was in front of him. She dropped to her knees and took his hand and kissed it. She was weeping. The preacher came forward and put his hand on her head and started to pray. She ignored him, staring as she was at the Gospel Singer. She crawled closer to him. One of her hands touched his leg. It was all doubly embarrassing for him because MaryBell was not only his friend and childhood playmate, but she was also his sweetheart.

"I seen the Lord," she said, still staring up at him. The Gospel Singer did not answer and he would not meet her eyes. "Glory Hallelujah," said somebody in the congregation, then "Amen, Amen." She suddenly gave a loud gasping sob and lunged for him, embracing his knees, jerking her head from the preacher's hand and burying her face in his legs.

The Gospel Singer sat up on the edge of the bed. He felt a momentary sadness, melancholy, as he thought of her dead now, lying this instant in Enigma Funeral Parlor. He knew finally that he had never loved her, but God knows she was good in bed.

He went to the window and looked out. The outbuildings, the small field of cleared ground, and the swamp beyond, swirled in a misting rain. But it would not keep them from coming; it would only make them come in greater numbers. There were already several wagons pulled up in the field, the mules taken out and hobbled. Occasionally he would hear a car horn or a motor. The lane in front of the house would be filled with the people of Enigma. There would be some there from Tifton or Albany too and some from as far away as Savannah. But mostly it would be the worst of his own people: the sick, the blind, the halt. And over in town the crowds would be coming in now, pouring into town in cars, in trucks, in touring buses organized by professional agents bringing people to hear him sing tonight and witness miracles from the hand of God. It was all so tiring. He sighed and pressed his temples with his hands. He was exhausted before it even started. He turned and his gaze fell upon Mirst's guitar. It was in the corner, slung from the back of a rocking chair by its red strap. He had no idea what time Avel and Mirst had come to see him during the night. But it was late, after his mother had left. He had been awakened with Mirst strumming in one ear and Avel humming in the other. It was not loud, but it was not music either. It came across his teeth like fingernails over slate-board.

"Please," said the Gospel Singer. "Please."

"It's a million dollars waiting on TeeVee for anybody what can play one of these things," said Mirst.

"We want you to see a little thing we worked up," said Avel, the dark hiding her bad teeth, her beautifully shaped mouth working just above his eyes.

The Gospel Singer put one hand across his face and with the other waved them away. "Don't show me. Take it to Didymus. He's the manager. He knows about radio and TeeVee and things."

Mirst took a vicious swipe at the guitar. It sounded as though he might have punched it with his fist. "Whatta we want to show him for? Who is Didymus? Ittas you makin money faster than a man can count. If you say O.K., ittas O.K. Who *is* Didymus anyway?"

"If you kindly set up there and lean back agin the head-board, why, it won't take but a minute," Avel said.

The Gospel Singer groaned and raised himself out of the bed. "O.K.," he said. "But hurry. Just hurry."

"Why, shore, brother," Mirst said.

Mirst came uncoiled like a spring, whipping the guitar with one hand, and urging his sister on with shouts of, "Git it down deep," and "Shake that thing! You better shake that *thing!*"

For Avel's part she stopped at the foot of the bed, faced the Gospel Singer, laced her hands behind her head, and with her feet anchored in one spot, moved all over. Her elbows and hips jerked forward forming her body in a bow. She grunted. Mirst shouted. Suddenly right in the middle of it she began to sing a song about a high school boy that looked in through the window one night and saw his grade school sweetheart kissing his best friend and he fell in the grass and cried like a dog because life was just passing him by.

But mostly she danced. Up and down the room, around his bed and back again. She whirled and grunted and sprang into the air, did deep-knee bends, flapped her arms, stretched her neck like a rooster, rolled her eyes, stuck out her tongue, then pulled it back and looked disinterested. All the time her hips were going ninety to the minute.

He was intensely glad when it was over. They both hung breathless at the foot of his bed waiting for him to speak. Their faces were flushed. They were both smiling widely.

"Well?" demanded Mirst.

"That was . . ." began the Gospel Singer. "It was different. That's what it was, different."

Their faces fell. "Different!" they cried. "That's no good," said Avel. "That's just awful. It caint be *different*. It's got to be just like theym othern. Theym on the TeeVee."

Mirst shook his head sadly. "She's been practicin weeks and weeks watchin theym gals git it on the TeeVee. Seem to me like she had it down purty good."

"I meant it looked better," the Gospel Singer said. "She was doin what the othern were doin so much better than they was that I thought it was different."

"We don't want to be bettern nobody," Mirst said. "All we want to be is famous and make a million dollars." He turned to his sister. "Avel, you been practicin too hard. You got to cut it down a shade and shake that thing like theym that shake that thing on the TeeVee."

"Do you think if I was to take in my natural talent a stitch, we could make it in the innertainment world?" asked Avel, looking contrite.

"Well," said the Gospel Singer. "I . . ."

"Sumpin like this I mean," said Avel.

Mirst struck the guitar with both hands and Avel started again, but this time she left off the embellishments. She didn't pump up and down doing knee bends or flap her arms or contort her face. All that was left of the dance was the hunch. She swayed slowly from side to side, but while she swayed her hips stroked forward with uncommon power and speed.

"That looks good," Mirst cried. "Now you gitten it. SHAKE THAT THING!"

When she had finished she asked, gasping, "Is that what *you* had in mind?"

The Gospel Singer flopped back on the bed. "I guess it is," he said softly. "Now you can show it to Didymus. He knows about the TeeVee."

"You hear that," said Mirst punching Avel in the side. "He thinks you do it good."

"Maybe we ought to show it to Mr. Didymus, too," said Avel. Her back was to the Gospel Singer as she talked to Mirst. It was as though now that they had his assurance, the Gospel Singer had disappeared.

"Why show it to him for?"

"Cause he knows how to git us on the damn thing," she said. "It's one thing to be able to do it, it's another thing to be able to do it where folks can see it. They don't give you no million dollars for doin it behind the door. You got to be right out there with the light on you."

They had been moving away from the bed. Mirst turned just as Avel was reaching for the door. "If it's all the same to you," he said, looking back at the Gospel Singer. "I'll leave this geetar in here with you tonight." He slung the red strap over the rocking chair in the corner.

The Gospel Singer was dressing quickly, trying not to think of the rain, or the people in the lane, or the revival that was waiting for him. The dining room was filled when he got there. Besides Mirst and Avel and his father and Didymus, all of whom sat around the table, and his mother, who moved between the table and the stove, there were four men sitting in chairs drying out in a line in front of the stove. Two of them were blind and all four of them were very old. One of them coughed in a slow, steady, quiet way into a soiled handkerchief. As the Gospel Singer walked around to his place at the table, the four faces in front of the stove followed him. The two blind ones smiled shyly, simultaneously as they listened to the sound of his feet enter the room, the scraping chair; then they stared at the quiet place they knew was he.

"I got your food all ready," said his mother.

She put a plate of ham and eggs in front of him. He looked directly into the four still faces by the stove. He saw that one of them had a leg that stopped at the knee. He was careful not to look too closely at the others.

"I ain't very hungry," he said.

"Try to take a little somethin," she said. "They's lots of people in the lane, more'n I can remember bein before."

"Must be the rain," said Mirst, stabbing a biscuit with his fork.

"Shut you mouth," said his father. "You the talkinest human being I ever seen." He turned to the Gospel Singer. "Son, you remember Uncle Ned Thurston, don't you?"

The Gospel Singer, in a reflex gesture that was too quick to stop, looked in the direction his father was pointing. A pile of wet clothes and old shoes moved on the floor at the back of the stove. A face appeared in the gradual unfolding. There was a sore where the nose should have been. The rheumy eyes blinked. A thin hand lifted.

The Gospel Singer pushed his plate away. "Yes," he said. "Sure, I remember." He tried to smile.

"You taken Mr. Didymus' eatin habits," said his mother.

Didymus pushed his plate away. He had eaten half a spoon of grits and was now sipping warm water from a coffee mug. "The body is a mirror of the soul," he said. "A man that fattens himself tempts ruination."

"And a man that ain't eatin caint be a man that's workin," said his father.

"There's work and there's work," said Didymus. "My work is souls."

"Mine's pigs," said his father.

"Didn't Gerd come home last night?" the Gospel Singer asked.

"No, and it ain't like him," said his father. "He don't usually like to git too far from the table and a place to lie down. If

he ain't to home by dinnertime, I'll put Mirst on a mule to go
lookin for him."

"Don't want to ride no mule," Mirst said sullenly. "Ain't
seemly for a rock 'n' roll singer to be on no mule."

"Then you can walk," his father said, "No mule of mine'd
want a rock 'n' roll singer on him anyhow."

"Caint you take the new truck?" asked the Gospel Singer.
"Is it torn up so bad it won't run?"

"Burned out," said his father. "That rock 'n' roll singer put
water in the crankcase and oil in the radiator and drove it to
Albany. Or as far as it'd go which wasn't very far."

Mirst looked at the Gospel Singer. His voice was apologetic.
"Me'n Avel got a chanct to try out for a TeeVee studio. Gerd
went with us. We was so excited I couldn't hardly get my
breath and somehow we done what Pa said. Coulda happened
to anybody about to sing on a TeeVee. I done the best I could.
I tried."

"Tryin ain't worth nothin. As my daddy used to say: try in
one hand and shit in the othern and see which fills up first."

"Pa!" said his wife. "You stop sich talk. What'll Mr. Didymus think?"

"He's at my table, I ain't at his." He got up and left the room.

"What ails Pa?" asked the Gospel Singer.

"He ain't been hisself lately," said his mother. "He worries
about you boys, about that geetar of Mirst's and . . ."

"I bet he wouldn't worry about no million dollars if my
geetar made that," said Mirst.

". . . and Gerd lyin around bein eat up by the sun, and you
away from home all the time among strangers."

His mother went to the stove and poured a cup of coffee,
put sugar and cream in it and gave it to Uncle Ned Thurston.
The Gospel Singer tried his best not to watch him drink it. His
mother came back and sat beside him.

"Son," she said. "I know you must be grievin over Mary-
Bell. Ittas most terrible."

The sore nearly touched the coffee when Uncle Ned drank
from the cup. The Gospel Singer cut his eyes down to his plate

in which the grits were cooling in a stiffening puddle of egg yolk.

His father had come stamping into the kitchen and sat in a chair in a corner diagonally across the kitchen facing the Gospel Singer. "It's rainin harder," he said. His face was flushed and he was agitated. He crossed and uncrossed his legs. He was staring straight at his son, his eyes bright and hard. The Gospel Singer knew the rain had affected him, perhaps even scared him. In his father's mind, just as it was in every mind in Enigma, the Gospel Singer had brought the rain. And that was good, but it was also frightening and unnatural, because a man that can bring you the rain can also take it away from you. It would do no good for the Gospel Singer to deny it. As a matter of fact his father would have been shocked if the Gospel Singer had said, "I didn't bring the rain," because said aloud it was obviously a stupid and unlikely possibility. Therefore nobody said it; nobody in Enigma would say it either, except in a joking, offhanded way, but that didn't keep everyone from knowing it and believing it. And so his father sat staring at him, a benevolent aberration, a frightening possibility for good that he had brought into the world and raised and loved but could not understand, and had now lost to the world.

His mother lifted a large wooden tray, some two feet in length. On the tray sat an iron pot with four or five tin cups beside it and an open bowl of sugar. "I thought I'd take a swaller of coffee to them folks on the porch and out in the lane."

She left with the pot and directly came back. The Gospel Singer had managed to eat a little biscuit and syrup.

"Son, ittas awful bad weather out there. They said did you reckon you could step on out to talk?"

"Sure, Ma," he said. "You tell them I'd be proud to step out there."

It was this time that he dreaded most. Sometimes word did not get out that he was home and nobody knew he was back until he stepped out of his Cadillac in Enigma. But even then it was the same. Slowly, out of the houses and stores, from both ends of the street, there slowly emerged those that were helpless, maimed and blinded. They would come to him there in the street and draw some curious, inexplicable solace from him. All he knew was that it bothered him dreadfully. He pushed back from the table and went down the hall. Didymus was at his elbow.

"That brother and sister of yours will make five million on TeeVee and personal appearances next year," Didymus said.

"But they're so awful," said the Gospel Singer.

"Maybe ten million," said Didymus.

He was at the door. He took a deep breath as though about to plunge into the sea and opened the door and stepped out onto the porch. There were perhaps twenty cars and trucks, ancient, some fenderless or without windshields, pulled up in the lane. Five wagons were bunched around the scrub oak to the right of the house. More wagons were in the field. Several people were on the porch but most of them were in the cars and cabs of the trucks or sitting on pallets under the wagons. Two or three people on the porch called his name. He did not answer but only smiled and waved his hand in their direction. The doors of the cars and trucks were beginning to open. A dog fight broke out suddenly at the end of the porch, the vicious snap and slash of jaws breaking over the quiet fall of the rain, and just as suddenly, stopped.

He stood on the porch and watched them coming out of the cars and trucks and from under the wagons.

After he had converted MaryBell, Mr. Keene had rushed forward and grasped him about the arm and shoulders and furiously whispered in his ear that he would go far, to the top of the gospel-singing business, that any man who could do what he had just done deserved the best of this world and he would get it. And so he had. The best beds in the best hotels serving the best food and women. But what was that beside having to face these poor maimed people whom he could not help, but who would not believe it even if he told them, and insisted upon the right to touch him and love him?

He sat in a rocker at the top of the steps. Didymus first put his elbows on the back of the rocker and leaned over the Gospel Singer's shoulder until the Gospel Singer told him to move, to get back. Didymus squatted to the right of and behind the rocking chair. The Gospel Singer did not want Didymus, who was unforgiving and insistent that every man should embrace pain and affliction as the kiss of God, listening to people who, while they might have said much the same thing as Didymus, only wanted relief.

The woman in front of him, the first one to reach the place where he sat, was old, toothless, her face inverted upon itself in numberless wrinkles. Her dress hung straight and gray over her fleshless, angular body. There were no socks inside the man's brogan shoes she wore. The heel was missing from one of them, giving her a slow, swaying limp when she walked.

"We glad you're home," she said.

"Thank you, Granny," he said. He could remember her looking the same as she did now when he was a boy. He had called her Granny then too. "I'm glad I am too."

"They ain't nothin like a coolin rain in a summer drought," she said.

"It does cool a body," he said.

"It's been now two months and more since it rained," she said. "I'm gone be there to hear you tonight. I been feelin most poorly ever since I broke my hip in the fall. Ain't even so much as been out of the house more'n a day or two since it happened but when I looked up and seen it rainin this mornin and they told me you'd come in the night, I said to myself that I was goin to hear you iffn it broke the other hip."

She had reached out as though to brush a piece of lint from his shirt but she had in fact only touched the cuff of his sleeve with her finger, softly, secretively, as an embarrassed maid might take the hand of her best beau.

"Granny," he said. "I'm as glad for it to rain as you are, but that's a mighty poor reason to come to the meetin. I just sing songs, you know, I ain't no weatherman."

She was turning to let the next person up to him, her face in profile, the long swelling nose hooking toward the chin, curving under a sunken mouth. She looked at him slyly out of the corner of her eye. "Sho now, that's what you do!" Then she winked.

She was followed by an old man wearing khaki pants and an undershirt stained almost the color of his body, with a stubble of gray beard about his face. Behind him the people were lined back from the house and around the single stunted cypress growing in the lane. The old man had a boy with him. The boy was in a wheelchair. He was wearing short pants and his legs were thin and white and slightly bent inward at the ankles. The boy's head was not steady. It was as though he were trying to keep it balanced up there on his neck and every now and then it would get away from him and flop to one side or forward. The wheelchair was old and rust grew through its chrome skin like fungus. It squeaked even when it was stopped, slipping first to the left and then to the right, a kind of counterpoint, it seemed, to the attitude of the boy's head. The padding had worn away from the seat of the chair and a croker sack was spread there for the boy to sit upon.

The door slammed behind the Gospel Singer and Mirst and Avel came out and sat on the edge of the porch with their legs hanging off. Mirst had retrieved his guitar from the Gospel Singer's bedroom. It was slung now about his shoulders by the red strap. He sucked his teeth and flipped a toothpick expertly from one corner of his mouth to the other. "Nice little crowd," he said.

The boy's eyes were steady, but unfocused, and the color of cornflower. They looked directly into the Gospel Singer's. The boy smiled and saliva slipped from his mouth. The old man bent with an automatic gesture and patiently wiped the front of the boy's shirt with a rag that he pulled out of his back pocket.

"I don't believe I know you, sir," said the Gospel Singer, looking at the old man to keep from having to look at the boy.

"We're from Adel," he said. "Me'n the boy been in Enigmer most a week waitin for you to come in."

"I'm sorry I was late," said the Gospel Singer.

"It ain't no matter," he said. "You here now. And I brung this boy all the way from Adel to see you. I'm his granddaddy. His daddy's dead and his ma couldn't come on account of she's married again and down in the bed sick with milk leg. So I brung him myself."

"I'm glad to see him," said the Gospel Singer. "What's his name?"

The old man leaned down until his mouth was beside the boy's face. "Tell him you name, boy," he said. The boy's head lost its balance and flopped over. His granddaddy was right after him saying gently, patiently, "Tell him you name. Say you name, NAME, NAME! Say it to the Gospel Singer."

The boy's mouth opened. His clouded, cornflower eyes squinted. His brow furrowed. A large red tongue rose and worked at random in his mouth. And a sound abrupt, hollow, but in two parts came forth. He smiled widely and the old man smiled with him. "Freddy, his name is Freddy," he said. "Fred-dy. You got to listen real close to git it."

Mirst leaned back and looked at the Gospel Singer. "You spose these folks'd like to hear me and Avel do a little number while they wait to sorta pass the time?"

"No," said the Gospel Singer.

But he spoke so softly that Mirst asked him again, and Didymus, sitting behind the Gospel Singer on the floor writing frantically in his *Dream Book*, told him to shut up.

"What you writin in that book?" asked Mirst.

"Shut up," said Didymus. "I've got to get this down."

"We gone be at the revival tonight," said the old man.

"I'm glad you can come," said the Gospel Singer. "Preacher Woody Pea is one of the best."

"Ain't no use to do a number for a audience like this no how," said Avel. "Half's blind and the other half caint hear."

"Between my playin and your dancin," said Mirst, "all of theym'd git somethin. A artist needs to practice as much as he can." He turned one of the strings down tighter and tested it with his thumb, then loosened it.

The old man went on, "I seen a man on the television— Freddy's ma is got a television cause her new husband works in the Sears in Albany—and I seen this man on the television that could make a blind man see or a cripple man walk. Just grab you by the head and send the power of God right through you."

The Gospel Singer stared back at the old man and did not

speak. Didymus, dabbing the pencil to his tongue, wrote rapidly.

The old man patted Freddy on the shoulder. "This right here is the last one of us. I ain't got no brothers and Freddy is the only child my boy had before the good Lord called him home, hit him in the field with a stroke of lightnin." He reached down and wiped Freddy's mouth with the rag. "That feller I seen on the television was way yonder sommers and he ain't never gone come to Adel, much less Enigmer, I know. But I heard him sing and he don't have near the voice you do."

"Didymus," said the Gospel Singer. "Write him out a check for a new wheelchair."

The old man's yellow face turned a shade darker. "Don't want no wheelchair. Freddy and me's comin to the meetin tonight."

Didymus handed the check up to the Gospel Singer. He tore it in two. "Write a bigger one, wheelchairs cost a lot."

"We don't want no money," said the old man. "We gone be at the . . ."

The old man left off because he heard what everybody else heard and turned as they did to watch a long black Cadillac, almost identical to the Gospel Singer's, emerge from the rutted road leading out of the pine and gallberry into the lane. It came slowly on up to the very front of the house. The hobbled mules turned their hindquarters to it and looked back over their shoulders with raised ears. A girl was driving, a young girl with bright red hair. Gerd sat beside her. His eyes were dark under his white hair and against the pallor of his face. The Gospel Singer had thought there were only the two of them, Gerd and the girl, in the car and then behind the sweeping windshield wipers he caught sight of a third head, an extraordinarily large head. The hair on the head was long and black and the eyes were protuberant.

The motor of the car was never shut off while Gerd opened the door and awkwardly got out into the rain and leaned forward between two crutches. His right leg dangled behind him, covered to the knee in a thick white cast.

The Gospel Singer's gaze had locked with that of the girl in the Cadillac. Her mouth was wide and heavy and well-made. Slowly, still looking at him, she smiled. Her teeth were small, slightly pointed and white.

"Why, he's been hurt," Avel said, getting to her feet.

She and Mirst rushed out to where Gerd stood leaning on his crutches. The Gospel Singer came down the steps and watched while the girl turned the Cadillac around and drove it back into the road leading out to the highway.

Avel and Mirst were on one side of Gerd, and Didymus, who had simply dropped the check on Freddy's lap when the old man had refused to take it, was on the other. They all began asking at the same time what had happened to him and Gerd without answering and staring straight ahead, his teeth clamped shut, started hopping toward the house, throwing his two crutches forward and then swinging through them on his good leg.

"What happened?" cried Avel. "What*ever* happened?"

"At least let us help you," said the Gospel Singer as Gerd came swinging past him.

"Hey," said Mirst, "how'd you git in that Cadillac? Whose Cadillac is that anyhow?"

Gerd hopped on, the knot of people at the porch separating to let him pass, struggling at the steps but refusing any help from the Gospel Singer or Mirst or Avel.

The old man caught the Gospel Singer and held him fast with surprising strength. He held the check out to him. It was in two pieces. "Here," he said. "We didn't come for no money."

"You should of kept it," said the Gospel Singer. "I would of kept it if I was you."

The old man walked back to the boy in the wheelchair. Didymus had stopped beside the Gospel Singer.

"That was him, wasn't it?" said the Gospel Singer.

"Who?" asked Didymus, looking across the steps and the porch where Gerd was tilting through the door that Mirst held open.

"Foot," said the Gospel Singer. "That was Foot in that car."

"Yes."

"Who was the woman with him?"

"His girl," said Didymus.

"She a freak?"

"No."

"She was beautiful," said the Gospel Singer.

"A most handsome woman," said Didymus. "As I recall."

"Foot's a freak," said the Gospel Singer. "A deformed freak. What's that beautiful girl doing with a freak?"

Didymus looked back at him a quiet moment before answering. "She loves him," he said.

Didymus bounded up the steps to the porch and the Gospel Singer followed him slowly, looking back over his shoulder to the place where the Cadillac had disappeared into the woods.

In the living room, Gerd was sitting on the couch, his cast stuck rigidly in front of him and partially resting on a stool.

"You gone tell us what happened or you just gone set there and look like you busted a gut?" asked his father.

"Foolishness," said Gerd. "Just foolishness."

"You ain't even told your brother hello," said his mother.

Gerd had not taken his eyes off the Gospel Singer since coming into the room but now he did to look at his mother and his lips were whiter than his face. "OOOOOHHH I did too," he said. "You didn't hear me but I already told him hello."

"I didn't know what in the world had happened to you," said the Gospel Singer. "We was all worried about you last night."

"Don't worry about me," said Gerd. "I can take care of myself. And if I caint I know who can. So just don't worry about me no more."

"Mind you mouth, boy," said his father. "You brother wants to help you."

"If he helped me much more I couldn't stand it," said Gerd.

"What?" asked the Gospel Singer.

"How come you to be in a Cadillac car with a busted laig?" asked Mirst.

"It was . . . It was over yonder on the hard road. That ol truck. Runned off the road to keep from hittin a hawg."

"Shoot, that ain't very innerstin," said Mirst.

"Why we must have come right by there," said the Gospel Singer looking at Didymus. "We must of went right by where the truck is."

"Shoot, Avel," said Mirst. "Let's go back out and look at that crowd some more. That's a nice crowd. Maybe do a little number for them."

"It was more'n likely too late by the time you come by," said Gerd. "Everthin was probably already done and I was probably gone. If that feller hadn't come by to care me to Tifton to git my laig fixed I don't know what I'd a done." He was looking at the Gospel Singer. "It ain't no fun to lie around in no ditch with a busted laig. Specially when it starts to rain."

The Gospel Singer's daddy was already saying that there weren't many Cadillacs on the Enigmer road and who was it that brung him, but Mirst had lost interest. After all it wouldn't be anybody he knew.

So he led Avel back out onto the porch where he found Hiram with his blind three-year-old daughter.

"Where's the Gospel Singer?" he asked.

"He's inside with Gerd," said Avel. "You know what happened to Gerd?"

"Would you ask him to step out here, please?" asked Hiram.

"He runned off the road and broke his laig on account of a hawg," Avel said.

"Listen," said Hiram, his face flushed, anxious. "Enigmer's run over with strangers. They all congregatin at my place around MaryBell. I took a awful chance comin here in the first place, leavin nobody there to mind my place but old lady Carter who ain't looked up from MaryBell in three days and wouldn't know it if they stole the buildin from around her. Please git the Gospel Singer out here and let my little girl see him."

"Oh, he's gone come out any minute now," said Mirst. "He's just talking to Gerd. Come on, Avel, let's shake the kinks outen this ol crowd." He slammed his guitar a couple of times and leapt to his feet, shaking his hips and knees, testing his joints.

There was no line now in front of the porch. Everyone had

sought some kind of shelter to await the return of the Gospel Singer. The crooked parallel lines made by the wheels of the chair were dissolving in the sand under the misting rain. Only Hiram stood before them, ignoring the rain, holding his little girl by the hand, her eyes from under the soaked hair looking nowhere.

Mirst spread his arms and legs and punched the shining guitar that hung free about his neck. Several car and truck windows slowly wound down. Some of the younger cripples came from under the wagons. The porch was a kind of stage and the people began filling the yard in front of it again. Even the old man pushing the wheelchair appeared. Freddy smiled happily as Avel began to stamp the boards under her feet. He slobbered and the old man patiently wiped him.

Mirst had already begun chording the guitar when the Gospel Singer came back out onto the porch. Didymus was just behind him, noting something in his *Dream Book*.

"What are you doing?" demanded the Gospel Singer.

"We thought we might sing a little somethin," said Mirst.

Hiram, who had come up on the porch now, leading his blind child, took the Gospel Singer by the elbow before he could say anthing else to Mirst and turned him around. "I took a chance," he was saying, but the Gospel Singer had not seen him and was not listening anyway. A man had shoved forward out of the crowd and stood now at the very edge of the porch. He was obviously a white man, but his skin was almost black. He was so thin that it seemed his neck was growing not out of a body, but out of a stack of old clothes suspended on a string. His eyes were solid and dark with no color demarcation between pupil and iris.

"You! You Gospel Singer!" he shouted, his voice coming like old glass breaking slowly. "I come sixty mile in a drivin rain—left my tobaccer crop in the field to burn up if it wants or to drown if it wants—I come sixty mile in a drivin rain because I heared tell you was a man weren't afeared a the layin on of hands and callin on the power of God. I heared you a healer. They tellin it in the country that you a healer. You gone lay on hands tonight and call on the power of the Lord?"

The Gospel Singer took a step backward. He saw death in the man's face. The wild, desperate, reaching-after-life in the man's eyes frightened him. The Gospel Singer had never put his hands on another man in his life with the intention of healing him. He'd never once said that he could do it. But he knew that people had been saying that about him, saying that he could and did heal the sick, and make the lame walk. And here was a man standing before him whose sickness was death, whose time was upon him. It showed in his dark colorless eyes and skin. The odor of it hung about him as distinct as smoke.

"So if you'd just kneel down," said Hiram, hanging onto his arm.

The Gospel Singer turned to Didymus and said in a lowered voice, "The Cadillac." Didymus shut his book and headed for the car. The Gospel Singer followed. He made it to the steps before he was forced to stop. Hiram was hanging onto his coat with both hands and the black-white man was below him in the yard directly in front of him.

Mirst slammed the guitar twice and Avel vibrated hugely.

"She caint feel you unless you kneel down," said Hiram, but the Gospel Singer did not answer him and continued to stare off toward the Cadillac where Didymus already sat with the motor running and the back door open. Hiram tugged again, "Just bend down a little, *kneel down.*"

"You didn't answer me," said the man, his clothes eddying emptily about his stick-like frame.

The Gospel Singer gathered his courage and looked down at him standing in the yard. "Whatever God will allow," he said, "will be done." He raised his eyes to the other maimed. "Folks," he said. "I've got to go on into Enigmer, now. Mary-Bell is there waitin. Her ma wants me to sing over her and I've got to do it. I'm sorry I ain't got to talk to all of you but there's tonight. I'll see you tonight." Without looking at Hiram, he shook him loose and went down the steps.

The black man had not moved. His face appeared to grow darker. As he passed, the Gospel Singer looked momentarily into the man's eyes, so hollow and depthless that it was like looking into a skull. The Gospel Singer, in spite of himself, broke into a run and as he did the man, as if invisibly hitched to him, broke after him. The empty clothes made a flapping noise.

The Gospel Singer turned in an act of outraged cowardice, afraid as he was that the man was going to touch him, and literally screamed in the man's face, "Get back! Don't you *dare* follow me in here!" The man stopped short. He seemed subdued, but his eyes were fixed upon the Gospel Singer. "You gone lay on hands tonight. You gone do it," he said. It was a statement, not a question.

On the porch Mirst chorded the guitar and he and Avel broke into a song about a teenage boy who rescued the corpse of his girl friend after she had been hit by a train and found his high school ring still clutched in her hand. Avel was also doing The Goat, a dance she and Mirst had made up.

"Hey!" shouted Hiram. "Hey wait!" But the Gospel Singer never stopped until he had plunged into the back seat of the Cadillac.

Behind Avel's voice, as she continued with the song, Mirst screamed hysterically: "SHAKE THAT THING! IT'S GONNA BE ARRIGHT! ARRIGHT! ARRIGHT! ARRIGHT!"

CHAPTER 6

The car rocked and careered through the dim road leading out from the farm. Bushes and the overhanging limbs of trees dragged the sides as Didymus fought to stay in the ruts, grown soft in the rain. Long sheets of clay-colored water shot out behind them.

"Where?" shouted Didymus. "Where are . . ."

"Away, away," cried the Gospel Singer. Didymus tried to say something else but the Gospel Singer shouted him down, waving his arms madly. "Drive the goddam car!"

But there were definite limits to where one could drive in Enigma. No sooner had Didymus spun out onto highway 229 at nearly fifty miles per hour and headed into town, than the Gospel Singer was screaming, "Turn around, turn around! The other way!" Didymus in a kind of inspired reflex action whirled the wheel, slamming the Cadillac across a ditch sending great spasms of water and mud flying, and was then carried back again into the road by the terrific momentum. Once the car was headed out of Enigma toward Tifton, the Gospel Singer lay back against the cushions and closed his eyes. "You can drive slower now," he said. Didymus slowed to forty. After a moment, Didymus said, "Would you like the vibrator?"

In the back seat, he stretched himself and said, "I guess."

Didymus touched a switch and the Gospel Singer swayed and trembled. "Music?" asked Didymus. When the Gospel Singer did not answer, Didymus touched another switch and made a tape selection and from ten different amplifiers situated about the car came the sound of a marching band: brassy,

with lots of drums. It was the Gospel Singer's favorite music.
After the first tape went off, Didymus tried again. "Where . . ."

The Gospel Singer waved his hand. "Out to U.S. 41," he
said. "Find me a place to eat, a restaurant or something." They
sped on to the strains of *Alexander's Ragtime Band*.

Myrtle and Bob's place was between Tifton and Cordele on
U.S. 41. It was almost hidden by trucks—flatbed and pickup—
carrying loads of all kinds: potatoes and cattle going north,
and double-stacked cars going south. It was a scarred place
with brilliant, various-colored signs stuck about over a thin,
one-storied block building advertising gas and oil and coffee
and tires and free ice water. A misting rain fell. A man in a
black slicker and rubber boots was buried to the hips in the
engine of a semi-tractor parked in front of an island of gas
pumps.

The Gospel Singer was out of the Cadillac almost before it
stopped. Didymus followed him. Inside, three tired-looking
waitresses hurried about with bored expressions on their faces
between tables of truck drivers who still wore crushed, black-
peaked caps while they wolfed their food. The faint odor of
gasoline hung over everything. A jukebox with small explo-
sions of red and green and purple lights going off in its cracked
plastic face screamed of love and dying at only sixteen. Behind the counter were stacks of doughnuts and NoDoz pills
and waxpaper-wrapped sandwiches and racks of Zippo light-
ers and postcards full of naked women and stunned-looking
Indians in full headdress wrestling alligators, and glittery
signs that said: WE DON'T PEE IN YOUR ASH TRAYS—
DON'T THROW CIGARETTE BUTTS IN OUR URINAL, and
WE DON'T ACCEPT PERSONAL CHECKS—WE STILL HAVE A
GOOD SUPPLY LEFT OVER FROM LAST YEAR.

"Yeah?" The waitress stood on one foot, her thin hip cocked
to one side, forming her body in a soiled question mark. A
kind of libidinous wax applied to her face was scaling off
around the nose and eyes. She was probably younger than
twenty.

The Gospel Singer looked up briefly, his eyes flicking lightly from the crown of her bleached, black-rooted hair to her thin, concave chest. "Grits," he said. "And ham and eggs and biscuits with lots of butter and pancakes on the side. Make the whole thing a triple order."

"To drink?"

"Milk, the biggest glass you've got."

"You?"

"A cup of warm water," Didymus said.

"We don't sell warm water, buster," she said, her caterpillar eyebrows crawling together and her jaws going into violent, hushed motion over a piece of gum.

"Coffee," said Didymus. "Black coffee then."

When the waitress had gone the Gospel Singer took a handful of coins out of his pocket and spilled them on the table in front of him. With one finger he pushed the coins about, arranging them into various patterns of pyramids, triangles, and diamonds.

"I'm starved," said the Gospel Singer. "I'm about to fall down from hunger."

Didymus lit one cigarette from another and sat staring at him. "You told them you were going to Enigma," he said. "Going to see that girl."

"So what if I did?" said the Gospel Singer. "I came to get something to eat first. Or I changed my mind. Maybe I changed my mind. Maybe I won't go to see MaryBell at all."

"You don't mean that," said Didymus.

The jukebox that had been quiet for a full minute suddenly flashed, trembled and burst into song again. Rather than try to talk over it, they waited for the food in silence. Toward the end of a three-for-a-quarter selection their waitress came back with plates and saucers and glasses balanced precariously down the length of both arms. She threw all of it onto the table in a great clatter of forks, knives and plates. The Gospel Singer rolled a pancake, and sawed it in two. It was undercooked in the center, white and stretchy, liquid rubber. He quickly slopped syrup over the whole mess and stuffed it into his mouth. "UUUmmmmm, that's good!"

"Looks dreadful," said Didymus.

"You don't have to eat, I do," said the Gospel Singer, mixing the uncooked yolks of three eggs into the grits. He leaned across the table and shouted to make himself heard. "I didn't eat anything this morning. Did you see I couldn't eat?"

Didymus leaned forward and shouted, "I saw."

The jukebox died in a crash of guitars and the Gospel Singer and Didymus sat nose-to-nose in terrific silence.

The Gospel Singer stopped chewing and swallowed. He blinked several times. "I think," he said, his voice a whisper without the jukebox, "that we ought to leave."

"You haven't finished," said Didymus.

"I mean leave Enigma." He glanced quickly about. Nobody was paying them the slightest attention. But a hipless truck-driver with an unbelievable stomach had his hand in his pocket and was headed toward the jukebox. "I've been thinking I ought to get in the car and head out. Head out."

Didymus took out another cigarette. "I don't think that's the thing to do. No, that's not in your best interest."

"I think it is."

"I don't," said Didymus. "We ought to stay."

The Gospel Singer crammed his mouth with food, chewed, swallowed. "We?" he said finally. "You can say that. They're not after *you*."

"After me? What do you mean? Is somebody after you?"

The Gospel Singer writhed in an odd way. "You know what I mean," he said.

"No, I don't," Didymus said.

The jukebox roared into life and the truckdriver leaned his enormous stomach against the machine and smiled dreamily.

"Everything's got too bad," said the Gospel Singer, having to raise his voice now to get over the volume of the jukebox. "All those terrible people showing up evertime I turn around," he shouted. "Everwhere I look somebody wants something. Well, to hell with them is what I say. I'm going up to Atlanta and check into the best hotel I can find. This whole thing was a bad idea. I shouldn't have come back."

"They always come," said Didymus, "asking whatever bless-ing you can give. It's no different here than it's been anywhere else."

"Did you see what was setting in the kitchen while I was trying to eat my breakfast?"

"God's unfortunates," Didymus said.

"And that one that showed up just before we left? The black one?"

"I've seen worse people than that come to you," said Didy-mus. "That's not what has you so edgy. It's that girl lying dead in Enigma. I can sense it."

The Gospel Singer sopped syrup with a piece of pancake and licked his fingers. "She has nothing to do with it," he said.

"Impossible," said Didymus. "Tell me about it."

"I would if it was anything to tell," he said. He packed his mouth with food and swallowed the rest of his milk. At a wave of his hand their waitress brought a carton to the table and filled his glass again.

"It doesn't matter anyway," said Didymus. "There's no use talking about it. You *can't* leave."

"Caint, hell!" he said, shouting through a song about a truck driver who left home and hearth for a honky-tonk angel. "I can do anything I want to."

"Sure you can," said Didymus. "But if you drive out of here now you ruin the image. I've signed with Woody Pea for you to sing. You've been advertised on three-minute spots on radio and television all over the South for the past week. What kind of Gospel Singer fills the largest tent in Georgia and then doesn't show up?"

The Gospel Singer's answer was to devour savagely an entire pancake in one bite.

"Of course," said Didymus, "as you say, you can turn your back and drive out of here and ruin your image and be back in Enigma next year up to your knees in hog manure because no-body wants to hear you sing."

The Gospel Singer's face balanced precariously over a frown, then fell into a smile. "I was only joking. Sure I never meant it." He belched loudly and sucked the butter and syrup from his fingers. "I'll go back into Enigmer. I'll do what they want and take their money and light out." He leaned forward. "But I'll tell you this, this is the *last* time. Never again. From now on it's the big cities—Yankee Stadium, the Cow Palace—or else on TeeVee. I never want to git close enough to an audience again to tell which ones is cripple and which ones is blind."

"You can do any way you want to," said Didymus. "You're the Gospel Singer."

"You damn right I am." He leaned back and rubbed his belly. The jukebox had quieted momentarily. He watched their thin waitress sliding toward them through the tables. "What I actually need," he said, "is a woman. I might even lay this dirty wonder coming here." He leered broadly across the table at Didymus.

"Repent, repent," said Didymus.

"Sompin else?" asked the waitress.

"How would a doll like you like to go for a little ride up the road in a air-conditioned Cadillac car?" asked the Gospel Singer.

She looked at him, continued writing, then tore the check out and put it face down on the table. She chewed her gum and stared at the Gospel Singer and said in a quiet, tired voice: "You yellerheaded son of a bitch."

The Gospel Singer sucked his teeth and watched her walk away. "It ain't no matter," he said. "She don't know who I am. She never heard me sing."

"*That's* a penance," said Didymus.

The Gospel Singer lip-farted and on the way out bought a postcard of a blackhaired girl with a brassiere full of oranges inviting anybody that wanted to to come on down and see her in Florida.

They walked across to the Cadillac. It had stopped raining. The air was steamy under the low, sunless sky. Beside the island of gas pumps, the man had disappeared farther into the mouth of the tractor. His legs, all that remained visible of him now, twitched erratically. A crow, in the very top of the single, wilting persimmon tree growing at the side of the restaurant, screamed in directionless anger.

The Gospel Singer settled himself on the seat and Didymus drove back onto U.S. 41 and headed toward the place where highway 229 turned toward Enigma. The picture postcard of the girl wearing narrow, triangular panties and oranges for breasts lay on the seat beside the Gospel Singer. He picked it up, glanced at it, and dropped it back on the seat.

"Funny," said Didymus.

"What?"

"Foot picking your brother up on the side of the road and helping him."

The Gospel Singer was silent. Then, "I guess so."

"Strange coincidence, wouldn't you say? Your brother and Foot? Makes Foot seem a little less like a monster, doesn't it?"

"I never said he was no monster. I said I didn't want him following me. He's got no right following me."

"It's a free country," said Didymus.

The Gospel Singer picked up the postcard and stared at it closely. "Let him be free someplace else. Evertime I look over my shoulder, I don't want to see him being free behind me." The Gospel Singer looked out the window at the flat, gray countryside. "You know where I want to go when we leave here? To Miami Beach." He looked back at the postcard. "I'm gone git the highest, biggest place in the jazziest hotel and lie on that sand and let that cool water lap up atwixt and between my legs." He touched the glossy, waxed surface of the postcard.

"You've got a penance," said Didymus.

"Aw, come on, Didymus, I just et!" He threw the card down in disgust.

"Twenty *Saving Graces*," said Didymus.

"Twenty! But I didn't say hardly nothing to that skinny bitch."

"Twenty," said Didymus calmly. "I'll drive slowly so you'll have time to finish before we get back to Enigma."

"Balls," said the Gospel Singer.

But Didymus prepared the Cadillac for penance anyway. He closed the glass panel separating him from the Gospel Singer. A switch on the instrument panel closed the air conditioning ducts leading to the back of the car. And then, because of the overcast day, he turned a knob which illuminated a small red bulb recessed into the ceiling. The light fell directly upon the Gospel Singer's scowling face. Didymus bent forward and brought his *Dream Book* from under the seat. He uncapped a ball-point pen, driving slowly, keeping an eye all the time on the back seat.

The Gospel Singer inclined his head. With the air conditioning off, the air was suddenly dead. The heat swelled around him. He could already feel the sweat slipping out of his hair, across his forehead, like ants crawling across his skin.

He knew Didymus was watching him, but he did not mind. Didymus was worth whatever he cost, because Didymus had saved him by stepping into the void left by his first manager. Mr. Keene had been gone two days when the Gospel Singer returned to his hotel room one night from Carnegie Hall where he was still appearing, having as he was, an unprecedented week-long revival, to find Didymus standing in the hallway in front of the elevator. He was short, very thin and dark, and wearing a hat that cast half his face in shadow. Coming as he did from a Protestant country, the Gospel Singer did not notice the clerical collar. It was late, past midnight. The Gospel Singer turned down the hall without looking at Didymus a second time. Didymus followed him. The Gospel Singer had his key in the door when Didymus spoke.

"Gospel Singer!"

He whirled, startled and took a half step backward. He was staring down a long brown finger pointing at him, fixing him where he stood.

"You are the unhappiest of men," said Didymus.

There was something in his voice that caused the Gospel Singer to relax immediately. It was heavy, profoundly concerned, like a father calling to a child. He stood still in his three-hundred-dollar silk suit with a hundred and forty-two dollars in his wallet, with the key to a Cadillac in his pocket, with his back touching the door to rooms in one of the finest hotels in the United States and watched this man behind the finger who had said what nobody else knew or even suspected.

"Who are you?" asked the Gospel Singer.

"I am Didymus and I have come all the way from California to help you. Do not be frightened, but you refuse to hear me at the peril of your soul."

"What do you want with me?"

"Many things," said Didymus. "Many things." His little hatchet mouth smiled. Relaxed, it was remarkably soft. "We can start with business. I understand you have lost your manager."

The Gospel Singer had told the police but no one else. "How did you know that?" he asked.

"Where you are concerned," said Didymus, "there is little I don't know. Let it be enough to say that you need me. I can help you if you will let me."

"I don't need any help."

"You know better than that," said Didymus. "Do not waste my time with bravado."

"Do I look like a man who needs help?" said the Gospel Singer.

"In a word, yes," said Didymus.

"All the help I need, I can get from Mr. Keene," said Gospel Singer.

"Mr. Keene never helped you, he only helped himself to the money you made. He won't be coming back."

"How are *you* going to help me?"

"Could we go inside?" asked Didymus. "Must we stand here in the hall to discuss this?"

The Gospel Singer was used to people demanding audiences. Everyone felt free to intrude upon his life at any time for any reason. He decided it would be less trouble to hear him than to turn him away.

The suite of rooms was large and Didymus paced through it looking in corners and closets and even into drawers of the chests, sniffing here and there like a dog on the trail of something that it does not quite have the scent of. All at once he would stop and stare at an ashtray, or a bed, or a lamp and then he would go on. The Gospel Singer, who had collapsed on a couch in the living room, watched him.

"You have a nice place," said Didymus finally. "And I don't have a thing to say against that. You don't really *need* it but I guess it's all right."

The Gospel Singer sat up on the couch. "That's nice of you to say it's all right for me to keep what I've already paid for."

Didymus came to stand before him. "The first thing you've got to understand is that you've *paid* for nothing! But you will. You'll pay for everything when it's over."

The Gospel Singer collapsed back onto the couch, sorry that he had not kept quiet. "I'm tired," he said. "I'm very tired. The revival tonight wilted me like a flower. Maybe you could come back tomorrow, and we could talk about whatever it is you want to talk about."

Didymus began breathing heavily. The color in his face changed. A vein emerged at the top of his nose and disappeared into his hairline. His voice came in a strained whisper. "There are three things you should know. One, you are not a flower. Two, it was not the revival that wilted you. Three, I am not leaving you."

The Gospel Singer, afraid that he had let a madman into his rooms, said the first thing that came into his head. "I'll call the police."

Didymus seized himself by the head and spun slowly three times in a circle, stopping with his face to the wall. He moaned. "I come to talk to him of his soul, and he says he'll call the police. Mother of us all, what have the police to do with his soul?"

"My soul?" asked the Gospel Singer, looking out of the web of his fingers.

"What else?" What else indeed! He snatched open the coat to his blue businessman's suit and took out a large book with hard covers. The Gospel Singer saw written on the front of it in square letters: *Dream Book.* "I've got it all written right here. Every bit of it!" He very slowly and deliberately opened the book, turned some pages, turned some more, then stopped. "The revival that wilted you is named Geraldine Flyer."

The Gospel Singer grunted like someone had hit him a solid blow.

"She wilted you not only tonight, but the last three nights. She wilted you once under the stage at Carnegie Hall, once in your Cadillac, once in a room on Forty-Second Street, and once in this apartment on the very couch where you lie!"

The Gospel Singer had stopped grunting. He lay on his back, pale, his hands pressed tightly over his eyes.

Didymus flung the *Dream Book* to the floor and screamed: "Geraldine Flyer sings in the first row, third seat, of the choir assembled behind you in Carnegie Hall for the purpose of doing God's work!"

"How do you know about her?"

"Not about *her!* Didymus knows about *them!* Didymus knows about all of them, about the long string of blasphemous insults in the face of God! Didymus knows that Mr. Keene, for nothing more substantial than money, aided and abetted you in the blasphemy."

"I didn't hurt nobody," said the Gospel Singer.

"When you were naked and coupled with naked Geraldine Flyer on the ping-pong table under the stage at Carnegie Hall, what do you think would have happened if that stage had rolled back and revealed you to those people sitting out there in the audience waiting for you to sing the word of the Lord? Do you think it would have done no harm for those who were waiting to thrill to your voice and see the mystery of God at work in one of His appointed creatures, for those same people to see you blindly hunching like a stinking goat on a deserted hill?"

"But they didn't see. I didn't hurt . . ."

"Are you sure you did no hurt?" Didymus' voice lowered again. The Gospel Singer sat up on the couch and Didymus came closer until he was half kneeling on the couch himself, his arms spread, hovering over the Gospel Singer. "When you took that child in your arms in whom you had caused a religious ecstasy, when you touched her flesh and felt her swoon, think! Did you do no hurt? When you knew you would have your way with her, when you saw her surrender to the love of God which you sought to turn into the love of flesh, think! Did you do no hurt?"

The Gospel Singer shrank from Didymus down the length

of the couch and Didymus followed. Finally there was no place to go, and he slid off on the floor but Didymus was there too, still talking, his eyes wide and burning. The Gospel Singer could only shake his head.

"When you loosened her clothes, let go the straps and peeled down the silk shielding her virginity, when you saw her open her eyes and saw her realize she was naked in the arms of the man who had sung of God and therefore could do no wrong, think! Was there no hurt?"

The Gospel Singer was half-crawling, half-sliding back across the rug and Didymus was after him, pressing his fiery face right against the Gospel Singer's.

"When you touched her there and found her suddenly wet, her body through no will of her own having turned the God-experience into the flesh-experience—was that no hurt? And who was responsible, if not you?"

The Gospel Singer had been sliding across the floor, and now both he and Didymus were in front of a closet. The door was open.

"And of course, I understand it all, how it is with you," said Didymus. "I don't expect miracles, but I do expect more than a dislocated and undirected self-pity. It isn't enough to feel sorry. What I do expect and demand of you is penance. You must contemplate the inadequacy of your heart. Dwell upon it. Do you understand?"

"Yes," said the Gospel Singer. "Yes, contemplate." But by now the Gospel Singer was in a daze, a kind of stupor, awed as he was by Didymus' incredible knowledge. He would have agreed to anything that Didymus had asked of him. If Didymus had demanded it, he would have jumped out of the fifth-story window of the apartment. But Didymus did not require anything so rare as that. Instead, he flung himself on the Gospel Singer's back and grabbed him by the scruff of the neck and the belt and flung him into the clothes closet on his knees. Fine linen suits and pastel shirts and calfskin shoes flew in all directions as Didymus stood above him in a frenzy, the bony finger drawn again and pointing directly into the Gospel Singer's upturned face.

"Sing, damn you," cried Didymus. "Sing, Barbarian! Sing forty *The World Is Not My Home*s and while you sing, listen to the voice God gave you and contemplate how you have used it to satisfy the base demands of your flesh!"

The door to the closet had slammed and he had been alone in the darkness and afraid. His throat was as tight as if a hand had been upon it. Beyond the door he could hear breathing, a kind of sobbing snort, and then Didymus had screamed: "Sing, Barbarian!" and the force of the words had jarred the song loose in his throat.

An hour and fifty-seven minutes later, soaked in sweat and shaking in every joint, he had opened the door and crawled out and fell into Didymus' arms who held him and crooned against his face, "There, there, my sweet master, you are purged."

The Cadillac crept slowly down highway 229. The Gospel Singer was in his last *Saving Grace*. Didymus, driving with one hand, glancing now and again at the road, wrote steadily in the *Dream Book*. The strain of twenty *Saving Grace*s was showing in the Gospel Singer's face. Finally he fell exhausted against the seat and Didymus put away the *Dream Book*. The sky was clearing, even though there was still a heavy line of clouds banked in the west. They were on the edge of Enigma now, and where before there had been only gallberry and dog fennel and scrub oak, there now was an enormous brown canvas tent with people milling around among shiny, late-model cars and old trucks with wooden side-bodies and wagons with mules unmoving and peaceful where they were hitched under the dripping trees. Across the top of the tent, which was at least one hundred fifty yards long, a line of triangular red, white and blue pennants had been stretched. They hung utterly motionless against the sky. A green panel truck with JIMMY'S ALL MEAT SANDWICHES AND ICE COLD DRINKS painted on the side of it was pulled up on the shoulder of the road in front of the tent. A line of people curled away from it. As they passed the tent the Gospel Singer saw two or three people raise their arms and point at him, then several people, then everyone in the entire clearing seemed to stop whatever

they were doing and whip their heads in his direction. Somebody waved a red shirt like a flag. Over the sound of the air
conditioning and the hum of the tires, there came a thin but
persistent roar of voices, like bees droning in a hive.

The Gospel Singer opened the glass panel between him and
Didymus. "Kind of early for so many people, ain't it?"

"What's a business manager for if he doesn't organize and
advertize?" Didymus said. "Radio, handbills, newspapers. You
deserve the best."

"Oh, you do a job, Didymus," said the Gospel Singer. "I
never said you didn't. Still, this is a strange crowd."

Didymus was suddenly sour. "They look too happy to be
coming to a revival. It's not a good sign."

"Maybe the preacher from Milledgeville drew them," said
the Gospel Singer. "They say he's real good."

"Anything could have brought them," said Didymus. "You
can't tell about people. You think you've got something fig-
ured out about them and then they go and do just the opposite." While he talked he eased his *Dream Book* out again.
"Why, this morning before I came to breakfast I was in the
lane talking to an Unfortunate, and we were talking about this
very thing. He said he'd never seen so many people in Enigma,
not even for one of your visits. And you know what he said?"

"No."

"Said the rain brought them. Can you imagine that, the rain
bringing them. There's been a drought all over south Georgia,
and seems like the minute we got in the state, it started raining. We were never in it because it would start just behind us,
but it was always back there. The Unfortunate in the lane said
one of the commercials that I paid for would come on the Tee-
Vee saying the Gospel Singer was coming home to Enigma and
CRACK! it would start to rain. Sometimes it would start to
rain right while the man on the TeeVee was saying that there
was no rain in sight. That's what the Unfortunate in the lane
said. Isn't that something? Just goes to show that you can't figure anything out about people."

The Gospel Singer had seemed to grow imperceptibly smaller
in the back seat while Didymus talked as though he were a

child's toy balloon that had a very slow but steady leak. Didymus made a notation in his book and closed it.

They were in the single main street of Enigma, facing the courthouse where the town stopped on the edge of the swamp. People that had seen them from the sidewalk turned to follow the car. Some of the cars that had been parked in front of the revival tent were now lined behind them in the street.

Didymus looked back at the Gospel Singer. "I hope this won't be too hard on you."

"I'll be all right," he said.

The car, when it stopped in front of the funeral parlor, was immediately surrounded by people. There was a great deal of noise and shoving out on the sidewalk. Someone held a baby up to the window. Its round blue eyes looked indifferently upon the Gospel Singer who sat breathing quietly, waiting for Didymus to come round and open his door. Didymus would be able to protect him if the crowd got too excited as it sometimes did. The Gospel Singer had had his clothes torn off him one night when he was scheduled to appear at a ball park in Elizabeth City, New Jersey. But that was when Mr. Keene was still with him. No such thing had ever happened with Didymus in attendance. Didymus was amazingly strong for a little man.

The door opened. A ragged, self-conscious cheer went up from the crowd. It consisted mostly of out-of-towners, people whom the Gospel Singer had never seen before. Didymus cleared a path to the door and the Gospel Singer was almost there, when a fat man in a brightly colored shirt, patterned in palm trees and girls in grass skirts, shoved forward with a small boy in his arms. The boy had a large head and stared furiously out from behind a pair of steel-rimmed glasses with eyes that were wet and red as though he had been crying. "There he is, son," shouted the fat man. "Touch him!" The boy reached out and caught the Gospel Singer on the back of the arm and pinched him as hard as he could. "Thataboy!" shouted the fat man. "Touch him again!" But the Gospel Singer had leapt out of his reach and was disappearing into the funeral parlor.

The room was not brightly lit. Flowers had been placed about the walls on the floor. There were four ladies in the room, one of whom was Mrs. Carter. They sat with their backs to the Gospel Singer. From where he stood in the door he could see MaryBell where Hiram had arranged her, half-propped out of her casket, her lips painted red, her eyelids slightly blue. The Gospel Singer put an expression on his face that he hoped was mournful. He walked slowly up to the casket. Didymus followed two steps behind. Mrs. Carter raised her head. Her face was heavy and very yellow. She looked as though she had not slept for a long time. The lady sitting next to her quietly raised a coffee can with the lid cut out of it and spit a long stream of snuff spittle into it. Mrs. Carter got stiffly out of her her chair and came to the Gospel Singer and embraced him. She smelled of sweat and snuff.

"Son," she said. "We've been waitin and waitin for you. I thought more than one time that we would have to bare her without you."

"Now, now," said the Gospel Singer. "You must try to stand up under this awful thing. You know what the song says: 'The world is not my home, I'm just passing through.' I come soon as I could. I didn't even know till I got here."

"You here now," said Mrs. Carter, "and that's all that counts." She turned to look again at MaryBell. "Don't you think Hiram done real good?"

"I do," the Gospel Singer said.

"Plumb lifelike," said one of the ladies.

"She talked about you the day before it happened," said Mrs. Carter. "She known it was time for you to be comin home. Poor thing. She was so excited, all she looked forward to was seein you from one visit to the next. She thought you was the sun in the sky. I'd always hoped that you and her . . . that someday . . ." She turned her head and made a deep ragged sound in her throat, but when she looked back her eyes were hot and dry. "Who'd kill my baby? Why? Why in the world? The nigger attacked her with a ice pick after she done so much down there in quarters."

"Ma told me it was Will . . ."

"I known that nigger to be a no-good. I allus said someday he'd come up to something like this," said one of the ladies.

There was a knock at the window. They turned to the sound. The shade was not quite long enough and there at the bottom of the glass was the round, blue-eyed head of the baby, its mother holding it up to look at MaryBell. The baby looked infinitely bored as though it might fall asleep at any moment. And on either side of the mother and child were other faces, pressed cheek-to-jowl the width of the glass pane in an immobile, blinking frieze.

"They just been like that all day," said Mrs. Carter wearily. "They started comin last night when I was settin up with Mary-Bell. They won't give nobody a minute's peace, not even the dead."

"They ain't from Enigmer either," said one of the ladies. "Ain't none of them people there lookin in, from Enigmer."

"It seems like people'd have common decency," said the Gospel Singer.

"They kept wantin to come in and look at her, to see the wounds. I let in one or two this morning, and they went out and told everbody else how purty she was and how she had them ice pick marks, and it weren't long before we had just such a crowd as you see now, all of them wantin to git in and look at her. I let them in to start with, but they was so rough and shovin around in here I was afraid they was gone turn her over."

"Caint we do anything about that?" the Gospel Singer asked. "Caint we git them away from there?" He had to raise his voice because the buzz of voices had risen at the window. Now that he was in the funeral parlor too, the crowd was growing outside in the street.

"Not that I know of," said Mrs. Carter. "They too many of them. If I known anythin, I'd done it before now."

"Yes, I guess you would have," said the Gospel Singer. "Didymus, can you think of anything?"

Didymus looked up from the *Dream Book* where he had been writing furiously. "Not really," he said. "Seems to me about what we could expect. We invited them here to see you.

You're here. And after all," he waved his hand at the casket, "this is a rather spectacular murder."

"Who's he?" asked Mrs. Carter.

"This is Didymus," said the Gospel Singer. "My new manager."

"What kind of a name is that?" Mrs. Carter wanted to know. "Where is Mr. Keene? I'll bet if Mr. Keene was here he'd know what to do. Where *is* Mr. Keene?"

"I'm afraid he disappeared, Mizz Carter, right after my last visit home."

Mrs. Carter looked hard at Didymus. "If Mr. Keene was here, he'd know what to do."

"I have no doubt he would, madam," Didymus said. Then to the Gospel Singer, "You could go out and *ask* them to leave or at least to stand back and be quiet. You know, as a kind of favor to you."

"Do you think they'd do it?" asked the Gospel Singer.

"No," said Didymus. "But you could try it."

Mrs. Carter was looking at him. "I want you to sing over her. It ain't fitten hardly to do it with them makin such a racket and lookin in the winder like it was some kind of circus they was at."

"I'll ask them," he said.

When he stepped out onto the sidewalk the crowd fell silent. Those pressed at the window turned to stare at him. The woman with the baby lifted it to her shoulder so it could see better. It was asleep. The Gospel Singer kept a careful watch of the fat man who stood at the very front of the crowd holding the boy with the steel-rimmed glasses. "Folks," he said. "I've come out here to ask you . . ."

"Is it true the nigger stabbed her sixty-one times?" shouted the woman with the baby asleep on her shoulder.

". . . to ask you," said the Gospel Singer.

"Sure it's true," said the fat man. "I been over to the jail to see the nigger, and the sheriff said it's true."

"Please," said the Gospel Singer. "The lady inside . . ."

As if by prearranged signal, the crowd in front of the Gospel Singer parted, and in the open space stood the man with the heavy black skin and solid eyes. With every movement of head and hand and foot, his clothes eddied about him as though filled with nothing more substantial than air.

"You Gospel Singer," said the man, his voice, though soft, sounding in the sudden quiet like a shout.

The Gospel Singer pretended not to see him. "Mizz Carter, whose daughter is poor dead MaryBell, asked me to come out here an see if you folks . . ."

But the crowd was not listening. It had its eyes upon the thin wavering figure which, even as the Gospel Singer was speaking, flew forward and fastened the Gospel Singer's arm with one of its black hands. A collective sigh came out of the crowd, and it pressed forward.

"You runned from me," said the man.

"I had to come here. I'm here," said the Gospel Singer, trying to keep his breaking voice from breaking.

"I come a long ways," said the man. "I thrown down everthin and come a long ways because they're tellin it in the country you a healer."

"I ain't responsible . . . I ain't responsible . . ." cried the Gospel Singer.

He was trying to say that he was not responsible for what they were saying about him, but he could not get it all out. The man was so close the Gospel Singer could see his own image shining in both flat, colorless eyes. The Gospel Singer did not want to look into them, but he could not help himself. They did not blink and he was as a bird struck still by the stare of a snake. The man leaned closer. His breath smelled of things long-enclosed.

"We is believers," the man said. "They ain't no doubter here. They better no man doubt you in my hearin. I know who you are, I believe."

The Gospel Singer chewed his random tongue, waiting for the man to release him, which he finally did, giving the Gospel Singer a little shove for good measure, causing him to stumble back into the funeral parlor through the half-open doors. A cheer went up from the crowd for the black man, who whirled in the instant and scowled it quiet.

Inside, the Gospel Singer had to concentrate to feel his feet touch the floor when he walked. He put his head and hip against the wall and leaned there trying to recover. Just as he was going in to join Mrs. Carter, Hiram burst through the curtain. He rushed so close to the Gospel Singer that his chin almost touched the Gospel Singer's chest. He was red in the face and sweating. His shirt showed dark half-circles at the armpits.

"Why the hell didn't you come back?" he demanded. "I waited. We all waited for you to come back? I had to come in the side way to git into my own place. That crowd out there ain't got good sense and all the time I'm waitin out yonder at you daddy's place for you to come back? Why the hell *didn't* you come back?"

The Gospel Singer put his hand over his mouth as though to keep from throwing up. He took a deep breath, trying to grasp what Hiram was yelling at him for. "Please," he said. "I try . . ."

Hiram seemed abruptly to get control of himself. "All right," he said. "All right, God knows I don't want to be mad at you. Of all the people on earth to be mad at, you the last one. I just wanted you to let my little girl see you."

"Yes, see me."

"She's in the backroom," he said. "I just want her to put her hands on you face. She's gitten old enough now to know what she's doin." He took the Gospel Singer by the arm.

The Gospel Singer pulled back. "I caint. I caint now. Mizz Carter's waitin. She's next. MaryBell's waitin. I promised her. Maybe then . . ."

"That's right," said Hiram bitterly. "Do everthin for everbody else. It don't matter how long I known you daddy, it don't matter that I had you own blood kin lyin in my parlor, dressed and laid out by my own hand. That don't count for nothin."

The Gospel Singer walked away from him saying, "I'm sorry, I'm sorry." As he was going to MaryBell he heard Hiram still talking. "Maybe after you through, then . . ."

Didymus, who had been at the window looking out and

taking notes, shut his *Dream Book* when he came in. The Gospel Singer went straight to the casket and knelt.

"The crowd did about what I thought it'd do," said Didymus.

The Gospel Singer had softly begun *Farther Along.*

Mrs. Carter backed away watching him. "Let's everbody go out and leave him with the poor thing."

"I never leave the Gospel Singer," said Didymus.

"You do now, Mr. Whatever-you-name-is," said Mrs. Carter. "Bein a outsider I don't expect you to understand nothin. You don't have to. All you have to do is get out of here and leave them alone. If you don't I'll pick you up like a sack of shucks and care you out." Standing in front of Didymus, her hands fisted on her hips, she was two feet wider and a foot taller than he.

"Whatever you wish, dear lady," he said. He left and directly a child's face that was peeping in the window jerked out of sight and Didymus' face took its place.

When Mrs. Carter stepped outside, she could no longer hear the Gospel Singer's voice. People were shouting and shoving, a car horn blew and blew again and off in the distance there came a sound like a string of firecrackers being exploded. Mrs. Carter had envisioned standing outside the funeral parlor and hearing the Gospel Singer's strong beautiful song echoing over her dead daughter and echoing through the quiet streets of Enigma. Instead, she was in the midst of a kind of confused holiday where people carried their Bible in one hand and a thick JIMMY'S ALL MEAT SANDWICH in the other. She sat down on a wooden bench across the street from the funeral parlor. The three ladies that had followed her there sat down too. They sat very still watching the crowd. Under her black bonnet, Mrs. Carter's eyes were flat and did not reflect the light.

"We'll never hear him singin now," she said.

"From the first time I seen the people start to come, I known we wouldn't," said one of the ladies.

Mrs. Carter said very quietly, "I wish God, hell would open up and swaller ever last one of them."

The lady sitting beside her sent a long stream of brown spittle into the street. "I don't misdoubt if it do," she said.

The calamity that Mrs. Carter heard was muted somewhat inside the parlor where the Gospel Singer knelt with his face on the same level as the cold, arranged features of MaryBell. At last, at long last, she was gone. And that she had gone straight to hell, he did not doubt at all any more than he doubted that he had been the one who had sent her there.

The night his singing had converted her she had stayed close at his side the rest of the evening, all through the preacher's sermon and the fellowship that followed. Her face was young and flushed and she kept whispering, "I'm just tremblin all over. I never known it could be this way, that I could be so happy." And afterward he had driven her home in the Ford coupe he bought with the money he made at the Tallahassee Gospel Festival, and no one thought anything of it, least of all himself, because it was generally known in Enigma that she was his girl. He had taken her plenty of times to the picture show in Albany or Tifton or Cordele with Gerd in the front seat of the Ford driving and them in the back. He had held her hand and kissed her before. Even once, at a candy pulling, he had touched her breast briefly and she had only blushed and looked away and had not stopped him, but that night after the conversion sitting under the pecan trees in front of her house with the moon incredibly big and yellow and still, hanging in the sky just beyond the fields, it was all somehow changed. They had not spoken more than two or three words since they left the church and they sat now quiet and embarrassed.

"How you feel?" she said.

"I feel all right," he said.

"I didn't know . . . tonight I . . ."

"Yes," he said. "I know."

She slid across the seat and sat close to him and touched his face with her hands. Her breathing was shallow and rapid. He could feel the heat coming off her in waves. "I didn't even know I was goin to do it," she said. "I didn't know it was goin to happen until I was out of my seat and standin there in front of you, and it was like God Hisself had touched me."

He kissed her. Not because he wanted to particularly but because he did not want to hear her talk of God. She held herself very still under his lips. When he drew back she said, "I caint explain it. I guess it was the song . . . and you. I was comin apart there listenin to you and God . . ."

He kissed her again. Gospel singing was a way to make money, a way to escape Enigma, a way to keep from having to spend his life wading around in hog slop. He had not planned on God getting into it. He was not even particularly religious, and to have someone tell him that he was responsible for saving a soul was confusing and scary. Her lips opened under his. She squeezed his arms with her hands. Then she drew back and said, "Have you ever thought of being a preacher?"

"No," he said. "Never."

"You so good," she said. "And they so much badness in the world. I know you could do the Lord's work."

He pushed her down in the seat. He was determined not to listen to talk of God and doing the Lord's work. In the morning he was going to Atlanta and sing on the TeeVee and have a room in the biggest hotel in the town and eat a steak. Mr. Keene had already promised. And he wasn't going to have it all spoiled by God and dull things like being a country preacher.

The moonlight caught and turned to a kind of mist in her hair. She smelled of blossoms and soap and a stronger, stranger something that he had never smelled before. Her face was damp with sweat and everywhere he touched her, her flesh seemed almost hot enough to burn. "In church tonight . . ." she said, and he kissed her again. He felt briefly, and for the first time ever, the tip of her tongue on his lips but then she was saying, "I know I was the only one brought to God tonight but everbody there felt the Lord in your voice."

"I love you," he said, touching her under her dress, not knowing what to expect as he did, perhaps for her to scream or slap him, but at least to stop talking of God. But she only gripped him more tightly about the neck. She made a sudden slipping movement and he was received into the cradle of her thighs. He looked about, amazed to find himself in such a position. Her dress was up around her waist, showing her square, white cotton pants and the fact that there was only a strip of cloth barely two-inches wide separating him from her seemed

the farthest thing from her mind. He was a virgin and therefore the mystery of woman was as deep and grave to him as
the mystery of God. But not nearly so frightening and, in his
own mind, without the far-reaching consequences.

"I love you, too," she said. "Oh, I do love you."

But that had not kept her from going on about God, about
him being a preacher and the fact that God shined through his
voice like the sun through clouds, so that finally he was forced
to tear her pants and tear her, almost against his will, there on
the seat of the Ford coupe sitting in her front yard. It was awkward and painful and brief, but startlingly real as no other
event in his entire life had been. To have sunk that small part
of himself out of sight and out of this world into another
human being seemed the best thing that had ever happened to
him. He was quite convinced three minutes later when it was
all over and she was crying against him, saying that she loved
him, that he also loved her. He looked up at the chrome door
handle glinting in the moonlight above her head and said in a
loud but incredulous voice: "I'm in love, I'm in love, I'm in
love."

The Gospel Singer raised his eyes and looked at MaryBell's
dead face in front of him. He stopped a moment and listened
to his voice singing *Farther Along*. It was full and firm and he
was in the middle of the song. If he could only have loved Mary-
Bell. If it had only been true. But of course it had not, and it
had only taken until the next night in the Atlanta Arms Hotel
to find it out. The TeeVee audition had been successful and
Mr. Keene had signed a contract full of money. After supper
he had brought a woman to their suite that was even more
beautiful than MaryBell, her skin was fairer, firmer, her eyes
bluer, her hair longer, and while Mr. Keene sat in the outer
room busting his guts laughing and reading the contract, the
girl took the Gospel Singer to bed and there showed him a
far wider, more excruciating world than MaryBell had ever
dreamed of because, unlike MaryBell, this girl was not a virgin. And when she had finished with him, she on top, her hair
falling about his face like a veil, he had looked up into her eyes
and said in a voice half dreaming, "I love you." And she had

exploded from the bed in laughter and refused to take any money from Mr. Keene for the job. Mr. Keene had taken him by the shoulder and waved the contract in his face. "Kid," he said. "You can have any like that you want, as many and as often as you want."

There had been nothing to do but tell MaryBell how it was. But he had not done that either. He had gone back to Enigma to tell her, got her alone to tell her, but she had lain against him, her hot breath as sweet as milk in his face and he, suddenly overcome with the moment and the memory of the whore in Atlanta, had taken her out of the Ford coupe and put her on a blanket under a pine tree. And she had gone with him, docilely, without protest, the same marvelous light shining in her face. He told her he wanted to take all of her clothes off.

"Out . . . out here in the woods this way?" Her eyes shadowed and she looked quickly about her as though expecting someone to step out of the bushes.

"I love you," he said, seeing in his mind the Atlanta whore strutting about the bedroom, the raven hair falling down the curve of her back.

And so she let him take off her clothes and later when he asked her to get up and walk round him naked while he lay on the blanket, she did that too, smiling all the time but keeping her eyes averted. He lay a long time, half-conscious it seemed to him, watching her go round and round the blanket while he lay dreaming of the contract Mr. Keene had waved under his nose and what he had said.

But later when he left her, when he went out of Enigma on singing tours to Tallahassee or New Orleans or up to the television studio in Atlanta to make tapes for future shows, he solemnly vowed that when he went back he would tell her the truth. He would say that what they were doing was wrong because he did not love her and because he was not going to marry her.

And he would have told her just that (he told himself) if it had not been that right about that time a greater and greater number of sinners began falling before his voice. He saved souls right and left. He couldn't open his mouth in church without some fool falling in a swoon, crying that he had found God. And worse, it was being rumored about that he could heal. Mr. Keene, who kept his ear to the ground concerning such matters, heard the rumor and brought it to the Gospel Singer, saying as he did that it would increase the fee they could command for personal appearances.

But this news did not cheer the Gospel Singer. He thought saving souls and healing the sick were things best left alone, especially in light of the fact that he was doing what he was doing not for God but for money: money to buy suits, money to buy silk underdrawers, and finally, money to buy powerful cars that he could jump into and roar out of Enigma. And even to the Gospel Singer, whose faith in God was not faith at all but an overwhelming superstition, it seemed obvious that a man could not have both silk drawers *and* God. He could have one or the other but not both.

And he knew, had always known, what his choice was, but he was not sure anymore he was free to make it. The more he demanded his right to sin, the more sinners flocked to his voice and found salvation. He was rapidly coming to the place where he believed, against his will, that he might be what the world said he was. It was frightening! It threatened to ruin everything!

Then in one marveling moment he had seen that MaryBell was his way out! It was during a revival in Waycross, Georgia, at the Church of the Tabernacle, when the first eight rows had given up to God in simultaneous conversion. He had not even finished his first gospel, and in exasperation he quit singing and watched them kneeling wet-eyed and penitent before him. As they began to amen and hallelujah, he suddenly had a vision of MaryBell, great-breasted and -hipped (she had grown magnificently over the months of their lovemaking) spread on a blanket in the woods, dappled with sun and damp with effort. It was a moment he would always remember when he realized that he could not be what they were saying he was if he was also taking every advantage of MaryBell, lying to her and laying her as regular as breathing.

MaryBell became his sure and steady defense against God. They could amen themselves to death, if they wanted to; they could save themselves and heal themselves and then point to him as having done it. But that didn't make it true. MaryBell proved it was not true. So from that time forward he had worked at MaryBell with a will, teaching her whatever delights he learned from whatever various whores Mr. Keene bought for him on the road. And she learned willingly and well, rushing into whatever tricks or postures he showed her with an enthusiasm that was fresh and spontaneous, talking all the while of the time when they would be married and of the children they would have and the house they would live in. She thought the house ought to be of brick with a green lawn and built in Atlanta, wishing as she did to get out of Enigma because it was not a good place to raise children. And he would say, Yes, that was true, all the while watching her move through whatever trick he was teaching her. And there was nothing she could not or would not do for him.

After a trip to Memphis, Tennessee, he wanted her to say some words aloud to him while they made love. He told her the words. For a moment it was as though she had not heard him. Her eyes went briefly opaque.

"You want me to talk profanity whilst we lovin one another?"

He pointed out to her that it was not profanity. And that was true. It was only filth. She was still hesitant. He said people that loved one another said it to each other all the time. But he could see that she still did not believe him. He had prepared for the possibility that she wouldn't. He stood up from the blanket and walked over to his Pontiac convertible, having long ago given his Ford coupe to Bigum Baptist Church in Foremost, Georgia, for a raffle sale to sponsor a Cub Scout troop, and brought back a book entitled: *Happiness in Physical Love—A Clinical Approach.*

"I bought this in a drugstore," he said. "Look what it says on page thirty-seven."

She took the book slowly, looked at it for a moment, then

opened it. She immediately closed it. "It's naked people in it," she said.

"I bought it in a drugstore," he said. "It was on a rack right beside the birthday cards. Look on page thirty-seven."

She opened it again, trying not to see until she got to page thirty-seven, but there was a picture there too and she could not help but look at it. The man, naked and smiling with a little black mustache, was as beautiful as the Gospel Singer.

"Read what it says at the bottom," he said.

She read it and it said you ought to whisper filth in your Love Object's ear if he likes it. "Do you like it?" she asked.

"I don't know," he said. But he was lying; he loved it.

"You want me to do it to you?"

"I do," he said.

And she did, singing out the words that she had always somehow known but had never said, singing them out in a monotonous, singsong fashion like a child chanting a nursery rhyme. He had to stop and show her how to say the words, the right inflection, the right pause, and the right variation in the pitch of her voice. She learned very quickly.

And that she was quicker than he had ever given her credit for, he realized later, was his undoing. Because it was she who finally began thinking of variations on the old perversions. The student rapidly surpassed the master. She took the initiative; she showed him where; she showed him how; she told him when. And in the process, a curious thing happened. He came more and more under the spell of her flesh. She did not need to be justified by God; she justified herself. He walked about in a daze at times thinking of her; he awoke in the night, soaked, straining for the touch of her. And even though he never knew when his control of her turned into her control of him, it was one day an accomplished fact.

They had driven straight to their place in the woods as he had been doing for more than a year, making no pretense anymore by going first to a movie or out to eat or anything else. She leaned back against the red cushions of his Cadillac, sighed deeply and said, "Well, you ready to fuck?"

He jumped on the seat. "What?"

She pulled her dress up and the sun caught the spot between her legs and turned it the color of copper. "There it is," she said. "You brought it out here to fuck, so fuck it."

He had heard her say worse things but she had never said them so coldbloodedly, so harshly, with nothing to preface them.

"For heaven's sake," he said. "Put down your dress. What ails you?"

"Why nothin, baby," she said, her face lighting with a cold humor. She patted herself. "You do want it, don't you? You not gone bring it out here all hot and wet and let it git cold, are you?" She rubbed herself.

He swallowed hard. "Of course I want you," he said.

"Not *me*, baby," she said. "*It*." She hunched herself forward in the seat.

His eyes narrowed. Blood swelled his heart. All he could see was round hips and round thighs and round stomach converging, sinking there in that shimmering copper of the sun. And beyond, above it, dominating it, were the twin mounds of breast rising suddenly from her unbuttoned blouse. His eyes fixed, he thought he could see it pulse, and it drew him as a magnet. "Listen," he said. "Listen."

He leaned toward her across the seat and she caught him by the ears and brought his face down into the copper smell of her and whatever he was going to say was lost. She twisted on the seat and above the beating of his heart, he heard her laughing softly and steadily and without pleasure.

It was almost dark when he brought her home. They sat in her front yard under the pecan trees in his Cadillac.

"Listen," he said. "I want to tell you somethin."

She smiled, but her face was too tight. It looked as if she were trying to bite something in two. "And I want to *ask* you somethin," she said.

"Sure," he said. "What?"

"When are you going to marry me and take me out of Enigma?"

He could not marry her. That would never do. It would only

prove that he had been on the up and up all along, that this had all been a courtship, a prelude to the holy bonds of matrimony. Besides, every preacher he had ever known had been married. A single preacher was to his mind an anomaly, a contradiction in terms. He was determined to remain without a wife.

"Well, now you know how much I have to travel around the country singing gospels," he said. "You know it's no fit life for a woman."

"Yes," she said. "I know. When are you going to marry me and take me out of Enigma?"

He didn't want to give her up, but he could see what was coming. She was going to make it impossible to continue.

"MaryBell," he said. "I've been thinking a lot about us."

"Am I a whore?" she asked.

"What? Are you a what?"

"Am I a whore? I never asked any money for it. Can you be a whore without askin any money for it?"

"You stop talkin about that," he said. "I don't want to hear you ever say that again."

"Do you think I'm a whore?"

"No," he said. "No I . . ."

"Does God think I'm a whore?"

"Don't talk that way. I don't know what God thinks."

"God don't like whores, does He?" she asked. "I bet He don't like whore-hoppers, neither."

He tried to remember if he had taught her the word "whore-hopper." "Why do you keep on talkin about God for?" he asked irritably. "I wish you'd leave God out of it."

"I don't think we can leave Him out of it," she said. "He got in it from the very start. Remember? He got in it the same night you got in it."

"That's blasphemy," he said. "You're blaspheming against the Holy Ghost."

"Ma says that's the one thing God never lets you out of hell for," she said. "Ma says once you do that, it's all over between you and God." The flesh of her face was fixed as stone. "Ma thinks it's a hell of a thing to blaspheme against that old bastard, if you do He'll hound you right into the deepest part of hell and there He'll break your back and watch you burn."

"MaryBell," he whispered. His hand went before his face in a gesture that was entirely reflex, expecting as he did for lightning to strike and melt the car around them there in the front yard. Because to the Gospel Singer's mind, God was a kind of enormous Black Cat that was continually threatening to cross the path just ahead. And if He did, the Gospel Singer knew the thing to do was to rush around and make the proper number of X's and spit over his shoulder the proper number of times and then sit back and hope that it would be all right. But under no circumstances must a man ever openly invite the Black Cat to cross in front of him, because then the X's and the spitting might not work.

"Ma thinks," said MaryBell, "that you ought to marry me and care me out of Enigma."

"MaryBell, listen to me," he said. "You're young and you're beautiful and you've got your whole life ahead of you."

"My whole life," she said.

"And you know . . . why, you know what's the most important thing in a person's life?" He was talking rapidly, turning a little on the seat, touching her with his hands. "Why, the most important thing is to be happy. A person ought to be happy. So I'll tell you what. You want to live in Atlanta? Then why not just up and go there? Sure! I can help you. You want a job? I know people at every TeeVee studio in the town. Right?"

"I don't want a job in Atlanta."

"But you just said . . ."

"I want *you*."

He sat up straight in the seat and held onto the wheel of his Cadillac. "Now MaryBell, it's time we had a long talk. I want . . ."

"It's past talk," she said.

". . . I want you to try to understand that I've just started a very important career. I'll be leavin Enigmer for . . ."

"I've got a right," she said. "God knows I got a right."

". . . leavin Enigmer for a long . . . You've got a right to what?"

"To *you*," she said. "That's all I got a right to, but I've got a right to that and I'm gone have you. If you want to stay in Enigmer then I'll stay with you. And if you want to leave Enigmer for good I'll do that too. But I ain't to be put off. I got a right."

"We better just wait and talk about it tomorrow," he said. He got out of the Cadillac and started around to open the door for her. She did not wait for him but opened it herself and got out. He stopped at the front of the car, waiting. The sky was heavy with heat clouds that caught and released the moon and in the splashing light she looked like something cut out of stone.

"I won't be askin you again to do what you said you'd do and be what you said you'd be," she said.

"We can talk about it tomorrow," he said.

"No we caint. You'll be gone tomorrow. But that don't scare me. You'll be comin back. And I'll be here. I'll always be here and you gone marry me and take me out of Enigmer, mark me sayin it." She went into the house without looking at him.

And from that time on she was at his back like the wrath of God. When he was in Enigma, she made his life a living hell. She had changed in a way that was frightening. You could not very well help but be frightened by a girl that, when you looked over your shoulder driving your Cadillac down the road at seventy miles per hour, you found lying in your back seat stark naked without even her shoes.

And yet that was where he had seen her the next time. He and Mr. Keene had been out of town for three months following that night in her yard and on his way into Enigma he had let Mr. Keene off outside Tifton to look over his tobacco crop. The next morning right after sun-up he had got into his Cadillac to drive to Tifton for Mr. Keene. He was about two miles outside of Enigma when he thought he heard singing. It was unnerving because he did not have the radio on. But he heard it so distinctly that he looked back through the glass panel separating the front seat from the back and there white and naked in broad daylight was MaryBell Carter with her hair down over her shoulders singing what sounded like a child's lullaby. He had only narrowly escaped running off the road. When he had finally fought the car back into the road, he opened the glass panel.

"What?" he said. "What! What!" That was all he could say and he sat spluttering while she smiled sweetly back at him. It was a long time before she spoke. "I'm ready," she said.

"Ready?" he cried. "My God! and what are you ready for?" He glanced nervously up and down the road. He was afraid someone would come along and find them this way. The Gospel Singer with a naked girl in the back of his car at seven o'clock in the morning on the edge of Enigma! That would destroy his image for good and forever.

"Ready for you," she said.

"But I don't want you," he wailed.

"You've got me though. Now come back here and make it right."

"Put your clothes on," he said.

"I don't have any clothes. I thrown them out the winder."

He collapsed against the seat. Frantically he searched for something to do and then he remembered his suitcases that were still in the trunk of the car from the trip he and Mr. Keene had just made. He leapt out and opened the trunk and found a pair of his trousers and a shirt. But as soon as he looked into the back seat, down upon naked MaryBell whose face was still set in the same rigid mask but whose body had shifted to receive him, all his best intentions melted. He forgot immediately that it was broad daylight and that he was on the road into Enigma and that he sang gospel for a living. All he could remember was the last three months during which he had tried to make other women—short, fat, tall, obscene, virginal, any kind whatever—take MaryBell's place. But they had not, not for an instant. And even though he had kept himself from admitting it, he knew now that he had looked forward to nothing but getting back to this moment with Mary-Bell. He dropped the clothes and sprang into the back seat and into her with a cry that was as much of anguish as of pleasure.

And later, as she stood naked from the waist up, his shirt

that she was about to put on trailing from her hands, her massive breasts shining solid as marble with the sweat of their
lovemaking still upon them, she said, "You gone remember
me," she said. "I promise you that. The last thought you ever
gone have on this earth'll be between my legs."

"I wish you didn't talk like that," he said.

"I do too," she said. "But I guess we stuck with it."

"You're not stuck with anythin ever," he said. "You can
change. You can stop talkin like that."

"Save anybody's soul lately?" she asked.

"Shut up," he said. "Don't."

"But it's important," said MaryBell. "Don't you think it's
important?"

"Of course, but . . ."

"Do you ever think of savin your own soul?" Her face went
soft in a curious way that he had not seen in a long time.

He had thought about it more than a little, and he knew he
could not save his soul at the expense of the world. It was too
much to ask a man born in Enigma to give up good food, and
fine clothes, and cars and hotels and women for the promise of
Heaven. But he also knew there *was* a chance. If it was anything the gospel songs made clear, it was the fact that every
man, no matter how evil he had been, had a chance in the final
moment of his life to gain Heaven. He just had to be lucky
enough to have the time and the inclination to make the necessary gestures that would turn the Black Cat out of his path.
And the Gospel Singer felt his luck would be with him when
the time came. But of course he could not tell MaryBell *that*,
because he himself only knew it vaguely, in a tentative way,
preferring as he did not to think about it at all if he could
help it.

"MaryBell," he said finally. "I want to help you."

"Yes," she said, and waited.

"But if you won't let me help you," he said, "there's not any
use in seein you anymore. This is the last time."

"Then don't come back to Enigmer," she said. "Go away
and don't ever come back. Cause if you come back, I'll always
be here."

But he did come back to Enigma because he had no place else to come back to, and she more than made good her promise. She wasn't just *there*; she was *everywhere*. It was as though she had somehow multiplied her kind and become a hundred MaryBells. He tried to hide from her, to evade her, but no matter where he went, she always managed to find him. If he slipped back to the spring that formed a clear pool behind his daddy's farm, he would have no sooner plunged into the water, than MaryBell, naked—and it was her special talent to seem nakeder than any other woman he had ever known—would step from behind a tree and plunge into the water with him. And they would end in the grass because as soon as he saw her without her clothes his will to resist left him. It seemed that everytime he saw her she was more beautiful and lewder than the last time he saw her.

And just to the degree that her sexual outrages with him became more numerous, the more her reputation for virtue in the community seemed to grow. It was not just going to church. *Everybody* in Enigma went to church. It was good works. It was helping the needy, caring for the sick and leading such an exemplary life herself. But mainly it was because of the Negroes. Enigma's Negroes lived in Quarters on the edge of town on a dismal little plot of earth with no grass and no flowers and no trees, with one-room shacks, unpainted and leaning, held up it seemed by the odor of human shit and dog shit. And nobody in Enigma liked the smell of shit which the wind would sometimes bring up from Quarters and they were delighted when it began to disappear and they said to one another how fine it was that MaryBell could do Nigras so good. MaryBell would say, "I think I'll go down and work in the Nigras," and off she would go and before long she had the Negroes burying their filth, cleaning their yards, sweeping, hammering, sawing and doing all the things they had never done before.

And while the people of Enigma thought it was a waste of time in the long run, over the short haul it made for a more pleasant town and sometimes they would take their friends from Tifton or Cordele by Quarters and show them Mary-

Bell's Nigras. "I bet you ain't got no Nigras like *them* in Tifton," they would say. "But then you ain't got no MaryBell in
Tifton." And they would laugh with delight and point with
both hands at the incredible and preposterous sight of a Negro's cabin painted a startling and flawless white.

It was about this time that the Gospel Singer began to see
the little Negro boys following him. As soon as he would drive
into Enigma, little black heads with tight caps of kinky hair
began to appear from behind trees, to raise out of bushes, and
to stare at him white-eyed from darkened storefronts. They
were MaryBell's special messengers to keep track of the Gospel Singer and at any given moment during the day or night
she knew where he was and where he was about to go. His
nerve began to fail him. He lost weight and looked drawn
about the eyes. He started carrying complete wardrobes for
MaryBell around in the trunk of the Cadillac because he never
knew when she would leap out upon him after first having de-
stroyed all her clothes. She once managed to sneak into his bed
in the very house with his mother and father and brothers and
sister. The Gospel Singer at first thought she had gone mad.

"MaryBell," he said. "I think you're crazy."

"I'm not," she said.

"I've got a right to think you are," he said. "Anybody that
opens the trunk of his car for a spare tire and has a naked girl
spring out on him has a right to think she's crazy."

"I'm not, though," she said.

"Mr. Keene thought you were crazy," he said.

"He shouldn't have watched us."

"He couldn't help it," he said. "He was right there in the car
and you had me in the ditch. He couldn't help it."

"You had *me* in the ditch," she said. "And a gentleman
would've turned his head."

"He ain't a gentleman," he said. "And you better hope he
keeps his mouth shut."

"*You* better hope he keeps his mouth shut," she said. "I
don't know what the people of Enigmer would do if they hear
tell of the Gospel Singer fuckin on the side of the road."

"He won't say anythin," said the Gospel Singer. "Even if he

wasn't makin twice as much off me as he's making off his tobacco farm he still wouldn't tell. He couldn't. Nobody would
believe him. They'd think he was crazy. That's how crazy it is.
And that's why you're crazy, MaryBell Carter, nuttier than a
pecan tree."

"That's a awful way to talk about a girl you've screwed . . .
How many times have you screwed me?"

"God!" he said.

"Ain't you kept track?" she asked. "Ain't you even kept account of how many times it is. It ain't anybody else that ever
screwed me, just you. You the only one."

He knew very well that he was the only one, that it had been
he who had taught her everything she knew. But he had never
thought it would go this far, nor had he thought there would
come a time when he was unable to resist her. But it had and
he was. At the same time it was obvious that she was purposefully trying to make their affair public, to have them caught
in the act. He had to do something; it was too dangerous to let
things continue as they were. That was when he had first
thought of trying to resave her soul, or if the other time had
just been a false alarm, to try to save it for the first time. And
so, while he was away from Enigma in Atlanta or Memphis or
some other city he would lie on the restful belly of one of Mr.
Keene's whores and try to figure out a way to save MaryBell.
After much thinking he decided there was not a thing to do
but to appeal to her sense of fair play.

"I was only jokin about you bein crazy, MaryBell," said the
Gospel Singer. "You a decent human bein. Right?" She smiled
down at him like a rock from the bottom limb of a pecan tree
where he had found her perched, naked as usual, when he
came home from Mr. Keene's farm in Tifton. "You know
you've got a place in my heart, that you'll always have a place
in my heart." While he talked he opened the trunk of his Cadillac and got a dress and some pants. "But I caint go on this
way. I caint." He threw the clothes in the front seat of the car.
Then he opened the back door and stood beside it. She gave a
little cry and leapt from the limb, striking him in the chest,

and they both fell backward into the car. She was tearing at his clothes and hunching before they hit the seat.

When it was over and she was dressed, they sat in his car while she smoked cigarettes, a habit she had only lately picked up. "Did you hear about me workin in the Nigras?" she said.

"Yes," he said. "That's how come I know down deep you a decent human bein."

"I don't do it cause I'm decent. I do it because I'm bored. They ain't much to do in Enigmer when you gone."

"MaryBell, I been meanin to tell you, I don't mind all them little Nigras you got watchin me, pokin their little wool heads in my life. They just cute as they can be."

"Them bigguns ain't all that ugly either if you git to lookin at them real close," she said.

He smiled weakly. "I know you wouldn't do nothin to hurt your dear old mother. Besides, that's the one thing Enigmer would never stand for, but Enigmer ain't worried cause it knows you a decent human bein. Why, I hear folks ever day of my life say that you one in a million."

"You know Enigmer don't know nothin about me," she said. "And what they don't know won't never send them to hell. All I know is you stay away longer and longer, weeks at a time and with you gone they ain't nothin here for me. I ain't sayin I'm gone do it but I know they ain't but one place for a white girl to screw and keep her reputation, and that's in Quarters." She smiled sweetly. "Unless of course she's screwin a gospel singer. But you the only gospel singer and you gone most of the time. You caint hardly expect to feed a girl candy steady, then take it away from her without her missin it."

There was no talking to her, he could see that. He didn't know whether she was crazy or what she was, but he knew his only peace would come from trying to avoid her. But he couldn't do that either. When he was in Enigma she was all over him. It was like being in a house of crazy mirrors where no matter which way you look you see yourself coming back at yourself from forty different directions. There was no defense against her.

"Everbody tries to do the decent thing," he would say.

"I don't," she would say. "I don't try to do the decent thing. I give up on all that shit. I just hang around Enigmer waitin for you to come home so I can . . ." She made a little snapping noise with her white, even teeth, and smiled. "So I can git you."

And nobody in Enigma ever suspected during all this time what she really was. She walked through the streets in her long white dresses and lovely smile, waving, talking, and doing good works with the sick and needy. In Quarters on the edge of town, blood red roses grew over yard fences. Only the Gospel Singer knew she was not normal.

"Ring your clapper in Mary's Bell!" she would cry with her legs wrapped about his hips. But she did not really enjoy sex. As far as he could see, she did not enjoy anything. The one possible exception was when she jumped naked upon him from a darkened doorway or onto his back from a low hanging limb or squirmed out from under his bed at two o'clock in the morning and leapt upon his sleeping form. And at such times when he awoke to find her staring into his face, she did have in her face a look of what might have been hysterical happiness.

And so the Gospel Singer had stayed away from Enigma longer and longer until finally in an inevitable ritual which he could not control, he had begun coming home every six months to hold a revival and to allow himself to be attacked by MaryBell.

"What are you trying to do?" It was Didymus that had him roughly by the shoulders, shaking him, his face jammed between his and MaryBell's.

"Leave me alone," said the Gospel Singer.

"I'll leave you alone," said Didymus. "But they won't." He pointed to the window where the line of faces still stared down at him where he knelt before the casket. But they were angry faces now, very red and sweating. Sometimes their mouths opened and he could see their teeth and the red insides of their throats.

"Why are you doing penance in front of everybody this way?" asked Didymus. "I told you that won't do. Not ever. The world won't stand for penance in public."

"Penance?" asked the Gospel Singer.

"They been watching you almost an hour in here on your knees singing *Farther Along*. And they've been out there on their knees too because that's the only way they can look in. They're hot. They're mad. If I've told you once, I've told you a hundred times, penance has to be in the closet. The public won't stand for it otherwise."

"I didn't realize . . ."

"I never heard a word of it," said Mrs. Carter. She came into the parlor trailing her three companions. "I listened and I never heard nothin. The longer you stayed with her the louder they got out there in the street. You might as well not even been singin."

"Come on," said Didymus. "Get up."

The Gospel Singer rose stiffly to his feet. Mrs. Carter stepped near the casket and looked down. "Do you think the poor thing heard?"

"I don't know," said the Gospel Singer.

"*You don't!*" said Mrs. Carter.

"She heard him," Didymus said.

"You think so?"

"Sure," said Didymus.

"I misdoubt it," said one of the ladies. "I misdoubt anybody hearin salvation or damnation with them yowlin in the street."

While Mrs. Carter was telling her companion that it took more than a crowd to keep the dead from hearing, the Gospel Singer saw Hiram watching him through a part in the curtain. Hiram raised his hand and crooked a finger.

"Mizz Carter, I hope it done some good," said the Gospel Singer. "I truly do."

Mrs. Carter had taken her seat beside the casket as had the other ladies. "Maybe we can dedicate a number to her at the meetin tonight," she said. "I caint help but think it would ease her mind if we did."

"It's no reason we caint do that," said the Gospel Singer.

"Son," said Mrs. Carter. "How come you reckon that nigger'd do a thing like this to MaryBell? What kind of heart must that nigger have?"

"Mizz Carter," he said. "I been wonderin that same thing myself." And truly he had. He had not seen Willalee Bookatee since he had started singing gospel regularly but he remembered him as a soft-voiced, gentle boy the same age as himself.

"I ain't seen the nigger, you know," said Mrs. Carter.

"Ain't none of us seen him," said one of the ladies. "Guess the only four ladies in the county that ain't seen him is us."

"We haven't seen him," said Didymus.

"They say he's calm as a cucumber," said Mrs. Carter.

"Say he don't move around hardly none," said one of the ladies.

"Don't see how he could be calm after takin a ice pick to my baby," said Mrs. Carter.

"That nigger is standin in that cell dead already," said one of the ladies. "He's been dead since the minute they caught him. That's how he can be calm."

"I'd like to see that nigger and ask him why," said Mrs. Carter.

"It'll all come out at the trial, no doubt," said Didymus.

All four ladies in a single movement turned their heads and looked up at him.

"I'm afraid he's gone go to God's justice without ever telling how he could a done such a thing," said Mrs. Carter.

"I could go over and see him," said the Gospel Singer.

"I was hopin you could," said Mrs. Carter. "I got faith in you. The only person that might could find out is you. They say he won't even talk. But I know if it's anybody that can do it, it's you."

"I'll try," he said.

"It's all a body can ask," she said.

The Gospel Singer left them sitting there and went through the curtain into Hiram's back room. Didymus followed him. He had taken out his *Dream Book* and was carrying it in his hand. Hiram stood by his desk where a light burned and beside him stood a little girl whose hair and eyes were the same off-color of red. She had pale skin and a pink mouth shaped like a bird in flight. Her face followed the sound of the Gospel

Singer as he crossed the room. Hiram looked embarrassed: a
smile that could not quite take hold turned on and off in his
face. Didymus walked up to an open coffin and looked in. Finally he closed the lid and sat down upon it. He opened the
Dream Book and wet the end of his pencil with his tongue.

"Hello," said the Gospel Singer.

"Anne, honey, do you remember the Gospel Singer?" asked
Hiram.

"No, sir," said the child.

"Think real hard," said Hiram. "You didn't git to feel of
him the last time he was home but the time before that, a year
ago it was, you felt his face. Remember?"

"No, sir," said the child, the same sweet smile never leaving
her face. "Do you remember me?"

"I couldn't hardly forget a little girl as pretty as you," said
the Gospel Singer.

"Am I pretty?"

"Yes," said the Gospel Singer.

"You have a nice voice," she said. "Daddy says you've got
the best voice in the world."

"Your daddy's a nice man," he said.

"Can I see your face?"

"I'd be proud for you to," he said.

"You'll have to kneel down," she said.

He knelt and the little hands came on his face warm and
soft and hesitant, then firmer, stronger until in places they almost pinched. And while she pushed and pulled at his face, he
remembered something MaryBell had said to him one of the
last times he had ever seen her alive. "Anybody that ever puts
a hand on you wants to pinch and ever mouth wants to bite
you. You got the smoothest roughest softest hardest body God
ever give a man."

"No," Anne was saying, "I don't think so."

Didymus stopped writing. "You don't think what, child?"

"I don't think he has the nicest face I ever seen."

"Anne!" said Hiram.

"It's all right," said the Gospel Singer.

"She's just a child," said Hiram.

"I told you I thought you were a pretty girl," said the Gospel Singer. "Now you have to tell me what you think of me."

"Well," she said slowly. Her hands moved on him again. "You face is nice, but it's more like everybody else's than not."

"She's only a blind child," said Hiram.

"Daddy said I might could see if I felt you face and believed real hard I could see," Anne said.

"Anne, I . . ." Hiram said.

"Hush, Hiram," said the Gospel Singer.

"It's awful hard to believe you can see if you ain't never seen," said the child. "You don't know how to try." She felt his face again, harder still, pulling at the cheeks. "You caint help me to see, can you?"

"No," said the Gospel Singer.

"What's it like to see?" asked Anne.

"Well it's . . . it's like." He wanted to tell her the color of the sun on trees, how flowers blossom and the sky blooms. But there was nowhere to start because she had never seen light. "No," he said finally. "I caint tell you what it's like."

She took her hands from his face. She looked inexpressibly sad, the broken wings of her mouth falling. She stepped back beside her father who touched her head.

"But I love you," said the Gospel Singer.

"We'll be out to hear you tonight," said Hiram.

Anne had half-turned from where the Gospel Singer still knelt on the floor. "I love you," he said again.

"In the front row," said Hiram. "Right in the front row listenin to you sing out the good, old-time gospels."

Didymus closed his *Dream Book* and stood up from the coffin. "Come on," he said. "We've got to go." He took the Gospel Singer by the arm and raised him. "Seems like I spend half my life getting you off your knees." The child was picking her nose as they walked through the parted curtain and seemed to take no notice of Didymus at all when he called good-bye.

"You going to see the Negro?" asked Didymus.

"Do you think I shouldn't?"

"Oh, I think you should! I wouldn't mind seeing that Negro

myself. Sixty-one times with an ice pick! But I wanted to know how come *you* told Mrs. Carter you would go see him for her."

"It's the only place I can think of where I might be able to git away from them people outside. This whole thing was a bad idea, and if they git close to me again, I don't know if I can go through with the revival tonight or not. If I go back home, they'll just follow me. In the cell with Willalee is the only place."

"That's good, God, that's good," Didymus was saying under his breath, fighting to get his book out again. "A sanctum in a murderer's cell."

The Gospel Singer was concentrating all his efforts on trying to feel bad about MaryBell's death. The poor lovely thing, struck down in the very beginning of her life. So kind and generous to so many people. Such a loving and devoted daughter. He kept saying these things over and over to himself but even while he said them he kept realizing that she was finally gone, that she was never going to spring upon him again in the middle of the night. He did not have to ever worry again about coming back to Enigma. He could, if he wanted to, never set foot in Enigma after this trip.

CHAPTER 7

The crowd was still packed tightly around Enigma Funeral Parlor. But thankfully the man with the black skin did not seem to be about. More cars had arrived. Some of them bore candy-striped stickers on their front and back bumpers: SEE THE FREAK FAIR—MARVEL AT HUMAN WONDERS! Hiram's brother Cash, who owned Enigma Seed and Feed, had sent out to Tifton for a cotton candy–making machine and across the street from the funeral parlor children sat on the edge of the wooden sidewalk eating tall pink sugar cones.

The Gospel Singer and Didymus stepped out of the funeral parlor and the swirling crowd stopped and turned to face them. Now that he had stopped singing over MaryBell, they seemed in a better mood. No one stood at the window looking into the funeral parlor any longer. They had shifted their attention to him. Many of them waved and a knot of teenaged girls suddenly chanted his name and squealed. There was music everywhere. All kinds of music. Car radios had been left on up and down the street. Many of the children held cotton candy pressed to their mouths and transistor radios pressed to their ears. The oiled, metallic voice of disk jockeys shouted through the streets of Enigma: YOU CRAZY MAD TEEN-ADULTS OUT THERE IN TRANSISTOR LAND GET READY FOR THE SWINGINGEST FLINGINGEST STOMPPINGEST ORGY OF SOUND *EVER* WHEN THE COLOSSEUM IN ATLANTA HAS THE SHOW OF THE YEAR! LISTEN TO THIS ALL-STAR CAST: MONSTER MAN AND THE BLOOD SUCKERS, ISAIAH MESSIAH AND THE MESSAGES, THE VIRTUE TRIO: HOPE,

FAITH AND LOVE! AND MANY MANY MORE OF
YOUR FAVORITES!

"Look at it," said Didymus. "God's love is immeasurable."

Something especially shattering came on a transistor radio
in the group of girls that had been shouting his name and they
all turned to face one another, their bodies abruptly coming to
life in a twisting, gyrating dance.

"Can there be penance large enough for this?" asked Didymus.

One of them was particularly pretty. She was wearing white
stretch pants and her hair was black and hung in a ponytail to
the small of her back. Her arms were round and pink. And
while her feet did not move at all in the dance, her bottom, impossibly round and incredibly taut, shivered and rippled like
water under a wind. The Gospel Singer's vision narrowed to
include only the quivering part of her that she now proposed
in his direction by bending forward to swing her ponytail
about her head like a windmill. She could not have been more
than fifteen. The Gospel Singer's teeth went quietly on edge
and his throat dried. There in the midst of that shouting and
waving it occurred to him that he had never had any woman
in Enigma except MaryBell. He couldn't *because* of MaryBell.
She had been as ubiquitous as the air he breathed. He took a
deep, comfortable breath and looked about. Gone! She was
gone! He was free!

He had just raised his foot to take a step in the direction of
the child with the black ponytail, when a man appeared in
front of him holding a microphone on which there were affixed the red letters WWWW. The man was small with spots
of color the size of a dime on his white cheeks, wearing a
brown suit, a tan shirt, and a round yellow straw hat turned
down in front and back. His eyes were very wet and his mouth,
which was formed well enough but sat on top of almost no
chin at all, seemed to tremble. A heavy black cord ran down
from the microphone and between the man's legs and finally
disappeared into the crowd. He reached out and touched the
Gospel Singer as though to convince himself that he was really
there, glanced up and got the angle of the sun, adjusted his tie,

turned around in the direction of the disappearing cord and
shouted in a startlingly loud voice: "You goddam people get
off that cord! Stand back there and knock off some of that
noise and douse those radios! Don't you know who I am! Can
you see?"

A hush fell and the crowd parted behind the man like bread
under a knife. The black cord ran back to a white panel truck
with WWWW painted all over it. A man in white coveralls
squatted on top of the truck with a portable television camera
on his shoulder. A few of the people waved timidly at the black
mouth of the camera as though it were a dear friend and this
were a sad parting.

The man turned his profile to the camera, took the Gospel
Singer by the arm with his free hand, and came suddenly to
life. His face brightened; his body quivered with small fluid
movements. His voice broke out of his mouth like something
pouring from a jar. Once it started, it had no beginning or end
but simply flowed. "No one in our audience needs an intro-
duction to this man. A man who has brought peace and joy
and happiness into the hearts of so many thousands. A man
known all over the United States and some say all over the
world." The Gospel Singer stood blinking into the whirring
camera while out of the corner of his eye he watched the girl,
now motionless and intent as granite leaning in the direction
of the magical box on the man's shoulder atop the WWWW
truck. "You are here today with WWWW network news in
Enigma, home base and birthplace for this man whose songs
have thrilled your hearts." The man on the truck suddenly
waved and took the camera off his shoulder.

"While he's getting set up again, how are you?" asked
the man.

"I'm all right," said the Gospel Singer.

"Looks like you got a real live crowd, Didymus," said the
announcer.

"You know how the Gospel Singer is," said Didymus. "He
draws the worst right along with the best. You can't be selec-
tive if you're in the gospel-singing business."

The man on top of the truck shouldered his camera and

waved to them. "Get back there like you were when we stopped," said the man. "We'll pick it right up again." He moved the Gospel Singer back into position. "Tragedy has struck here, and the man with me today, the man near and dear in the hearts of so many of you out there in the audience, this man is at the very center of that tragedy. I know this is a bad time for you, but I wonder if we could have just a few words with you?"

The Gospel Singer, who had been watching the child in the white stretchpants, realized that the announcer had stopped talking but he did not know what had been said to him.

The Gospel Singer shook his head. "I know, I know," he murmured.

"Of course you can," said Didymus, who had just seen the girl with the black ponytail and consequently knew that the Gospel Singer wouldn't know what he had been asked.

"In your own words could you tell the folks—all your friends—out there what it's like to be the Gospel Singer and . . ."

". . . tragedy, tragedy," said the Gospel Singer.

". . . and have a thing like this happen? Yes, a tragedy. Certainly that. Nothing if not a tragedy. Did you have any inkling that such a thing might happen?"

"None," said the Gospel Singer.

"And now that it has, what do you propose to do?"

"I think," he said, pausing just briefly, glancing in the direction of the girl who had raised her radio to her ear and was now pulsing softly from the waist down. "I think I'll raise a monument to MaryBell," he said. It was an inspiration of the moment, but once he had said it, he knew it was right. "I think I'll raise a monument for that dear, sweet girl right here in this very Enigma, something for the whole world to see."

"I understand that your relations with MaryBell went all the way back to childhood."

"We were very close," he said.

"Did you know the Negro?"

"I known him a long time ago."

"How about motive? Any speculation about why he did it?"

"Why, rape," said the Gospel Singer. "Why else would a Negro kill a poor girl like MaryBell?"

"Yes, of course," said the announcer. "Why else?" He turned from the Gospel Singer to face the camera. "And that's the story from here, a sleepy little town where the country's own Gospel Singer was born and raised and has now returned to find only heartache and . . . tragedy. This is Richard Hognut in Enigma, for WWWW News."

"Are you really going to build a monument?" asked Richard Hognut, sticking the microphone into his hip pocket.

"Yes," said the Gospel Singer.

"Why don't you build a goddam hotel instead?" asked Richard Hognut. "And . . ."

"Watch your mouth," said Didymus.

"Sorry, Didymus," Richard Hognut said. "Build a hotel and air-condition it. I drove all the way out here last night, not a hotel in town, couldn't find your folks' place—somebody said it was in a goddam . . . sorry . . . swamp—and finally wound up driving all the way back to Tifton to find a place to sleep."

"She's been dead four days," said Didymus. "Why are you just getting here?"

"Wasn't news until the Gospel Singer got here, not network stuff anyway. Putting *him* on tape talking about it, that's the thing." He turned suddenly on the crowd pressing at his back. "Get off that wire, goddammit! Man, is this a crowd! Think I'll drive in to Tifton and send this out and come back tonight for the revival. God, they're restless. *Get back!*" He walked slowly back to his truck, winding the electrical wire about his arm like a lariat.

A large part of the crowd followed them down to the courthouse at the end of the street. The sun came suddenly, brilliantly, through a hole in the overcast sky. The Gospel Singer had lost track of the girl in the white stretchpants. He wondered briefly whether or not she would be at the revival that night, and if she was, where he would take her. Now that he had made a public statement about the monument, he'd have to be sure and build it. Didymus could take care of it. He had no idea what kind of monument it should be, but Didymus

would know. He must not neglect to tell him to start on it
soon.

The sheriff was sitting at the desk in his office reading an
old newspaper comic strip and drinking a diet-rite cola. About
twenty people came right through the door with the Gospel
Singer. The sheriff got heavily to his feet, rubbing his belly that
swung like a half-filled sack under his shirt. He set his diet-rite
cola down on the desk and waddled across the floor to the
Gospel Singer. His head bobbed rapidly up and down as
though he were agreeing as hard as he could with something
or somebody. He touched the Gospel Singer on the arm and
then as if he were seeing them for the first time, he turned on
the people who had come into the office with him and began
herding them back through the door. "Out," he said. "Out,
out, out, out." He took Didymus by the arm and tried to push
him out too. "Out, out."

"He's with me, Lucas," said the Gospel Singer.

The sheriff was embarrassed. "Oh, I *am* sorry." He brushed
Didymus off and patted him variously about his body. He
closed the door and fell against it. "Madhouse, madhouse!"
said the sheriff. "They been pilin through here like that since
last night. Once they git a look at MaryBell, they caint git
enough of lookin at him." He walked slowly around the Gospel
Singer, looking him up and down, reaching out as though to
brush something off his shoulder, but ending by gently squeez-
ing him on the arm. "This is a pure pleasure," said the sheriff.
"I didn't know if you'd be able to git by or not. But we was
comin to the meetin tonight, wife and me. Was." He stopped
to breathe, looking at Didymus. "Terrible thing! Terrible. Just
awful. Soon's it happened I thought of you. Terrible for you!
MaryBell and all. Yes." He was still staring at Didymus.

"This is my new manager," said the Gospel Singer. "Name
Didymus."

"I'm pleased to meet you," said the sheriff. "Name Lucas."
Didymus stuck out his hand and the sheriff caught him by the
wrist and commenced to pat and rub him. "I known you'd git
rid of that Keene one of these days," he said to the Gospel
Singer. He still had Didymus in a half-embrace. "Notice you

smoke, Didymus. Really suck'm down. Use to do that. Keene's a tobacco farmer, you know. Yes. Cancer farmers I call them. You know I had cancer. Or maybe *have* cancer. I won't know until I die or don't. Say, you really *do* puff, don't you!" He leaned forward and wet his lips and stuck his nose into the pillar of smoke pouring from Didymus' mouth. "Opened me up and took a lung right off like it weren't no more'n a wart." He turned to the Gospel Singer. "Let me call Martha out. She's gone be happy, real happy to see you." Without taking his eyes off the Gospel Singer he screamed, "MARTHA!"

And from somewhere back in the granite recesses of the courthouse there came an immediate and direct reply like an echo: "GODDAMMIT THEY AIN'T KNEE-MORE!"

The sheriff smiled shyly at the Gospel Singer. "She don't know how come I'm callin. Thinks I want more sandwiches and coffee. We run out. Sold everthin we had. It's not another loaf of sliced bread or slab of baloney to be bought in Enigmer. This crowd's cleaned us out, et everthin. Martha's a little frazzled on the edges cause of it. We could of sold four times what we had."

"I come to see Willalee," said the Gospel Singer. "I promised Mizz Carter."

The sheriff screamed again. "It ain't *them*, it's *him!*"

There came the sound of breaking glass and a happy little squeal and presently the door behind the sheriff opened and a woman burst upon them. She was built along the lines of a pencil, with old skin and iron-gray hair brought together at the base of her skull like four Brillo pads. It was tied with a red ribbon. She came flying directly at the Gospel Singer, busily wiping her hands down the sides of her hipless, breastless body. She looked as though she would throw herself on his chest, but she managed to stop, half-curtsying, nervously touching herself.

"I know you're shocked!" she said. "I know that. But to the end of my rope is where I've been since this thing started. Right at the end of it, holdin on with nothin but my teeth. You know I don't usually say a word out of the way usually. Lucas, yes, but not me. And MY, DON'T YOU LOOK GOOD!" She stepped back to look at him and threw her hands on her hips which weren't there so that she ended by rubbing herself again.

"I guess I ain't said goddam more'n forty times in my life but thirty of em must have been since that poor child was struck down by the nigger."

"I come by to see him," said the Gospel Singer.

"Everbody and his brother's been by," she said. "And that's the God's honest. Guess Lucas told you. He ain't much to look at. He won't talk. Ain't et a handful since we had him in there and he's a big nigger too."

The Gospel Singer stretched his neck as though to breathe or to see over her head. "I really don't see what I can do but Mizz Carter wanted me to stop by. It's the least I can do. I've got to git on back to the place too and git ready for the meetin tonight. But I wanted to see him before I did."

"Did you know I git on as well on one lung as I use to on two," said the sheriff. "I got good color and eat like a hog. You think I got good color?"

"You lookin fine, Lucas," said the Gospel Singer. "Now could . . ."

"You think so? Martha thinks I'm too fat. Says I'm too fat for one lung? Do you think one lung can do a man stout as me?"

"You'll be all right," said the Gospel Singer. "Now I got to see Willalee. I ain't got much longer."

"All right," said the sheriff.

"It ain't nothin you can do, I don't think," said Martha. "You might as well stay out here and talk a while. You still got that Cadillac? I got some coffee I saved back. I can make it in a jiff on the hot plate. You want a cup?"

"I better see Willalee."

The sheriff opened the door and they all followed the Gospel Singer back to the cell where Willalee still stood with his back to them looking out on the street through the barred window.

"That's the way he stays mostly," said the sheriff.

"Are you positive he killed her?" asked the Gospel Singer.

"Oh, he killed her. They never been any doubt."

At the sound of the Gospel Singer's voice, Willalee turned from the window and came to face them at the door. He was a big man, three inches taller than the Gospel Singer, but lean and well-made. He was very black, and his features were good: strong chin, deep eyes, high prominent cheeks, a broad, smooth forehead. They might have all been logs or not have been there at all for all that showed in his face. The Gospel Singer had not seen him in years, or if he had seen him, he did not remember, and he was struck immediately by what a handsome man he was.

"Hello," said Willalee. "I been waitin."

"He's probly crazy," said Martha. "Most everbody thinks that's what it is, he's crazy."

"Open the door and let me in," said the Gospel Singer.

"I don't think you oughten do that," said the sheriff. "He ain't a thing if he ain't dangerous."

"I'll talk to him anyway. I promised."

The sheriff opened the door and the Gospel Singer went into the cell, along with Didymus who had his *Dream Book* out and opened with his pencil at the ready. The sheriff closed the door again. Willalee looked at no one but the Gospel Singer. Didymus sat down on a chair and the Gospel Singer sat on the iron cot. The sheriff and his wife remained close to the door, intent, slightly bent forward from the hips, as though expecting to witness something extraordinary, perhaps a miracle.

"Be careful," said the sheriff.

There was a sustained shout from the crowd outside as though it were cheering a horse race.

"He's not gone bother me," the Gospel Singer said. "You go on out and watch those folks. They liable to tear down your front door. Didymus and me'll be all right."

"I guess you the only one in Enigmer that could go in there and feel safe," said the sheriff. He handled the heavy, tobacco-colored pistol hanging below his paunch. "If you need me, you call. And, nigger, if you put a hand on him, I'm just gone stand out here and shoot you six times through the guts."

As soon as the sheriff and his wife were gone Didymus went to the window. "It's going to rain again," he said. "Maybe it'll drive those people out of the street, back into their cars or somewheres."

A heavy droning rose out of the street. Someone hawked sandwiches above the voices and music from radios. On the table in front of the Gospel Singer a swarm of flies fought over a plate of food. The air was a hot humid weight that pressed about them from the walls and ceiling. The cell smelled of sweat. Didymus went back and sat upon the chair. He examined the point of his pencil and made a mark in the margin of his book. He crossed his legs and uncrossed them. "Well," he said. "Well."

Willalee still stood at the door. Sweat was shining on his face and on the backs of his hands. His blue workshirt had darkened on the back and at the armpits. It was sticking to his chest. His face was calm but his eyes were very bright and skittered about the walls of the cell as though expecting some frightening thing to leap out upon them.

"I hoped you'd come," said Willalee. "I's afraid you'd come too late. They gone kill me tonight."

Didymus leapt out of his chair. "Kill? Kill?" He stared up into Willalee's face as though trying to see the word itself. "Kill! Kill! Tonight?"

"They wouldn't do that, Willalee," said the Gospel Singer.

Willalee brushed Didymus out of his way. "They is," he said. "I known it. Tonight after the meetin they gone care me out and hang me on a tree. I ain't studyin it. I's just hopin you'd come before they done it."

"Willalee, I don't think I can do anythin," said the Gospel Singer. "I don't know what I can do. Do you know when your trial's set for? Do you have a lawyer?"

"I ain't studyin it. Ain't gone be no trial. They gone do it to me tonight."

"Now stop sayin that," said the Gospel Singer. "You don't have to be afraid. I know the sheriff. He never lost a prisoner to a mob."

"Ain't afraid of gitten hanged," said Willalee. "I . . ."

"You're not afraid of *dying?*" cried Didymus. Once more he was pressed almost against Willalee, staring up into his face.

Willalee gently pushed Didymus out of the way. "I's afraid of losin myself to hell. I ain't afraid of dyin, I's afraid of God.

I don't want to die till I know how come I killed Miss Mary-Bell."

"Did you rape her?" asked the Gospel Singer.

"That's white talk. A lie. They say I did, but I ain't raped that girl. I ain't touched her with nothing but that ice pick. But I touched her with that. I killed her."

"Why did you kill her?" asked Didymus.

There was a long silence. The noise from the crowd in the street flowed through the barred window and slowly swelled to fill the cell. "Don't know how come," said Willalee finally. "And I's afraid I'll lose myself to hell, if they hang me thout me knowin. It ain't the dyin, it's the knowin."

"You wrong. Nobody's gone hang you tonight. I know that, but just so you know it, I'm goin out and talk to Lucas," the Gospel Singer said. He shook the cell door. "Lucas! Open up!"

The sheriff burst through the door clawing for his pistol. "What is it?" he demanded. "What?"

"Open the door. And put that damn gun up before you shoot me."

Back in the office the sheriff was not inclined to say definitely one way or the other. "Now it's a complicated thing, justice," he said. "Why don't you have one these diet-rite?"

"I don't want one," said the Gospel Singer. "I want an answer. Are you tryin to tell me you don't know if someone's gone try to hang Willalee tonight?"

"No, I ain't tryin to tell you that," he said, inspecting the top of his belly where it swelled out to hide his holstered pistol. He paused. "I *know* they gone kill him. It ain't sure yet if they gone hang him or if they gone shoot him."

"Lucas, NO!"

"I tried to talk them out of it," he said.

"A southern lynching!" Didymus said, writing furiously in his *Dream Book*.

"But you caint do that," said the Gospel Singer.

"Well, if he's guilty . . ." said Didymus.

"I tried to talk them boys out of it," said the sheriff. "I tried real hard. I mean it ain't gone be no picnic for me. The governor'll be sendin people down here and the FBI and all them organizations for the protection of the nigger—all of them'll be down here askin me how it happened."

"He ought to have a trial," said the Gospel Singer.

"Well," said Didymus. "If he's guilty . . ."

"The boys is all stirred up on this one," said the sheriff. "You know what the boys thought of MaryBell. They so goddam mad about that nigger killin her, they ready to lynch anybody."

"Lynch, lynch," said Didymus.

"Somebody in Enigmer would've got MaryBell sooner or later if that nigger hadn't killed her. You gone have to forgive me talkin like this but it ain't nothin but the truth. I mean, you was gone from Enigmer a lot of the time and . . . Well, more'n one of the boys had they eye on her. It ain't nothin but the truth. She couldn't stay a virgin forever. Then that nigger gitten in her pants after ever man in the county had dreamt—it ain't nothin but the truth—a hundret times about him bein the one to . . ." The sheriff trailed off, shaking his head sadly.

"Willalee says he didn't rape her."

The sheriff stared, his eyes widening. "Then it don't make no sense at all," he said. "None at all." He held up a hand and counted on his fingers, "He didn't take her money, and he didn't take precious jewels. What else is they? Not but the one thing. Besides," the sheriff looked down and stroked his belly softly. "Besides, she didn't have on no pants. Ittas the first thing I checked when I got there." He sighed. "And she didn't have a thing on under that dress. That nigger'd done taken her pants."

The Gospel Singer opened his mouth and then closed it. He couldn't tell the sheriff that MaryBell did not wear pants, that she had not worn any for over a year.

"I must talk to Willalee," said the Gospel Singer.

"Again?" asked the sheriff. "What all you got to talk about with him?"

Just then the door popped open and several people stared into the office. "Get back," shouted the sheriff. "We closed. Go on, git out of here!"

A man stopped in the door. His voice was belligerent. "We

want the Gospel Singer. We drove a hundred miles and we want to see him."

The sheriff pushed him through the door and closed it. Somebody on the other side shouted, "He's in there all right." A cheer went up.

"Madhouse, madhouse," said the sheriff.

"Come on, open the cell for me," said the Gospel Singer.

"If it weren't you, I wouldn't do it. You the only one I'd do it for."

"I'll stay out here," said Didymus. "And help the sheriff keep these people out of here."

As the sheriff and Didymus were going back out into the main office Didymus was asking, "You ever seen a man lynched before?"

Willalee sat on the bed and watched the Gospel Singer standing across the cell from him. There was a Bible open on Willalee's knees.

"They gone do it, ain't they?" asked Willalee.

"They might," said the Gospel Singer.

"I known it," he said. "It ain't no matter." He got off the bed and walked to the window. He carried the Bible with him. There were perhaps two hundred people gathered directly below his cell. They swelled back and forth, eating, talking, turning the radios louder.

"Willalee, if they . . . if they do it tonight, it'll be because they think you raped her. That's what they're so stirred up about."

"I didn't," said Willalee.

"How do you know?" asked the Gospel Singer. "How can you be so sure if you don't remember . . ."

"I remember it all," said Willalee. "All what I done." He held the Bible in his left hand, extended in front of him. The hand was thick, massive, blacker than the black Bible. "I taken her by the throat. I remember. I reached my ice pick offen the wall and I struck her the first time. I remember. She couldn't scream. She couldn't make a word. When she was dead, I got in the bed and went to sleep. I ain't touched that girl with nothin but the ice pick."

"The sheriff says it don't make sense if you didn't rape her, and it seems like he's right," said the Gospel Singer. "I mean, why else did you do it? Was you mad at her?"

Willalee frowned slightly. "I ain't no crazy man. If I hit her with a ice pick, I musta been mad at her."

"Why?"

"I don't know," said Willalee. "That's the part I caint remember. Everthin I done, I can remember. I just caint remember why I done it."

"I wish I could do somethin."

"You can pray," said Willalee.

"What?"

"Pray with me. You can axe the Lord to forgive me what I done."

"If He's gone forgive you," said the Gospel Singer, "it'll be because *you* pray, not me."

Willalee came to where the Gospel Singer sat on the bed and slowly sank to his knees. "I know what I done to you."

"Get up, Willalee."

"All the colut folks know how it is with you and Miss Mary-Bell."

The Gospel Singer straightened on the bed. "They do?"

"I know I killed you sweetheart, but I known you'd forgive even that. I known you wouldn't turn me down. You gone help me git it straight with God."

"Get up, Willalee," the Gospel Singer said. "I caint help you get nothin straight with God. I don't know what you did or nothin about it."

"Everbody knows you power and you glory," said Willalee. "White folks know it, colut folks know it. You the way and the salvation. The only hope I got."

The Gospel Singer now was tugging at Willalee, trying to pull him to his feet.

"Miss MaryBell known it. She use to say it. She use to sing it. It's all she use to say in Quarters."

The Gospel Singer quit pulling at Willalee. "What did she say?"

"Say, Willalee, he the Lily of the Valley. Say, paint up you cabin and nail down the roof cause he the Sun in the Sky and he want it, and then she laugh cause she so happy. Just laugh and laugh and laugh. She tol all the colut folks in Quarters you sent her. Say, plant that rosebush and let it grow cause the Gospel Singer like a rosebush. He like a rosebush. He like swept yards and he don't like no dirty chillun nor no dirty houses. Then she laugh and laugh and laugh cause she happy doin what you want her to do."

The Gospel Singer was shaking his head to the rhythm of Willalee's words. "No," he said. "She didn't do that. She couldn't do that. Nobody in Quarters would care if I wanted one thing or another. It was no reason for them to care."

"Yes it is," Willalee said. "The best reason in this world. I tol them what she say was the true gospel accordin to the Singer, and it was right to do it. That made Miss MaryBell happy as she could be. Evertime I tol'm, she'd near break laughin, you could hear Miss MaryBell laughin all over Quarters."

"But why would *you* tell them that?" asked the Gospel Singer. "I never done nothin to you. How come they'd listen to you anyhow?"

"Because I's a preacher too," he said.

The Gospel Singer paled. "Not *too*," he said. "Not *too*."

Willalee got to his feet and held his Bible out to the Gospel Singer with both hands. "I's a preacher and I built my church on you."

"Willalee!" cried the Gospel Singer. "For God's sake!"

"It was the only thing I could do," said Willalee. "You saved me on the TeeVee." His voice became dreamy. He brought the Bible nearer his body. "I was just a ordinary man, workin in the woods, dippin tar and chippin boxes. Evertime you was on the TeeVee, I watched you, an evertime I watched you, I known what you was. Then in the dead of night, lyin in my cabin, you come on the Muntz and I seen how it was gone be. The seventh day of April, on a Wednesday. You was in Nu Yawk City. And as soon as you come on, I was ready. Miss MaryBell tol me. She done tol me agin and agin how it was gone be if I just kept watchin you. So I did and it was. I laid my hand up on that glass and . . ."

Seventh of April. A Wednesday. She had red hair and very dark nipples. That was all he could remember about her except she had been pretty and he had dallied with her for almost three hours before the show, which was done at Radio City Music Hall, and then again until midnight after the show. He could not remember her name but she had been uncommonly good—clever, ingenuous—and he had thought about her during the show. And while he thought about her white, enormous sandwich, spread and waiting for him when he was through singing, Willalee's black, stretched hand had touched his glass image and found God. The Gospel Singer felt his lungs collapsing. He did not think God would stand for that. That just about cut his last chance.

". . . so Miss MaryBell say, why not build the church on the Gospel Singer? And it taken all the money you given her to help us with to git the church started. All that money and you was the best man we known and you done so much to help us, so we done it."

The Gospel Singer remembered the first time she had asked him for money in a letter. It had been about four months ago and he could not remember now why she said she needed the money, but he could remember distinctly how relieved he was. He sent twice as much as she asked for and then left instructions with Didymus to add her name to the long list of people to whom he was already sending money regularly.

"How many in Quarters belong to the church?" asked the Gospel Singer.

"Most half the colut folks in Lebeau County," said Willalee. "They sees you on the TeeVee and Miss MaryBell done told us how you gone make it right with God."

"Where's the church?"

"Down from the Shackleford place." Willalee went on his knees again before the Gospel Singer. He took the Gospel Singer's hand and pulled it down on his head. The hair was coarse and damp. "How come I killed Miss MaryBell? She brought the money. She tol me what to do. Ittas her that thought of the name for the church."

"The name for the church?" breathed the Gospel Singer.

"She thought it up and drawn the letters and . . ."

The Gospel Singer lunged to his feet almost upsetting Willalee. "No!" he cried. "No don't! Listen, Willalee, I got to stop this, I . . ."

Willalee shook his head sadly. "Don't think you can stop it. No, tonight they gone hang me on a tree and that's all they is to it. And the good Lord knows I's ready. I killed Miss Mary-Bell and they ain't no tree He ever growed that can hang me high enough for that. No. I only want to say on the Judgment how come I done it, to say to *you* how come I done it. Me, a preacher in you own church, killin the girl you loved with a ice pick. When they put me on that tree I want to look up to God and know I'm goin home. But a man with a sin hid like a thief in his heart is headed straight for hell. God don't take none that ain't washed clean. No."

Willalee sobbed with his eyes closed and he rocked on his knees. The Gospel Singer, stricken with the growing knowledge that he was responsible for Willalee's plight, stared at him, unable to speak. Finally he took Willalee by the shoulders and said, "Hush, hush now. Listen, they ain't gone do anythin to you. You hear? I'm with you. Now stop that and get up. I'm with you."

Willalee got up and sat on the edge of the iron cot. The Gospel Singer went to the window and looked out. Below, down the entire length of Enigma, the crowd now swirled, a continuous wash of color and sound. Behind him, Willalee was talking on in a flat, spiritless voice. "You allus been with me. Since I been saved, it ain't one time you left me, never one. And I's saved, I known it when it happened. And I's still saved, that's gospel and I know it. But I got the blood of Miss MaryBell on my hands . . . on my heart."

"Listen," said the Gospel Singer, turning from the window, wanting to comfort Willalee, wanting to tell him the truth, but knowing the truth would hurt even worse than the fantastic tissue of lies. But what he saw as he turned made it unnecessary for him to say anything. There on the iron cot was his ragged and tattered image, carefully smoothed out, but old and quartered by creases. Willalee, his lips moving, talking on, was looking not at the Gospel Singer but at his picture.

The Gospel Singer walked slowly across the cell to the cot. "Where did you get that?" he asked.

Willalee did not look up. ". . . her done errythin. If she ain't come to Quarters, I still be lak I was. A mean nigger, razor cuts on my back, laying up with yeller girls. She showed me the way." Willalee's tremendous, calloused finger traced the outline of the Gospel Singer's face on the magazine cover as he talked. "She helped a mean nigger git right, no more cuttin, no more takin the Lord's name, no more yeller girls. Tol me about the Gospel Singer. Tol me how it was. Miss MaryBell, Miss MaryBell. Got the church. Got it fixed. Got it goin. Miss Mary-Bell." He looked briefly at his hands, turning them both palms up, shaking his head as he did, still talking, softly in a sleepy monotone, "Meetin. Meetin in the church when he come home. We got it fixed, we got it ready and he gone stand in his church and he gone look out on us and say ittas good. Yes. We ready, for he comin home. Yes. Miss MaryBell say she gone come to tell when the Gospel Singer comin home the minute she know. She come in the middle of the night. They ain't no man know the day or the hour. She . . ." He paused, turning his head slightly, as though to listen. He pressed the middle of his forehead with one finger. "She say, I come to tell you about the Gospel Singer. I say, when he comin? She . . ." A grayness the color of wet ashes moved in Willalee's face. A vein leapt in his temple. "No," he whispered. "I's a preacher. I's saved." He sank down upon the limp picture of the Gospel Singer. "No, Lord, no, no. *She say, you saved on a lie, the church a lie, the Gospel Singer a lie. She say, God is a man with his pants down, God is a unbuttoned fly.* She say, the Gospel Singer . . . and I hit her with the ice pick. I taken her by the throat and hit her and hit her and hit her." He sobbed face down on the cot, his fists balled.

The Gospel Singer did not so much kneel as he collapsed. He put his arm around Willalee. "Please," he said. "Please."

Willalee looked out of the cot. He had stopped shaking. He no longer wept. He looked almost as though he would smile. "I known it," he said. "I known you'd know how come I killed her and git me right with the Lord. I's ready now. It ain't nobody can hurt me now cause I know what I done and I know I wronged the Lord. I's goin home."

The Gospel Singer stood up and turned toward the cell door and saw Didymus squatting there on the other side of the bars, motionless, his head down, his *Dream Book* open on his knees, his short bitten pencil flying across the page.

"I's a mean nigger with a mean temper," said Willalee. "When I heard the lies, that ol Devil got me agin. Yes. Got me. But I's right with the Lord now." He sat up on the cot. "Why Miss MaryBell tell them lies?"

The Gospel Singer heard Didymus' pencil stop on the page. The noise from the crowd in the street rose. "I don't know," he said.

"But they ever one lies," said Willalee.

"Ever one," said the Gospel Singer, facing the cell door. Then in the same breath: "I got to go, Willalee."

Willalee stood up behind him. "I know it," he said. "But thank the Lord you come. I known all along you couldn't stay but a little. It's one good thing though."

"What's that?"

"They can still have the meetin in the church tonight. It ain't no matter that I ain't there."

The Gospel Singer shook the cell door and screamed for the sheriff, who burst immediately through the door searching his underbelly for his pistol and demanding to know what was going on, what?

"Open the door, Lucas."

"Did you find out anything?" asked the sheriff. "Did . . . Say, you look pale. You better set down. What did he say? You want me to go in there and rap his head one time?" He waved vaguely in the direction of the pistol he could not see.

The Gospel Singer could only shake his head. He could not seem to get enough air and his legs were prickly with sweat. He was overwhelmed by what MaryBell had done. He could still scarcely believe it. He, who had always been loved, found the prospect of hatred incredible. And only now was he beginning to see how much she must have hated him. Back in the office, he leaned against the sheriff's desk.

"Lucas," he said. "You caint let anythin happen to Willalee. I want you to give me your word you won't let anybody take him out of that cell."

Lucas opened a styrofoam ice chest beside his desk and took out a diet-rite cola. "Would you care for one of these? They refresh real good and don't put on the flesh like the othern do."

"Will you give me your word?"

Lucas took a long drink and belched. "Sure," he said. "I can give you my word. But the boys ain't gone hang my word, they gone hang the nigger. What I tell you ain't gone make a bit a difference to them." He made an angry noise into the neck of his diet-rite bottle.

"You could stop it if you wanted to," said the Gospel Singer.

"Listen," said the sheriff. "He'll tell you hisself he killed MaryBell, don't even deny it. Me? I got one lung, and I'm overweight. Should I git in the way of anybody wantin to hang the nigger?"

"I'm askin you too," said the Gospel Singer.

"I'm gone tell you somethin else cause I like you," said the sheriff, the color rising in his neck and hanging jowls. "You the Gospel Singer. But this is Enigmer. Nobody cares what you think of the nigger. Even if you like him nobody cares. But I swear I wouldn't go around talkin about how he oughten to be taken out and killed. I swear I wouldn't do that if I was you."

"I just want him treated fair."

"The boys gone treat him about like he treated MaryBell. And they subject to treat anybody that gits between them and him the same way."

"I wish you wouldn't let them take him."

"I wish you'd have a cup of Martha's coffee or a diet-rite," said Lucas. "Martha's gone to fix it now. We can have a good talk about all them places you been, and the things you done and forget about the nigger. Ain't no use talkin about him. You caint run a dead horse."

"I got to go," said the Gospel Singer.

"Martha's gone be real disappointed. She's making that coffee special for you."

"Tell her I had to go. Come on, Didymus."

The crowd that had been under the window of Willalee's cell, in a kind of spontaneous intuition, swirled around the corner of the courthouse and gathered at the door where the Gospel Singer emerged. More people had arrived in town for the revival. The Gospel Singer stood on the top step of the courthouse and looked down upon them. The street was a jammed mass of faces turned up like masks with black open mouths sucking and expelling a collective breath. Two Good Humor trucks had come in from Tifton and were parked now on each side of the street between the jail and the funeral parlor. On top of the trucks were small, rotating megaphones out of which poured music that sounded like Christmas carols. After each song, a mechanical voice came on and read ice cream flavors and names of sundaes, like a conductor calling stops on a commuter train.

"We'll never get through that," said Didymus.

For an answer the Gospel Singer plunged into the mob. Didymus fastened his *Dream Book* inside his coat and followed. Getting back to the Cadillac was like running the gauntlet. Hands sought to pat and touch and caress the Gospel Singer, but there were so many hands they had to hurry, and in their haste the caresses became slaps and digs and finally outright punches. Or so they felt. A squirming wall of flesh squeezed in from all sides. Didymus tried to help him, tried to fight them off, but the crowd summarily ejected him, and the Gospel Singer had to struggle on alone. A pocket was torn from his coat. Wet and feverish mouths hummed hymns about his head. Others whispered parts of impossible demands in his ears. Here and there a curse fluttered among the supplications to God.

After a long time during which the Gospel Singer was never sure he would make it, he reached the Cadillac. He jerked open the back door and flung himself inside. He touched a switch that automatically locked the car. He lay panting hoarsely against the cushions. The windows and windshields were solid with stretching faces, distorted mouths and eyes brightly glazed. Far off, a group of young girls was chanting his name in time to something playing on a radio. Finally Didymus' face pressed through to the window. His eyes didn't seem to focus, giving his expression the slightly distorted look of a funhouse mirror. He was very red and sweating. The Gospel Singer opened one of the doors. A young girl had him about the legs and the Gospel Singer had to help get him get loose and into the car. Didymus locked the door behind him.

"Wild, they're wild out there!" he said when he could get his breath.

The Cadillac swayed gently.

Didymus shook his head. "Usually I can keep them back. I don't know, they're not normal." He was agitated, bouncing on the front seat as he talked, bending his head to look first this way and then the other. "The combination of you, murdered MaryBell, and the Negro locked up at the end of the street has done something to them. I was right behind you and then these hands had me and the . . . Say, are you O.K.?"

"I'm all right," said the Gospel Singer. "You did the best you could. Now crank it up, get us out of here."

Didymus did not try to go back up the main street since by now it was impassable. People milled about between the wooden sidewalks as though forming for a street dance. It was just beginning to rain as Didymus eased the car through a back street that paralleled the main street. Even there, they were recognized, and people kept trying to head them off, shaking autograph books and Bibles and various maimed and deformed limbs in their direction. Didymus had to go slowly while they were still in the town because he was afraid someone would be badly hurt, or worse, killed. Every now and then one of the more enthusiastic of the people ran blindly into the side of the car like a bug slamming into a night screen.

"You lied to Willalee," said Didymus, stopping momentarily because people were swarming over the front bumper and hood.

"Would you have told him the truth? Would that have been better for him?"

"No," said Didymus losing his composure and sticking his tongue out at a face jammed against the windshield. "I just thought I'd point out that when a man tells a lie, it's because he's ashamed of the truth, or because he wishes the lie were the truth."

"Can't you go any faster?"

"Not unless you want to kill somebody." Didymus was driving with one foot on the gas and one foot on the brake, literally pushing people out of the way. He expected at any moment to mash the life out of somebody. "Say, that sheriff is something. You know him long?"

"All my life," said the Gospel Singer, watching a small boy on the sidewalk eat a cotton candy.

"He told me all about lynching and such," Didymus said. "Did you know a man can die from being tarred and feathered? You'd be surprised what that man knows about lynching. Says they almost always do something to a man before they lynch him. You'd think lynching would be enough. But they tar, castrate, blind, and emasculate. It's something. There's no telling what they'll do to Willalee tonight."

"They not gone do anything to him. I'm gone stop them."

They were free of Enigma now and the car gained speed.

"How?"

"I don't know. I've got to find a way. And don't turn up there, we're not going back to the place yet."

"Where are we going?" asked Didymus, driving with one hand and getting the *Dream Book* out on the seat beside him with the other.

"You'll see."

"You're going to that church, aren't you, to Willalee's church?"

"Yes."

"That's a good sign."

"Shut up about your goddam signs," said the Gospel Singer. "And turn in that dirt road by the pecan tree. I'm coming out here to see what it is MaryBell's done. She was crazy. I see that now. It's all this church business that got her killed, stirring up Willalee like that. Crazy bitch. Go slower."

"What Willalee said didn't make much sense to me," said Didymus.

"It made plenty of sense," said the Gospel Singer. "She filled Willalee full of lies, got him to believing them, then told him the truth. He had ever reason to do it. I wish he hadn't, but he had ever reason. This is the Shackleford place up here. The church ought to be just beyond it."

The mule-and-wagon-road they were in was dark and narrow with a dense growth of weeds pressing in from both sides.

"There's something up ahead," said Didymus. "Yes, and it has a steeple of sorts. This must be it all right."

The Gospel Singer, hunkered down in the back seat, had not looked. He was gazing up at the still, oppressive sky. The rain was light and steady. The clouds appeared to him like the fabulous undersides of a mountain range. In order not to have to look at the approaching church, he concentrated on the impossible fact of being buried under a mountain.

"Say, now," said Didymus. "That's not a bad-looking building to be stuck out here in the . . ."

The Gospel Singer heard the change in the pitch of his voice and jerked his head round and stared himself. It was an oblong, dog-run structure, the front door of which was painted a brilliant red so that it glowed like a light. The room was covered with shiny tin. Then the Gospel Singer saw what had changed Didymus' voice. It was a sign nailed at the apex of the roof: THE FIRST CHURCH OF THE GOSPEL SINGER.

"It's a Sign," said Didymus.

"It's a nigger church," said the Gospel Singer.

"But a church, a church with your name on it."

"MaryBell did this to me," the Gospel Singer said. "She did it because she hates me, as a joke, as a blasphemy!"

"God's church," whispered Didymus.

"MaryBell's church," insisted the Gospel Singer.

"Your church," said Didymus, his voice firm. "God's church founded on *you*."

"Is that what you think?"

"You wouldn't be so angry if there wasn't truth in it," said Didymus. "You wouldn't be afraid either."

"I'm not afraid."

And truly he was not. He had been, but a curious serenity had settled in him. From the moment he found out that Mary-Bell was dead, he had dreaded what he might find as the cause of her death. There was no limit to what she could have done. She was crazy. He guessed he was lucky that it was not worse.

"You've been acting as though you were," said Didymus. "You going inside?"

"I got no reason to."

"Do you still think you're going to save Willalee?"

"I . . . I want to. *Really*, more than anything, I want to. See, they gone kill him, hell, I know that. He killed MaryBell, so they have to kill him. But I don't want them to lynch him. I wouldn't care if they hung him for killing MaryBell, but they're going to hang him for something he didn't do . . . raping her. He didn't . . . well, you heard what he said."

"I heard him. But what I asked is do you think you're going to save him?"

"I been telling myself it doesn't matter if he dies now or dies later or what he dies for if he's got to die anyway . . ."

"But you find it does matter," said Didymus.

"Yes."

"Then I think we better go inside," Didymus said.

"Why?"

"Don't you see that this is at the heart of everything that has happened. The church killed her; the church will have to save Willalee."

"How?"

"I don't know. Just trust me. Let's go inside. Trust me."

The Gospel Singer watched him open the door to the car and approach the church slowly, stopping for several moments at spots along the way, gazing warily about him, at the sky, at the dense wall of weeds. Finally, he disappeared inside. The Gospel Singer waited, not sure himself whether he would follow or not, and then got out and went through the rain to the door. The church was in deep shadow. He stared a long time before he saw Didymus sitting halfway down the aisle on one of the benches. The Gospel Singer sat beside him and immediately Didymus stood up and turned slowly around and around saying: "This is real, this is real."

"You don't know how MaryBell come to do this," said the Gospel Singer quickly. "You don't know all of it."

Didymus stopped and looked down upon the Gospel Singer. His voice was soft, dreamy, "I know you."

"I fucked her," the Gospel Singer said.

"That would hardly make her unique," Didymus said.

"But it was different. This was different. She was clean . . . innocent. I had to show her . . . a lot of things." The Gospel Singer told Didymus all the things he had to show her, leaving nothing out. "Don't you see, she did it to get back at me and poor Willalee Bookatee got caught in the middle."

Didymus raised his head from the attitude of prayer in which he had been listening. He was smiling, but tears streamed down his face. "It's beautiful. Beautiful. God's will *will* be done. Not desire, or flesh or even death can get in the way of His plan."

"You're crazy," said the Gospel Singer. "She didn't even believe in God."

"But she founded a church, and your name is on it. Is God so weak He cannot protect His house? I think not. Rather, I think that God does not ask which roads a man walked down, only where they finally led him. Your name is written there; you cannot argue with that."

"I don't want to argue. I'm not arguing. You said if we come in here we might be able to save Willalee. I just want to save him and get away. I want to get out of Enigma and never come back."

"I think," Didymus said, "that the only way is the truth, to admit the truth."

The Gospel Singer stood up. A flash of lightning gave the Gospel Singer's face, white, rigid. "The truth? The truth about MaryBell! about Willalee? You *are* crazy. You don't know what you're asking!"

Didymus averted his eyes shyly. "I mean the other truth. Tell them who you are."

"Didymus . . ."

"Before you answer, let me show you something I saw before you came in."

Didymus went down the aisle and the Gospel Singer followed him. There was a low altar built there.

"Look," said Didymus.

There was a square of paper on the altar. It had thumbtacks
in it. The Gospel Singer had to bend to make it out. He leaned
down and looked into his own face. It was the same picture
Willalee had spread out on the cot in the cell, another cover of
Life. The Gospel Singer stayed bent there a long moment, feeling not fear or even anger, but rather a kind of numbness. He
finally straightened, only to find Didymus pointing to some
spot behind him. The Gospel Singer turned. On the near wall,
looking out of the shadows, was his face. The pointing arm
moved. His face again. And again. And again. All over the end
of the church behind the altar, his face stared back at him. He
turned to look at Didymus, who shyly averted his eyes. The
Gospel Singer turned and walked back out into the rain.

In the Cadillac, he said: "She did it because she hated me.
She did it as a joke. It's all a joke."

"What are you going to do about Willalee? You can't very
well save him by telling everybody it was a joke."

"I'm not going to save him. I thought I could, but I can't. It's
gone too far. I wouldn't even sing tonight except you're probably right about it ruining my image if I didn't. I've got to save
myself and my career if I can. Come on, let's get out of here."

"You need to get back and rest, get a nap, for tonight," said
Didymus. "You're not going to hold up to sing if you don't."

"We're not going back," said the Gospel Singer. "Go where
Gerd said Foot was set up. I'll get more rest at Foot's than I
will back at the house. There's no telling who they got waiting
for me back there."

Didymus was silent driving out of the tight, rutted road.
When they were back on the highway, he said, "I know why
you're going to see Foot."

"Good, then we won't have to talk about it."

"It's the nature of the gift," said Didymus. "You do everything for the wrong reason."

The Gospel Singer told him to put on *Stars and Stripes
Forever*.

CHAPTER 8

The Freak Fair had been set up in a clearing just beyond highway 229. It was neatly and symmetrically laid out in an eight-sided figure having eight equal angles, and in each angle there stood an eight-sided brown canvas tent from the top of which flew red pennants stamped with the black outline of a foot. A wide path had been cleared and smoothed to join the tents together. Power had been brought in from the REA lines running along highway 229 which eventually went to Enigma. Across the entire front of the enclosure a string of red bulbs had been affixed to a wire and strung between two poles. In the rain the unlighted bulbs looked almost black.

The Gospel Singer stared from the rain-distorted window of his Cadillac in disbelief. He didn't know what he had expected, but it certainly was not this. The camp looked like it had been set up by a group of Senior Eagle Scouts under the direction of a knowledgeable Scoutmaster who was probably a deacon in the church. There was no litter on the grounds. Smoke curled slowly from small flues in the tops of two of the tents. There was something very restful in the whole scene.

"That's his place in there," said Didymus as the Gospel Singer rolled his window down so he could see better.

In the center of the area delineated by the tents, like a giant toadstool in a fairy ring, sat an enormous house trailer. Beside it was a Cadillac of the same model as the Gospel Singer's. On the end of the trailer that faced the road a coat of arms was inscribed. It consisted of two heralds with bugles and swirling flags and crossed swords. The Gospel Singer stared at it a long time before he saw that at the center of the design and integrated with it was a foot.

"What are you going to say to him?" asked Didymus.

"I don't know," said the Gospel Singer.

"You better decide pretty soon."

"I'll talk to him about Gerd. I'll tell him to leave my brother alone."

"Awkward," said Didymus. "He hasn't done anything yet except take him out of a ditch and bring a doctor to have his leg set and put in a cast. I don't see how you can fault that." Didymus started the car. "Maybe while you're here you'd like to go through the tents and see what Foot's got. It's a lesson for us all."

"I've been stared at enough to know I don't want to stare at anybody else," the Gospel Singer said.

Didymus drove into the compound and stopped by the trailer. They got out of the car and stepped under a long narrow awning that stretched some twelve feet away from the front door. Stone squares had been laid neatly under the awning to form a walk. It was very quiet. The Gospel Singer smelled baking bread. Rain drummed steadily on the awning. Over the falling rain and the stillness came a voice, singing. It was a woman, high and pure and sweet. Didymus stood staring curiously at the Gospel Singer who did not move, bemused as he was momentarily by the peace and the pleasant orderliness. He could easily forget what the bland quiet faces of those tents hid, forget that here, organized for the entertainment of the rest of the world, were God's most unfortunate creatures.

There was a noise behind them and the Gospel Singer snapped around and looked, and looked again, then took two steps backward which put him out in the rain. In the door was a short, fluid creature with a low, square head and arms and legs that seemed reversed. It wore no shoes and whatever was coming out of its trouser legs looked like they might have been hands. "Don't you do it!" cried the Gospel Singer. "Get back, geeeeet back!"

Didymus frowned at the Gospel Singer and said something

sharp about being unkind. He turned to the thing in the door. "How have you been, Randolph? How's the fair business?"

Randolph's pink underlip rolled down in a smile exposing a solid terrific jaw-tooth. "Oh," he said. "Fair."

"Randolph," Didymus said. "I'd like you to meet the Gospel Singer." He turned to the Gospel Singer. "This is Randolph Drayton, body servant and personal handyman to Foot. You remember me telling you about him, don't you?"

The Gospel Singer put his hands down. He was trying to compose himself. "I guess I do," he managed to say. "Sure, I remember. It's a . . . it's a pleasure to meet you."

Randolph quit smiling and became very still. "The Gospel Singer," he said, his voice softly awed. He flowed down the steps onto the cement walk. "Now, I do admire to make your acquaintance."

The Gospel Singer forced himself to come in out of the rain. "We've come to see Foot."

"Now that's good of you," said Randolph. "A man like you comin all the way out here." He had stopped right in front of the Gospel Singer and out of the folds of his clothing there came a thick, club-like thing with buttons of flesh on the end of it. It was an arm. He wanted to shake hands.

The Gospel Singer took it. It was smooth and hard as polished wood. But it was warm too. After they had shaken hands, Randolph turned smartly and flowed back up the steps of the trailer talking all the while. "Many's the time I've seen you on the TeeVee, and I wanted to meet you right off. But I guess everbody does and just like me they don't ever think they really will. Course, I've seen you time and again from a distance when they was a revival and we was settin up the fair makin ready for the crowds. You shore do draw a crowd."

They were inside the trailer now. It was very large and richly furnished. There was a television built right into one wall and into the facing wall, a sliding door, which was open now to reveal crystal glasses of various sizes and whiskey bottles lined in rows, some with the seal unbroken and some nearly empty. A heavy black leather couch, built very low, ran entirely around the room on three sides. A low teakwood table was in front of the couch, and on the table, gold-tipped cigarettes pointed out of a molded hollow foot. The foot was done in great detail, showing veins and the indentation of muscle and ligament.

The door leading deeper into the trailer was of folding, laminated wood, supported on runners in such a fashion that it would entirely collapse into a specially built recess in one wall. Randolph opened the door only wide enough to admit himself.

"If y'all would wait here, I'll git Foot. He's restin right at the minute."

"Certainly, Randolph," said Didymus. "Take your time." He turned to the Gospel Singer. "Well?"

"It's not what I expected," he said. "Not at all."

"You owe it to yourself to go through the tents, too."

The Gospel Singer ignored Didymus and said he bet you couldn't find a room as nice as this one in half the hotels on Miami Beach.

"We might as well sit," said Didymus. "There's no telling how long he'll be. Foot rather moves at his own speed."

They sat upon the black leather couch but just as they had settled themselves comfortably, the door through which Randolph had gone slid open and they were looking at the bottom of a tremendous, naked foot supported on a stool. The foot was fully twenty-seven inches high and eighteen inches broad under the toes. It was very well-shaped but incredibly white, as though it had never been stood upon or even touched the ground. The midget himself was hidden behind the foot and it was a long moment before Didymus and the Gospel Singer could raise their eyes, transfixed as they were by what they saw. A girl was standing behind the foot holding on to a chrome bar, which served as the handle to the flat, padded dolly on which Foot was half-reclining, his magnificent deformity enthroned, as it were, on a low stool built onto the dolly.

Didymus and the Gospel Singer leapt up, not for the girl, whom they both knew to be a whore, but for the foot itself, which had about it the presence of royalty.

"Sit down, sit down, gentlemen," said Foot. "Randolph, bring towels and coffee. This *is* an unexpected honor. Although I must admit that I had some notion that I might be seeing you after talking with your brother, Gerd. Oh, I *am* sorry, gentlemen, may I present my assistant, Miss Jessica Worth. Jessica, you remember Didymus from the previous visit, and I'm sure that like a great many people all over this great country and even the world you feel you already know the Gospel Singer."

Didymus, still standing, as was the Gospel Singer, bowed stiffly from the hips. "Miss Worth," he acknowledged. "It's good to see you again."

"*Jessica*, please," she said. She had come from behind Foot. She was delicately built, small boned and fragile, but rather too full in the hips and breasts. Her eyes were round, skillfully but not heavily accented with mascara, and so green as to appear almost transparent. Her hair was brilliant, shimmering red. "I am, of course, very glad to meet *you*."

She put out her hand and the Gospel Singer took it. He had smelled her the moment the door slid back, smelled her even before he had seen her, while he was still looking at the foot. It was soap and the faintest touch of perfume that he smelled, but it did not serve to conceal the odor of her own body, as the most skillfully applied commercial fragrances never do. "Thank you," he said. "It is my pleasure."

"Well, do sit down," said Foot. "And please smoke if you will." He gestured to the replica of the foot on the low table holding cigarettes.

Didymus ground out his own cigarette and out of courtesy lit one of Foot's. Jessica pushed Foot into the center of the room near the table, fluffed up the pillows on which he leaned and made his foot more comfortable where it rested on the stool. To do so, she had to bend, and in bending she put the rounded curve of her rump inches from the Gospel Singer's face. Furry, legged creatures crawled up the inside of his stomach. He could feel himself drowning in her, slowly letting himself down into the sight of her as into a warm bath. Then she shifted the weight on her feet and her rump shifted inches in front of him and a most intense ache settled in his jaws.

"There," she said, patting Foot on the top of his head. "That better?"

"Fine, thank you," Foot said.

Randolph flowed in with the coffee, a huge silver pot steaming on a tray between cups and sugar and cream and heavy silver spoons. There were also two thick white folded towels.

"I'm sorry you had to get wet," said Foot. "But do dry off the best you can. It certainly wouldn't do for *you* of all people to come down with a sore throat just now." He laughed pleasantly.

The Gospel Singer took a towel and made two or three pats at his head and then dropped it in his lap. "Actually . . ." he began.

"Oh, *really*," said Jessica. "Isn't that like a man. You haven't begun to get your hair dry." She had risen while she talked and come to him, made him turn slightly so she could take the towel out of his lap and stand behind him. "May I?" she asked, and the Gospel Singer felt her fingers individually through the towel moving in his hair, the long curling blond hair that fell to his neck, and the delicately strong ends of her fingers went right down the sides of his face and over his chest and stomach and loins. And all the time she rubbed him, Foot talked.

"No sir, not a sore throat tonight of all nights. That would surely disappoint a lot of people, not the least of whom would be us right here at the fair. If you have a real good revival over there tonight, why tomorrow that same crowd will just drift over here to the Freak Fair for a little entertainment. As a matter of fact we had a nice little crowd last night when they started coming in after you got here."

But the Gospel Singer was not listening. The smell of her standing this close to him was overpowering. It was a beautiful and complete feeling, one which, if it had been possible, he would have extended into eternity. Lust rose in him like a live thing, and it swept everything before it: altars, lynchings, churches and revivals.

"Randolph, pour more coffee, bring more cream," Foot was saying. "Didymus, you're looking well. I believe you've a little more color in your face than you had the last time I saw you. Don't you think, Jessica?"

"Uh huh, I think so," said Jessica. She stopped rubbing the Gospel Singer's hair with the towel. "There now, maybe you won't catch your death of cold."

The Gospel Singer looked up at her, unsmiling, his eyes shot with blood. "Thank you," he croaked.

Didymus looked disappointed. He touched his cheek. "I can't imagine what it could be," he said. "I *certainly* haven't felt any better. Maybe I ate too much this morning."

"I came about my brother," said the Gospel Singer, desperately trying to take his eyes off the strip of thigh that winked at him from where Jessica sat now on the opposite side of the room.

"Ah, yes," said Foot. "Gerd. Marvelous boy. Too bad about his accident. I'm sorry I had to meet one of your kin under such circumstances."

"He said you'd offered him a job."

"I thought I might make room in my organization for him. It seems the least I can do inasmuch as you've done for me."

"As much as *I've* done for you?"

"Listen," said Foot. "I want you to know how thankful I am to you. Everything I have, I owe to you. Before I discovered you I could barely stay alive. All of this," he said, waving his hand, "the trailer, good food, the Cadillac outside," he smiled at Jessica, "being able to afford an assistant, everything I owe to your wonderful voice."

"A great many people are in the Gospel Singer's debt," Didymus said.

"But not like me. I was with a children's fair in Tampa, Florida. Strictly nickels and dimes when I first saw the Gospel Singer on television. It was like something from Heaven, a bolt from the blue, so to speak. I knew there was nothing for me to do but follow him."

"Follow me," the Gospel Singer, not asking a question but simply repeating the words.

"Sure," said Foot. "What else? I could see what kind of

crowds you were drawing, and if it's anything I know it's crowds. So I got some freaks together—actually there are so many on the market today that I could pick and choose, nothing but the best ones—and bought an old truck and took out after you. From there on, it was nothing but gravy. You're shocked. The word 'freak' bothers you. Don't let it. Anybody that's hauled something like that," he nodded at his huge extremity, "as far as I have can call himself by his right name."

"I thank you for your concern for my brother," said the Gospel Singer. "But I don't think he wants a job in your fair. Not really."

"If you'll forgive me, I think you're wrong," said Foot. "He does."

The Gospel Singer was trying to keep his mind on the conversation. But at the same time, Jessica's translucent green eyes met his, openly, frankly, everytime he looked in her direction, so that even as he and Foot discussed Gerd, he knew that he was going to have Jessica if he had to grab her and rush out to his Cadillac and speed away while they watched him.

"Gerd's got everything he needs," said the Gospel Singer. "He lives in a good house—I built it myself—has plenty of food to eat and money to spend."

Foot smiled kindly, patiently. "Yes, everything. Except he doesn't want to be in Enigma. He wants out, more than anything, he wants out."

"Why would Gerd want to leave Enigmer?"

"For the same reason you did," said Foot. "There are Enigmas all over this country, all over the world, and men everywhere are struggling to get out of them."

"I left Enigma because I had a voice," said the Gospel Singer.

"Vanity, vanity," Didymus said.

"I know what it sounds like to say it," the Gospel Singer said. "But if you have a voice like mine, you can't just ignore it, you can't pretend it isn't there. The only thing you can do is leave Enigma and use it."

"Ah yes," said Foot. "I know exactly what you mean. I too as you can see have a gift, a special . . . how shall I call it? . . . consideration under God. I was born of parents who were wealthy and socially prominent (I have even dropped my name to save them embarrassment). I had the best education money could buy, all private tutors. But alas, what was I to do with the education, having as I did, a foot twenty-seven inches long. You see, that was my Enigma, being in that rich house full of servants and well-formed parents and graceful friends. I couldn't very well stay, could I? No, of course not. You say: Oh, but you could become a successful man using your mind, say a stock broker or some such thing. True. But my business associates and friends would still have had the fact of my being a freak to deal with. You can't imagine, you really can't, how a man with a foot twelve inches long reacts to a man with a foot twenty-seven inches long. So my only alternative was to leave and use my gift after its own nature—the nature of the gift and the nature of the world."

"Yes, I see that," said the Gospel Singer. "But that has nothing to do with my brother Gerd."

Foot was very serious, no longer smiling, leaning forward from his pillows. "You must know," he said, "that every man invents the world and justifies everything in it through the miracle of himself, in the same way that every man is convinced that his name appears first on the scroll of Heaven. True, nobody will tell you that, but it doesn't keep everybody from believing it." He lay back on the pillows. "In your case and mine, it is easy to see how we are special under God: your beauty and voice, and my foot. Incidentally, I'm sure you won't mind my being candid, you are not nearly as beautiful as I had once thought, now that I see you in the flesh."

"Thank you," said the Gospel Singer. "And you are not so ugly as I thought you must be. Actually your foot is well-formed, nice in its own way."

Foot fell serious again. "But large, very large."

"Yes, true," said the Gospel Singer.

"To get back to the point though," Foot said. "Because our gifts are obvious does not mean that Gerd does not have one, or at least that he doesn't fancy he does. Every Catholic knows that he could have been Pope, had circumstances just worked out right; and every criminal, even the pettiest, knows in his heart that he is really Pretty Boy Floyd or John Dillinger. Every man knows that his gift will set him free if he is just lucky enough. Or unlucky enough, depending upon your point of view."

"Didn't I tell you he was amazing?" said Didymus. "Isn't he fantastic?"

"I'm glad I came," said the Gospel Singer. "It sounds silly sitting here in this comfortable room looking at you, but you can't imagine how I've been bothered by you following me."

"I'm sorry for that."

"It was senseless, I see that now," the Gospel Singer said. "But it was sort of . . ." He laughed. "It was scary. Everywhere I went I'd see your sign, and all I knew was that you had all those poor, unfortunate . . . unfortunate . . ."

"Freaks," said Foot.

"All right, freaks then, and I couldn't figure out why you were following me," said the Gospel Singer.

"For the crowds," said Foot. "It was all for the crowds. I know a man of your . . . dedication doesn't like to speak of money, but I dare say that the crowds give us as much as they give you. And that, as you know, makes for some very rich freaks. Poor and unfortunate as they may be in your eyes, my people have a place in the world, a certain prestige, a kind of prominence that they could never have had if they didn't have me to organize them and you to follow. It's one thing to be a freak out in the normal world surrounded by normal people; it's quite another to be surrounded by your fellow freaks in a fair for just that purpose and have the world come to you."

"Didymus told me you had a man that could eat a live chicken in two minutes," said the Gospel Singer.

"I see what you are asking without asking," said Foot. "Yes, I do have such a man. The question you did not ask is how can I do such a thing to a man or allow him to do such a thing to himself. I deplore clichés as much as any man but my only answer can be that I did not make the world. The crowds want to see it (he is our biggest draw) and the man is willing to do it if they will pay him for it. Would it be better if he were lying drunk and starving in some ghetto or gutter, than it would be for him to have, as he does now, a warm bed, good food, and a doctor when he needs one to sober up? No, I think not."

"I could be your friend," said the Gospel Singer. "When Gerd told me he might leave with you, I was horrified. Now I feel almost as though I could go with you myself."

Foot smiled. "I'm afraid you wouldn't fit into the organization, at least formally and out in the open. That doesn't mean, of course, that you aren't an important part of it."

Didymus, who had been smoking steadily while they talked, lit the last cigarette from the holder on the table. He looked at the Gospel Singer. "Since we're here, maybe I could go through the tents again. It's not often a man's treated to such things."

"I'd love to show you," said Foot.

"But it's raining," said the Gospel Singer. "You'll be soaked and besides . . ."

"It's no matter," said Foot. "Wouldn't let a thing like rain stop me." Jessica, at the first mention of Foot showing Didymus through the fair, had gone into the rear of the trailer and come back shortly and helped Foot into a bright yellow rain slicker, a rubber for his left foot, a huge, specially shaped cellophane wrapper for his right foot and a wide-brimmed, water-repellent hat. "No sir," said Foot. "Not rain or anything else, for that matter. Didymus spoke earlier about vanity, about you being vain about your voice. Well, there's vanity and there's vanity. I am more than a little proud of what I've been able to put together in this fair. Never pass up an opportunity to show it, especially to a connoisseur like Didymus."

"The Gospel Singer can't get wet," said Didymus. "He'll have to stay here."

"Heavens no," said Foot. "Wouldn't have him out in this weather for anything. No crowd for the Gospel Singer, no crowd for me." He grabbed a wheel on the side of his dolly and spun himself around. He hit a switch near the floor beside the couch. A motor whirred. The door opened and a ramp slid down over the steps to the cement walk under the awning. "Randolph can hold the umbrella and Didymus can push me. You just relax. Have more coffee. Jessica will entertain you while I show Didymus around." He shot himself down the ramp with Didymus following, hurrying to catch the chrome handle and Randolph behind him, his stubby, fingerless arms miraculously blossoming the umbrella and holding it expertly to shelter Foot. The dark slanting rain framed Jessica where she stood in the door watching them go. Finally she touched the switch that closed the door and turned to face the Gospel Singer.

"There's not many like Foot," she said.

"He seems like a remarkable man," he said.

She sat beside him on the couch and through the window at the back of the trailer watched the bright yellow slicker disappear into the first tent. He could not take his eyes off the tight green fabric covering her body, the rounded, swelling flesh of her hips and thighs. It was as though he were slipping into, or out of, a dream in which he would lose himself in her flashing, lacquered body. She would drive Mirst and Didymus and the revival and even God out of this world, leaving the two of them, coupled and anonymous.

"Did Didymus tell you about what Foot has in the Fair?"

"He told me some of it," he said.

He had not had a woman since Roanoke, Virginia. She had been tiny and white and hot and she had come to him helpless, like a moth into a flame, while he still burned after a service on the rough pine altar at the front of the revival tent. And she had, as he knew she would, made him forget that he was on his way back to Enigma.

"The tent they just went into belongs to a man whose bones don't fit right. He sort of comes apart. He can fold up like a jackknife, put his legs in under his arms and his arms in under his back and make his head disappear."

He knew he might have trouble with her. She had never been present at one of his performances, never seen him come alive with a gospel.

"They're coming out," said Jessica. "They're going on to the next tent."

Only four of the tents were visible from the back window of the trailer. He watched the three men escorting the huge, upright foot to the next tent. They were moving faster than he had anticipated. If he was to have her, he too must move.

"The one in this tent is a little better than the one in the last tent," said Jessica. "They get better as you go around the circle. Foot planned it that way. By the time the crowds get to the last tent, they're willing to give anything they got—money, rings, watches—to see what's in it. The last tent is where Foot keeps the Geek, the one that eats the chickens."

"Do you think," he asked, "that my hair is dry enough? In this air conditioning I might come down with a sore throat or something." He tossed the long curling hair with the ends of his fingers and then inclined his head for her to feel. She laid her hands gently on his head and then very quickly drew them back.

"I'd better get you another towel," she said.

He made no move to take the towel when she brought it but sat still with his head turned to her. She put her hands in his hair, standing this time in front of him so that her stomach was just there in front of his face.

"They're staying in the second tent a little longer," she said. "That's the way the crowds do, too." Her voice had the barest tremor in it.

The Gospel Singer raised his hands to her hips. It was like palming two cantaloupes. He put his face against her stomach, catching the fabric of her dress gently in his teeth. He could feel the mound of her pussy against his chin. He heard her breathe deeply and felt her tremble.

"They're coming out of the tent," she said. "There's only six more to go. They'll be back in a minute. They might not stay to see the Geek do his trick."

The Gospel Singer kissed her through the dress. He felt his mouth sink in the little cushion of hair. "I'd better take off my shirt," he said. "It's wet. I must save my voice for tonight." He turned her loose. She took a half-step back and dropped the towel. Slowly he slipped the pale, bone-colored buttons of his shirt and shrugged out of it and sat watching her eyes cloud with the sight of him. He was white as milk, and almost thin, but with perfectly symmetrical muscles standing in his chest and shoulders. He knew the contrast his yellow hair made against his skin as it fell below his ears.

"I love Foot," she said. "I love him."

He took her hips again and pulled her down beside him. She twisted her head to look out of the window and his eyes followed hers and they watched Randolph flowing along the path, his crippled arms impossibly holding the umbrella, guiding Foot and Didymus into the next tent. She was limp beside him saying, "Foot took me out of a house where I was bought and sold by the hour and I came with him for money but I've stayed because I love him."

Her breast came into his hand a live thing, its little nipple-nose hard through her thin dress. Her odor had changed. The acrid smell of love squeezed up from her lap, her flesh breathing it into the room, and he caught the scent, trembling, knowing that his own escape from the world was imminent.

"They'll be going into the next tent," she was saying. "It's raining harder. They might not go to the others. They might come back. Do you know what's in the tent where they are? Do you?"

His answer was to open his mouth and let out against her ear his voice singing softly of God's love, of the Bridegroom of Heaven and the bride of the world consummated in spirit when the flesh is gone.

"A man with solid bone for eyes," she was saying. "His face stops at his nose." She stopped to breathe. "You don't believe I love him, do you? I do! I swear I love . . ."

Her zippered dress came apart under his hands and she was all pink legs and stomach and nippled breasts and pinker panties wet and clinging there where the world stopped. In the expert way of all desperation, the Gospel Singer, without ever losing contact with her body slipped out of his own clothes and lay against her naked and beautiful.

"Foot!" she gasped. "Foot, Foot!"

And the Gospel Singer sang on, singing now not only with his voice but with his long curving legs, his hands, his tongue. Her pants were gone and he felt her, wet, warm, swallowing him out of the world.

"They are with the Geek," she said, but her hands were on

him now holding him fast, submerging him until he was no longer himself. "Oh, touch me God, deep and deeper touch me!"

Over the sound of the drumming rain and her breathing, a chicken cackled long and loudly, ending in a screech, a kind of scream. "There's time," she said. "There's time. The crowd only thinks the Geek can do it in two minutes because it scares them so they never want it to end. There! There!" she cried. "God, there!"

But the Gospel Singer heard neither the scream nor her nor his own pounding heart, but swam quietly away into a vast warm sea, vaster than the eye and without direction.

CHAPTER 9

They were in the Cadillac again. The Gospel Singer, soaked to the skin, lay across the back seat. His wet hair covered his head like a cap of thin, tarnished gold. His breathing was shallow. Through slitted eyes, he concentrated on the sagging brim of Didymus' hat. An occasional drop of bright water broke from it and ran down Didymus' neck. Drops and rivulets hung quivering on the other side of the glass just as they had on the window through which he and Jessica had watched Foot's journey from tent to tent.

Whenever the Gospel Singer had come back from wherever he had been, Jessica was crying against his chest, holding him tightly to her. She was saying again and again that she loved Foot, that Foot had taken her out of the house where she had been sold by the hour, but she would not turn the Gospel Singer loose, and she murmured as she kissed him that she had waited for him all her life. When a chicken cackled the second time over the raining silence, she pressed him still more tightly between her breasts and told him there was time, all the time in the world, for him to love her again. But for his own part it was over and he rested between her strong thighs with his face buried in the angle of her neck and shoulder.

The wind had died. Rain fell in straight, solid sheets. The sound of it came into the car as a drum roll of unbroken roaring. On either side of the road, the ditches overflowed and the ground rose with dark, standing water.

"The Geek was most wonderous," said Didymus.

"You shouldn't have stayed so long," said the Gospel Singer. "You should have come back."

"The strength in a human's jaws is fantastic," said Didymus. "Foot is knowledgeable in these things and he says a human mouth is capable of exerting five hundred pounds of pressure. That chicken was still alive in the Geek's mouth and hardly dead in his stomach. Why would a *man's* jaws be given that kind of power?"

"So men like you can watch it," said the Gospel Singer bitterly.

"Or so men like you can avoid watching it," said Didymus.

"You couldn't be satisfied to see one chicken eaten," the Gospel Singer said. "You had to have him tear up three."

"Four," Didymus said. "But he couldn't eat the last two. He got them chewed up pretty good, though."

"One would have been enough."

"None would have been enough," said Didymus. "I'd seen him do it before. I just wanted to give you as long as you needed."

"You gave me too much." He forced a smile as Didymus looked back at him from the front seat. "I don't like to deal with a woman after I've had her. Take it and leave, that's the thing. But I couldn't hardly leave with you out there watching a monster. The chicken would cackle and she would beg me to take her away with me, to take her away from Foot."

"What did you tell her?"

The Gospel Singer forced out of his throat the smooth chuckle that he knew irritated Didymus. "I lied to her, what else?"

The back of Didymus' neck reddened. "What did you tell her."

"I told her I'd pick her up tonight, that I'd come by in the Cadillac as soon as the revival was through."

He chuckled again. But it had not been funny. She had wept and he had lied to her out of the same wild compulsion that had driven him to seduce MaryBell again and again. She had caressed him and pressed him to her and the fabulous lies had rolled out of his mouth one on top of the other. He would take her away from Foot. She would be a mother with beautiful children and he would love her forever.

But it had not been the same as it had been with other

women. He had to concentrate to keep from trembling. If he lifted his hands away from his body, they shook in spite of everything he could do. And he kept glancing overhead in a gesture that he could not control, but instead of a sign of God's displeasure all he saw was the ceiling of the trailer covered in cubes of acoustical tile in the shape of a black foot with tiny white toes. He kept telling himself there in the trailer that what was happening to him was just a reaction to MaryBell's death and that it would be all right as soon as Didymus gave him penance. But Didymus had stayed out in the rain and chickens had cackled and he had trembled, and Jessica had told him he was a dream come true.

"Give me a penance," said the Gospel Singer, when he could wait no longer.

"Are you going to save Willalee?"

"I can't," said the Gospel Singer. "I told you."

"Then I can't give you a penance."

"But you've got to," said the Gospel Singer. "I wronged that girl. I told her as many lies as I could think of. She's going to be waiting with her suitcase tonight, waiting for me, and I knew I wasn't coming when I told her I was. Give me a penance. Give me twenty *Saving Grace*s . . . no, twenty's not enough. Give me forty, make me sing it backwards."

Didymus, who had been slowly shaking his head while the Gospel Singer talked, suddenly cried: "*Nothing* is enough!" He twisted to face the Gospel Singer with an abrupt, erratic jerk of his shoulders. "*Nothing* is enough. Nothing will *ever* be enough. Someday when it's all over you'll find out what's really enough. Don't think it makes you any less miserable in the sight of God, not twenty or forty or five thousand *Saving Graces!* Penance is just for the moment, to let you live to do God's work." The car slipped on the shoulder of the road. Didymus went back to his driving.

"All right, Didymus, all right. Give me penance just for now, then."

Didymus, who was still jerking and twitching, went calm. "I can't," he said.

"But you've got to."

"I can't because of Willalee. He's God's penance. If you let them hang him, I can never give you penance again. We're finished if you let them take him out of that cell and hang him for raping MaryBell."

"If I let them?"

"They'd listen to you."

"It's nothing I can say that'd keep them from Willalee."

"If you gave it some thought, there's probably something that would make a difference."

"Well, I'll never find out," said the Gospel Singer, "because I'm not going to think about it. I'm not even going to the revival. I've decided. To hell with it, they can do without me."

Didymus stopped the car by the side of the road. He turned on the Gospel Singer. "That really finishes it. I'm not going to try to get you to go. If you don't want to, don't. But that shoots the image, ruins it, kills it for good! They know you're here. You've been interviewed for the television. That newsman is still around. It'll get out that you purposefully didn't go. This time next year you'll be back in Enigma grubbing on your daddy's farm, wondering what happened."

"I'll tell them I was sick," he said, "that I was too sick to go."

"And I'll tell them the truth. I'll say you didn't go because you didn't want to. I'll tell them you said to hell with them, too."

"You said you wouldn't try to make me go," whimpered the Gospel Singer. "If you not going to give me a penance, you've got no right to try to make me go. I can't sing without a penance."

Didymus lit a cigarette and considered this. "All right," he said finally. "You sing tonight and I'll give you penance for Jessica."

"How many *Saving Graces*?"

"No," Didymus said. "You've got to sing first. I'll give it to you after."

"What about Willalee?" asked the Gospel Singer.

Didymus hesitated and then, "He'll have to take care of himself."

"You can see I can't help him."

"Yes," said Didymus.

"And we'll leave Enigma after the revival?"

"Yes."

"And never come back?"

"Yes."

"Let's go pack our clothes," said the Gospel Singer.

When they pulled up in front of the house, Gerd called the dogs off, and Didymus and the Gospel Singer came onto the front porch. Dark puddles formed where they stood. There was not a light on in the house and they could barely make out Gerd where he sat in a ladder-backed chair with his casted foot propped up on a cardboard suitcase.

"Where is everbody?" asked the Gospel Singer.

"Town," said Gerd. He kept his eyes fixed on his injured foot.

"Everbody?"

"They didn't know what happened to you," Gerd said. "After you went runnin out of here like a wild Indian and didn't come back, they got scared. Finally Reverend Woody Pea come by an told them they oughten stay here, but go there. So they went, ever blesset one of them."

"And left you here?"

"Settin right in this cheer," said Gerd. "But I didn't want to go nohow."

"Why not?"

"Cause I'm going sommers else. Caint you see my suitcase?"

"You caint go nowhere," the Gospel Singer said. "They ain't nobody here to take you."

"Thought on the way to the revival you might drop me by the Freak Fair."

The Gospel Singer stared at the water pouring from the eaves of the house. He refused to look at Gerd. "All right," he said. "I've got to git my things first."

In his room the Gospel Singer opened his alligator suitcase and threw his dirty underwear into it. He collapsed onto the bed beside it. One more time to sing in Enigma, and it would all be over. He would never come back. Come to think of it, he couldn't come back. Enigma would more than likely find out about the church with his name on it. And if it found out about that, it might find . . .

Gerd was tilted in the door like a ghost between his leaning crutches. He was looking in the direction of the Gospel Singer but his eyes were focusing past him on the far wall.

"Care if I come in?"

"No," said the Gospel Singer. "I've just about got everthin together."

Gerd jerked into the room and sat on the bed. He let the crutches fall to the floor. He looked at the ends of his fingers. "Preacher changed the program."

"Did?" said the Gospel Singer.

"It's a special idee of his to honor the fambly. He's gone have Ma and Pa set up on the stage in the tent tonight. He even got Mirst and Avel on the program with they geetar. Everbody gits to do something but poor ol Gerd, I reckon." He kicked gently against the cast with his good foot.

"You oughta go over there too, Gerd."

"No," he said. "It ain't no use in it if I'm gone go with Mr. Foot and work in a freak show." He tapped the cast. "It don't make no difference to you if I go with the Freak Fair or not do it?"

"I did think about it some," the Gospel Singer said. "That's how come I went over there. I talked to Foot and he didn't seem like a bad sort. I want you to do whatever you want to do, though."

"Did you go through them tents and see them freaks?"

"Didymus did," he said.

"Did you?"

"No."

"I did. I can tell you what's in them tents."

"I already been told," said the Gospel Singer.

"Do you want me to be in one of them tents?"

"You keep askin if *I* want this? If *I* want that. Quit blamin it on me!"

"You ain't got to shout at me," said Gerd. "I might be crippled but I ain't hard of hearin."

"I'm sorry."

"I ain't blamin it on you. It's just that I been lying in that croker sack hammock under the cotton shed for so long that I caint stand it no longer. One way or another, I'm gone git out there where Rock Hudson and Doris Day is. They's a better world than Enigmer and I'm gone find it, even if I have to go in one of Mr. Foot's tents."

"But you don't *want* to go that way."

"I purely don't," he said. "It ain't the kind of thing that a natural man wants to do."

The Gospel Singer said something, but it was so soft that Gerd couldn't hear it and had to ask him what he said.

"I said, what is it you want to do?"

Gerd sat studying the big toe sticking out of his cast. "Well," he said. "I know I ain't gone be no whoppin big help to nobody. I mean I caint play the geetar like Mirst or dance like Avel and they ain't nobody can sing like you so I ain't, as I say, gone be no big help to nobody. They ain't many things I can do. I don't guess nobody'd want to just have me around to help do any little thing I could, pick up they clothes, help git they suitcase in them big hotels, or help Didymus drive that ol big car and stuff like that. But I shore would ruther do that than I would be in one of Mr. Foot's tents."

It was clearly impossible. He could not take Gerd in the Cadillac with him on singing tours. Gerd, standing in the lobby of the Waldorf Astoria, would be more of a freak than he would be with Foot. Gerd had no place, no function, no purpose, no anything. He'd be in the way. He would, almost certainly, be more uncomfortable and unhappy on Fifth Avenue than he was in the hammock under the cotton shed. Yet Gerd wanted to go. The Gospel Singer had the *fact* of Gerd's existence to deal with. There he sat, unaccomplished, diseased and unhappy, but his brother still. And he was asking to be taken out of Enigma. To leave him was the greater impossibility. Besides, it had occurred to him that it might be a good penance, and, God knows, he felt he needed every penance he could get.

"Gerd," he said. "I've been thinkin and I've got an idea. Why don't you come with me and Didymus and forget about Foot?"

Gerd's breathing changed. It became quick and short, like the panting of a dog. He took up a fist full of quilt off the bed and twisted it in his hands. "Shoot," he said. "Shoot amighty!" His eyes were bright, but his face was caving and trembly. His lips could be still only if he pressed them together. "I didn't never suppose you'd want me to go with you."

"Sure," said the Gospel Singer. "You'll be a big help to me."

"Boy, wait'll I see the look on Mirst's face when I tell'm you're takin *me*. I'm gone set right up there in the front of the tent with the rest of them, too. I'm gone set up there and show myself off and if anybody asks me I'll tell'm I'm leavin Enigmer. Mirst can talk about his geetar and Avel can go on about her dancin, but I'm the one that's leaving Enigmer. Say! Say now! Listen, you know what? You know?" Gerd could not talk fast enough; his arms and head jerked about. The cast on his foot was all that kept him from jumping up and racing around the room. "I forgot to tell you. You know? Revered Woody Pea said he had a surprise for you. He said a *big* surprise."

"For me?"

"That's what he said. He said if you come home before you went over to the revival for me to tell you shore. You ought to be lookin for a big surprise cause he's got it for you."

Woody Pea was a huge man who had been a turpentine worker outside Milledgeville, Georgia, before he got the call to preach. He had never had a church of his own, but rather, stamped up and down the South preaching to whatever crowd he could draw. He had been after the Gospel Singer for years to hold a meeting with him, but Mr. Keene would never accept because, as Mr. Keene used to say, Woody Pea was just small-time religion. But that was before Woody Pea got his tent.

Two months ago Didymus had received a letter from Woody Pea saying he had a tent that would hold three thousand immortal souls and that he was willing to haul the tent to Enigma itself if the Gospel Singer would appear with him. Without consulting the Gospel Singer, Didymus had agreed that the next time the Gospel Singer was in Enigma he would sing in Woody Pea's tent if it was in Enigma and set up to hold a revival.

A surprise? A surprise for the Gospel Singer? He didn't even know Woody Pea, had only met him once, by accident, at a tobacco auction in Tifton where Woody had suddenly stepped from behind a pile of wooden, saucer-shaped baskets and taken the Gospel Singer by the arm.

"Praise God, I seen you from the door and known it was you," said Woody.

"Who the hell are you?" asked Mr. Keene, who had been a little ahead of the Gospel Singer inspecting the stacks of tobacco they had just brought to the warehouse from Mr. Keene's farm.

"Who the hell is he?" asked Woody Pea, gesturing at Mr. Keene with a thumb as big as a banana.

Mr. Keene tried to force himself between Woody and the Gospel Singer, but Woody gripped the arm more tightly and the Gospel Singer had to bite his lip to keep from crying out. Mr. Keene repeated his original question.

"I'm somebody that's twice as big as you," said Woody Pea. "That's all you got to know." And he was. He was as big as the Gospel Singer and Mr. Keene and several of the warehousemen put together.

Mr. Keene said something else, but not much, because Woody Pea was as violent as he was large and he turned the Gospel Singer loose and took Mr. Keene by the head and threw him across four rows of tobacco where he landed on his back. There followed a fantastic rout in which four of Mr. Keene's warehousemen had been hospitalized. Woody Pea fled in a doorless Dodge car, and none of the policemen in Tifton had felt inclined to go after him.

"He didn't say what the surprise was?" asked the Gospel Singer.

"No," Gerd said. "Just it was a big one."

Didymus appeared in the door. "You ready?"

"Yes," said the Gospel Singer.

It was still raining when they got to the tent. They could not get the Cadillac closer than five hundred yards to the entrance. No one had directed the parking and every imaginable sort of vehicle was interlaced in the field surrounding the tent. There was no order or pattern. Each driver had maneuvered his car or truck or wagon as close to the tent as he could possibly get and there he had parked in whatever position he found himself.

"We're late," Didymus said.

They sat in the car and watched the rain. It was so heavy that from this distance, the tent was no more than a ring of light at the center of the field.

"Well," said the Gospel Singer. "If I'm going I might as well go."

"Gerd," Didymus said, "with it raining like this maybe you better wait in the car."

"I ain't gone miss settin on that stage to set in no car."

The Gospel Singer and Gerd stood in the rain and waited while Didymus opened the trunk of the car and got out the velvet-lined metal case containing the singing robes. It had been Mr. Keene's idea to have the Gospel Singer wear special clothes when he sang. "Packaging is part of the product," he would say. And by the time Didymus came along, the special clothing was so well-established in everybody's mind that Didymus had allowed him to continue wearing it.

They were met at the entrance to the tent by Reverend Woody Pea, huge, red-faced, short of breath and sweating. Without a word he grabbed the Gospel Singer by the arm as though he were a truant child and rushed him up the center aisle, bowling people out of his way as he went, stepping on toes, shoving faces. Gerd was immediately lost in the crush of the audience, which rushed forward when it realized the Gospel Singer had come. Didymus held onto Woody Pea's belt and was towed along like a swimmer. The babble of voices rose to a sustained roar. Every person that the Gospel Singer could see was soaked. The sawdust floor stood two inches deep in water and small waves were washing in around the edge of the tent. The heat was unbelievable. A vaporous steam rose out of the audience and swirled in the brown ceiling among the strung lightbulbs. At the far end of the tent was a raised platform on which the waxen figures of his family sat under the glare of specially rigged lighting. His mother and father sat on one side; Mirst and Avel sat on the other. They faced the audience, unmoving.

In one corner of the front of the tent, portable wooden screens had been set up to form a small enclosure. It was there that Woody Pea dragged them, Didymus and the Gospel Singer, and flung them inside like two drowned chickens. There was a wooden table with chairs around it. The Gospel Singer fell exhausted into a chair. Didymus put the clothes case on the table and opened it.

"I thought you wouldn't git here," Woody Pea said. His immense chest rose and fell. "Scared my pony," he said, grinning. "Yes, sir. I don't know what I'd a done if you hadn't got here." He went to the screens to peep out at the people. "They wet, they tired, they hot, they been fist fights breakin out there in the middle of the tent. You know how much this tent cost? Why, it cost . . ." He turned and saw the Gospel Singer still sitting in the chair watching him. "Well, for God's sake git dressed will you! They waitin! Cost a lot. I mean it. I had to hock my soul to git ahold of this tent. And them fools out there shovin and pushin, I already had to bust a couple of them to keep them from tearin the sides out. That's what I want to talk to you about. The tent! Cost!" He rushed over and helped Didymus with the Gospel Singer. They stripped him to the skin, dried him, and dressed him in the white robes, tied at the waist with a silk rope.

Woody Pea cupped the Gospel Singer's face in his palms and patted him affectionately. His hands held the Gospel Singer's head like an orange. "I know this ain't the time to talk to you about it," said Woody, "but I been waitin a long time. Did you brother tell you? The surprise? Well, it's this tent. My idea is to throw in together. You sing, I preach. We haul this tent with us. No overhead, no rentin halls. No cut to nobody. Right? You see? Don git me wrong though! I can see in you face you gitten me wrong." He appealed to Didymus. "Tell him it's on the up-and-up. I explained in the letter. Tell him."

"It seems . . ."

But the Gospel Singer cut him off. "I can talk," he said. "Tell me the deal."

"The deal," said Woody Pea. "Yes, the deal . . . but it ain't the money. We ain't interested in the money."

"No," said the Gospel Singer.

"Forty–sixty then," said Woody. "With you taking the sixty cause I ain't ashamed to admit you a better draw than me. Everbody knows you got the best draw in the country."

The Gospel Singer said nothing. He had sat down again in a chair. He was listening to the roar of voices beyond the wooden screen. Like a river, he thought.

"All right then," said Woody. "Thirty–seventy." His voice turned peevish. "But I didn't expect you to want everthin. When I heard tell you'd lost that Mr. Keene I thought we could deal."

They were out there waiting for him and in here this man— this Woody Pea—was talking a deal. It had all been a deal. Deals for as long as he could remember. A deal with his family, a deal with MaryBell, a deal with Mr. Keene, a deal with television studios, and finally a deal with Didymus. He, the Gospel Singer, was a deal. The sound of money, of folding paper and jangling silver, had played over it all.

"Twenty-five–seventy-five is stealin," Woody said. "Robbery." He beat the air with his enormous balled fists. "But I'll do it. I got to. I'm spread and you gone put it to me. But I caint go no lower. Twenty–eighty is out of the question. I got everthin in the world tied up in this tent. My brother mortgaged his farm to help me git it. My payments . . ."

But the Gospel Singer was no longer listening. He had not rested or eaten since morning. The day had been a long sustained shock. In a kind of detached, euphoric mindlessness, he regarded his hands, lying palms up, in his lap. They were white and soft, the fingers relaxed and curling. He could not even *imagine* himself being able to go out on the stage and sing. His throat was tight and gravelly, his vision blurred. Something inside himself seemed to have given way, broken. His white hands moved on his lap and he stood up. "O.K.," he said. "All right."

He meant: all right, let's go on out and get it over with, but
Woody Pea took it to mean that he was consenting to the
twenty-five–seventy-five proposition. "That's more like it," said
Woody. "It's a bad deal but it's somethin. Maybe I can at least
keep my tent. Without you, I'd lose it sure. I ain't never seen
such a draw as you, maybe some of you'll rub off on me." He
went to the section of the screen that swung open like a door
and peeped out. "We got to get out there," he said. "You line
up behind me. We'll go out one behind the other, with me
leadin and the Gospel Singer in the middle. *That* ought to be a
sight." He was still talking as he led them out into the short
aisle joining the raised platform to the section sealed off by the
wooden screens. As the Gospel Singer ascended the steps, a
special light burst blindingly around his white robes. The
voice of the audience hushed. A chair, very large with heavy
wooden arms, was placed in the center of the stage for the
Gospel Singer. Didymus remained standing just behind the
chair. Gerd was on the stage, too, by this time, sitting over by
Mirst and Avel. Strangely, Gerd looked frightened. His shirt
was split neatly down the back, the two parts hanging open to
show his scabrous, purple skin. His gaze swung nervously
from the audience to the Gospel Singer and back again.

The audience was divided into three distinct parts. In the
very front were the maimed, and the sick. Several wheelchairs
were lined side by side; crutches protruded from an assortment
of angles; the overhead lights caught and were reflected in
the metal of various braces and supports. Behind the afflicted
were the people of Enigma. They were dressed mostly in dark
colors, black suits, overalls, felt hats in their laps. Some of the
women wore bonnets or black scarves. Their children sat beside them on the collapsible benches, still, subdued, the young-
est of them sucking sugar tits, staring with their parents toward
the stage bathed in light and crowned with the Gospel Singer.
The remainder of the audience, something more than two-
thirds of it, was composed of people who had driven into
Enigma from other towns, drawn by the commercials and ad-
vertisements Didymus had placed in newspapers and on radios,
and by their own insatiable curiosity about the word-of-mouth

rumors which, in some parts of the South at least, approached legend. Their clothing was more fashionable, brighter. They looked better-fed; they were fatter. It was they who had brought the transistor radios—some of which were still playing, but softly. They had cameras and binoculars slung about their necks. And of the entire audience, at the moment, they were the angriest. They were wet, their good shoes were ruined, they were tired. And none of them was sure the Gospel Singer was going to prove to be a large enough entertainment to off-set their uncomfortableness. They could have gone to a nice dry movie or stayed home and watched television.

Reverend Woody Pea approached the microphone at the center of the stage. "This going to be a greeeet night." His voice boomed through the tent. He stretched his arms and held himself in a fat crucifix. "*He* has come to share with us *his* great gift." He launched a shouting history of the Gospel Singer's accomplishments, of where he had been, of what he had done, of what he was going to do.

The audience endured him, but all the time its eyes were focused past him on the Gospel Singer. He could feel the force of its collective gaze fixing him where he sat like a weight. In the very front, between the first row of wheelchairs and the stage, was the man who had grabbed the Gospel Singer in front of the funeral parlor. He was standing, slightly inclined in the direction of the stage. His wet clothes were only slightly darker than his discolored skin and they hung on him in descending folds like clothes someone had carelessly hung up to dry.

His eyes locked with the Gospel Singer's and they, the Gospel Singer and the man, balanced each other there in a bright, dry gaze. The expression in the man's eyes alternated between a fierce, blazing determination and a whipped, dog-like suppli-cation. For the Gospel Singer, he became in that moment, the symbol not only of the rest of the audience but of every person who had ever heard him sing. The man was asking, as plainly as if he had shouted it at the top of his lungs, for an impossible benediction, for an intercession between the world and the flesh that the Gospel Singer could not make. Instead of pity or love or compassion, the Gospel Singer, staring into that blackened dying face, felt the strongest stab of hatred he had ever known. *Damn you! Damn you to hell!*

The Gospel Singer jerked out of the trance-like stare. The words had exploded with such force in his skull, he thought he must have shouted them. But no, he had not. Woody Pea still lied about him through the microphone and the audience still made him a lie with their eyes. If he could have touched a button and killed them all, he would have. The injustice of his life brought tears to his eyes, but they were tears of rage.

A thundering ovation shook the tent. The preacher beckoned him forward. The afflicted strained in their harnesses. The man at the front of the tent, his black skin absorbing the light like polished wood, had come close enough to touch the stage.

The Gospel Singer rose slowly to his feet. A piano player, half-hidden by the far wall of the stage, looked up expectantly at the Gospel Singer and let his hands run explosively down the keys. He had no music, nor could he have read it had there been any, but he was ready to follow the Gospel Singer into whatever hymn he cared to sing.

The Gospel Singer opened his mouth and the entire tent leaned and stopped breathing. But Didymus suddenly stepped before him, put both hands on his chest, and pushed him back into the chair. Didymus stood looking down upon him and he could see his lips moving but he couldn't hear what he was saying because the audience was rumbling again. Didymus turned to the microphone. "Ladies and gentlemen," he said. A stillness stretched after his words. Then a collective exhalation, a drawn sigh. "The Gospel Singer has something he must tell you before he can sing."

The Gospel Singer came out of his chair as though shot by a giant, uncoiling spring. He landed on his two feet, rigid, his face as white as the gown he wore. He stared incredulously at Didymus, who was still talking but whom he could no longer hear because the audience was making such a noise. Didymus turned and held out his hand to the Gospel Singer. The Gospel Singer stood where he was, refusing to approach the microphone and said in a strangled, inaudible voice: "Judas! You bastard Judas!" He was beside himself with anger. It was suddenly clear that Didymus had insisted that he come to the revival only so he could betray him. And the hatred for his audiences that he had managed to contain for so long, burst free. He was blindly furious and he was about to lunge at Didymus to take him by the throat when someone screamed: "Sing!"

The Gospel Singer looked over the microphone at the cadaver touching the stage in front of him. "What?" he asked angrily. "What did you say?"

"I said sing!" cried the cadaver, his black mouth swelling.

"Sing, sing," chorused the first row of cripples.

An old man pushed a wheelchair up behind the cadaver. The wheelchair had a boy in it. He was too fat and too soft and too white. His head bobbed like a cork. "We come to hear you sing," the old man said. "We been wadin around in the wet since sun up. We ain't ready to wait no more."

Several other wheelchairs jerked erratically in the soggy sawdust; crutches waved; metal braces creaked.

"Get back!" cried the Gospel Singer. "Get away from me!" The rest of the people in the audience droned noisily. They were glad for some diversion and craned their necks to see what the cripples would do next.

Woody Pea, a horrified smile frozen into his face, sidled up to the Gospel Singer. He kept the cast iron smile turned toward the audience and spoke out of the side of his mouth. "What are you trying to do? Done stirrum up! For heaven's sake, SING!"

The Gospel Singer jumped away from him as if touched by fire. "May God strike you!" he flared at Woody Pea. "You *and* your damned tent!"

When he jumped back he collided with Didymus, who had come forward to stand beside him. Didymus had his *Dream Book* out. The Gospel Singer whirled and stared wildly at Didymus as though he had never seen him before. Didymus would not meet his eyes and looked at his *Dream Book* instead. The Gospel Singer turned to face the audience, hesitated, then ran up the stage and back again, his white robes billowing on either side of him, resembling nothing so much as a huge moth fluttering for a source of light which it cannot find. Finally he fell in the center of the stage; then rose to his knees. "Who do you think I am? You that always talk to me about sinnin evertime I stop and turn my head. Who do you think I am? *Who Am I?*" His voice had risen at every word until finally he was screaming. "Who am I? Sin? You want to talk about sin? Is it any man here I caint teach about sin? Is it any woman here I caint give lessons or who wouldn't take them?"

There was no sound in the tent except his voice and the steady drum of the rain.

"I'm the biggest sinner here, if you want to talk about that. God knows I am. I've done everthing you can think of and some you caint." The dark rows of Enigma tensed. Their mouths went white; their backs straightened. The Gospel Singer saw them. "That's right," he said. "Did you think I could be what you said I was? Didn't you know from you own black hearts what mine must be like?"

Woody Pea rushed to the microphone and drowned out the Gospel Singer's voice. "Friends! Some terrible thing has happened. Strange is the workins of the Lord! The Gospel Singer is . . . he's . . . I think we'd better pray! Yes, let us pray . . ."

The Gospel Singer lunged to his feet and hit Woody Pea where he stood before the microphone and, surprisingly, because the preacher was several times over as large as the Gospel Singer, Woody went flying from the stage and landed on a man who had only one leg. The Gospel Singer threw the microphone after him. He turned on the people of Enigma. "That's right, you sonsabitches, stare at me! You've hounded me as far as I'm goin. Now it's my turn! The biggest whore that ever walked in Enigma or anywheres else was MaryBell Carter— *and I made her the whore she was!*"

The entire people of Enigma rose out of the audience. It made a savage noise. Woody Pea had fought his way out of the cripples and regained the stage. "Somethin awful is happened," he yelled. He was no longer smiling. "We better pray! Let us pray! All right, everbody *pray!* Watch out for the tent! Watch the tent over there, don't press up agin it that way."

All of the people were on their feet now. The crowd surged and swelled. The visitors had pressed in to get a closer view of the people of Enigma.

"You want nothin but lies!" the Gospel Singer was screaming.

"Watch the GODDAM tent!" yelled Woody Pea.

"Drag that crazy bastard down from there," shouted somebody from Enigma.

A fight broke out among the visitors who were stepping on each other trying to get closer to the action. A whole side of the bottom edge of the tent went down in a tumult of bodies. The wind had picked up and water sprayed into the ballooning ceiling.

"You're gone hang Willalee Bookatee because he wouldn't screw MaryBell Carter. He could have and didn't. She wanted him to and he wouldn't. If he did, you'd left him alone." The Gospel Singer flapped and screamed, beside himself on the stage.

"Sing, damn you, *sing!*" cried the cadaver, his face the color of dried blood.

The old man directly behind the cadaver suddenly bent and embraced the fat, giggling idiot child and wept. "He ain't gone heal you, son. He ain't gone heal you."

"Heal? Heal?" demanded the Gospel Singer. "I caint heal and I caint save. I never said it. You said that, damn you." He pointed to the people of Enigma. "I caint do nothing but sing gospel songs and lay your women, your wives and mothers and daughters—*all your MaryBells!*"

Enigma moved as one man, not out of the benches, but through them, over them. Babies thudded from laps, old people lost their footing. The cripples in front were pushed aside, tipped over and stepped upon. Crutches, wheelchairs and pieces of brace and harness flew in all directions. The visitors rushed forward to see what would happen. They were laughing and shouting. Somebody hit somebody with a transistor radio and was in turn thrown into a tent brace, causing it to collapse.

"Pray! Pray!" screamed Woody Pea as he disappeared under the irresistible crush of the first wave of people gaining the stage. A large woman with a triangular mole growing in her chin was the first to reach the Gospel Singer. With a savage cry she fell upon him, her immense bosom wrapping his head, her frantic hands clawing at his back, ripping the robe. She smelled like something shot in the woods, a heavy, musky scent of hide and hair. There were other hands at him now, poking, punching, digging. The Gospel Singer felt himself smothering in the press of her flaccid body. He was trying to bite her when she was suddenly jerked from him and he himself was seized by strong hands and pulled back.

For an instant he was free. Between him and the mob was a flash of fists and flying hair. It was his mother. There was a livid tear in the flesh of her right arm and on the side of her head a great splash of blood. She fought silently and with incredible fury. There was blood around her mouth, but it was not her blood. She clawed and bit and kicked, but finally the mob simply opened up and swallowed her.

Lying flat on his back, the Gospel Singer watched her disappear. He had been kicked at the base of his spine and he could not get up. The bodies and faces swelled about him and he drew inward upon himself. The anger had completely deserted him and he was terrified beyond breathing.

In the final second before they would have had him, Didymus miraculously rose where his mother had stood. He had the leg of a collapsible bench gripped tightly in both hands, laying about him on all sides and screaming something that sounded curiously like singing. Then the side of his neck splattered and he went down like an empty sack.

From the moment they really had him until they got him to the tree on the edge of the clearing, the Gospel Singer never stopped saying he was sorry. He screamed that he had been lying, that it was all a mistake. He first said MaryBell was a virgin; then he said she was a saint. He told them if they would just turn him loose, he'd save every one of them; he'd heal the sick, make the blind see and the cripple walk. But the people of Enigma, joined now by the visitors, roared and raced with him across the field to an oak tree where a rope already swung from a limb.

The Gospel Singer had to force himself to breathe. It was some kind of nightmare. He cried and writhed and begged. He tried to pray and God's name stuck in his throat like half-chewed food.

When he saw the rope he fainted. The robe had been stripped from him when he regained consciousness. His hands were crushed and he was bleeding from cuts in his stomach. Directly above him, sitting straddle of a mule with a rope around his neck, was Willalee Bookatee Hull. He was naked too. Blood poured from a wound between his legs and ran down over the mule's shoulders. The Gospel Singer could feel nothing. Even his face was numb. He opened his mouth to tell them to leave him alone but screamed instead. Somebody brought a second mule up and they threw the Gospel Singer straddle of it. He fell off. They threw him on again and steadied him this time with a rope around his neck. The Gospel Singer was close enough to Willalee now to hear him saying, "Lord forgive them." His voice was as calm and soft as if he had been sitting in the woods alone watching the sun go down.

The Gospel Singer watched Willalee Bookatee and tried to say, but could only think, "I'm sorry." Then summoning his last bit of strength he looked down upon the faces staring up at him and cried, "Damn you, damn you all to hell!" Then he heard the crash of a limb across the mules' rumps.

The Gospel Singer and Willalee fell together. The ropes were tied badly and they strangled. They writhed at the end of the rope and were finally still. The mob watched dumbly. The rain fell. Suddenly the man who had hit the mule and who still held the limb in his hand said softly, "My God," and turned and dashed away from the tree and out across the field toward the ring of light. The mob dashed after him.

Didymus was left where he lay at the foot of the tree. It was a long time before he stirred. He stared at the Gospel Singer's body where it hung as still as the pendulum of a stopped clock. Beside him on the ground was the white silk robe, blood-stained now and muddy. Didymus rolled it carefully and put it under his coat. Then he took out his *Dream Book* and opened it and wrote: *Tonight they hung a man on a tree in Enigma and ...*

It was raining too hard and he had to stop. He put the book inside his coat with the robe. He stood up and had to lean against the tree to keep from falling. The dark field in front of him tilted, then settled. He touched the coagulated wound on the side of his neck. His hand came away with fresh blood on it.

He stood trying to remember which way the church was from where he was standing. Willalee had said they were having a meeting there tonight. He did not know if he'd be able to get there or not. He was not sure of the direction and it was raining and dark. He stood breathing against the tree.

EPILOGUE

Enigma reminded Richard Hognut of a battlefield. The town lay in complete and oppressive silence under a brassy sky. None of the stores was open. Nothing moved. The streets were deserted and littered with sandwich wrappers, crumpled cardboard boxes, colored bits of paper and drinking cups. On the sidewalk in front of the bank someone had abandoned a crushed baby carriage. And out on the edge of town the largest tent in the state of Georgia was ripped to shreds and stood now in a deserted field with strips of canvas hanging from its center standard like streamers from a maypole.

Richard sat at his portable typewriter in the back of the white panel truck trying to work out some outline of what he should say on the news tape. Sweat poured down his neck into his shirt collar. The air seemed to steam around him. He had to file a story; he had to say something. But what? He typed: "A whirlwind of violence has swept through this small southern town . . ." But there he stopped. What the people back in the studio would want to know—and what the world would want to know—was *why*.

It was not that the studio or the television audience expected him to solve anything. But they expected him to put it into some kind of context. And he did not even know how to begin talking about what had happened here. Church congregations don't riot. Gospel singers aren't hanged with rapists. And yet, the ruined tent was in the field and the Gospel Singer's white naked body had hung from the tree that morning while FBI men walked round and round it taking pictures. Richard suddenly remembered clearly the Gospel Singer's awful, black face twisted in death, and he got up from the typewriter and bolted through the back doors of the truck into the street. He stretched his neck to breathe, and tried to shake the face from his mind.

When he had started as a newsman years ago, Richard Hognut had told himself that he must learn to expect the unexpected. But he had soon seen that there is nothing so predictable as the ritual of catastrophe and tragedy. If you've seen one flood, or fire, or explosion, you've seen them all. If you've seen one mutilated corpse, or raided whorehouse, or busted crap game, you've seen them all. So by now he knew that there was nothing so monotonous in its sameness as man's vice.

The cameraman came around the truck. "That's open," he said, pointing to the funeral parlor. "I looked through the window and somebody's in there."

Richard looked up. He had not noticed that they were parked in front of the funeral parlor. "Let's go in and see," he said.

They went quietly through the door into the parlor where MaryBell was propped out of her coffin, glowing softly under the naked overhead light. The room smelled of decaying cosmetics. A woman in a black bonnet sat in a chair beside the coffin with her back to them. Flowers potted in cans were wilting along the wall. Richard cleared his throat and scraped his feet on the gritty floor. The woman in the chair did not move.

"Pardon me," said Richard Hognut.

The woman shifted in the chair and the two men came to stand beside her. She looked up. "I didn't think it was any tourists left." Her voice was flat. She bent to the side and drained her mouth into a can.

"I'm not a tourist," said Richard Hognut. "I'm a reporter. And this is my cameraman." The cameraman, staring down at the dead, serene face of MaryBell, blinked and said hello. "We're trying to get the facts."

"It's a fack my daughter is dead," she said in the same flat voice.

"And it's a tragedy," said Richard. "I know how you must

feel at a time like this." The woman glanced up at him briefly and drained her mouth again. "But what we're trying to do is . . . Well, were you *there* last night?"

The woman's body went rigid. The hand outstretched on her knee stiffened, the fingers curled.

"Would you tell us about the Gospel . . . ?"

The woman stood straight out of the chair and put herself between the two men and MaryBell's coffin. Her arms were slightly extended from her body as though to shield something. In a net of red veins her eyes were stretched and starting. She made a strangled noise in her throat. "It's a fack my daughter is dead."

"Yes, ma'am," said Richard. He was suddenly afraid of her.

"If it's anything else you want to know, you go sommers else."

"It would help us a lot if you could just tell us a little about . . ."

"No," she said.

"You won't even talk to us about him!"

"Not to you nor no man," she said, looking fondly down upon MaryBell's cold arranged features. "I got one fack and I already given it to you. My daughter's dead." She looked at Richard. "She never deserved it, you know."

"No, she didn't," said Richard. Did she think he thought MaryBell deserved being stabbed in the neck sixty-one times?

"You can ask anybody in town and they'll tell you she didn't deserve none of it." She took a heart-shaped fan out of her clothes and fanned herself with it. "You from the television, ain't you?"

"WWWW network news," said Richard Hognut. Neither Richard nor the cameraman were looking at her now. Instead they were staring at her hand and the heart-shaped fan with the face of Jesus in it, because Mrs. Carter had begun fanning MaryBell. The yellow hair lifted and fell on MaryBell's forehead.

"We gone bare her this afternoon," said Mrs. Carter. "Some of the men already left for Tifton for two white horses. And her coffin's gone be on a white wagon and them horses'll pull

206

her. And we gone lay her in the ground this afternoon." She quit fanning MaryBell and looked at Richard. "It'd purely make a picture."

"A picture?" said Richard.

"For the television," said Mrs. Carter. "My MaryBell was struck down and never had a chance for no television nor nothing else. And it'd purely make a picture, MaryBell on that white wagon and them white horses."

Now Richard and the cameraman were looking at one another. "It's a natural," said the cameraman. He held up his hands, the thumbs extended and touching. He looked through the frame of his hands at MaryBell's face. "And maybe we could get the people of Enigma to follow along on foot behind the wagon."

"It ain't nothin folks in Enigmer would ruther see than Mary-Bell on the television being pulled by them white horses," said Mrs. Carter. "They'd foller that wagon to the cemetery and back again. They'd foller it anywhere."

"It might even rain again," said Richard. He was smiling. He saw a news tape taking shape. A burden lifted from his heart. "Can you imagine all those people in black clothes behind white horses *in the rain?*"

"It'd make a picture," she said.

"You stay right here, Mrs. Carter," said Richard. "We've got to see the sheriff. But we'll be back."

Out on the sidewalk, the cameraman stopped Richard. "I thought she was crazy in there for a minute."

"She may be," said Richard. "But that doesn't change anything. It's still a natural. Get the truck and let's go."

The sheriff was sitting behind his desk in the courthouse chain-smoking Camel cigarettes and sipping diet-rite cola. "You've come to the wrong man," he said as soon as he knew who they were and what they wanted. He leaned forward in his chair and turned his head to show a red swelling behind his ear. "That's where I spent the night. Just me and that bump. Hit me right in the head, they did, and taken the nigger. And you know something? I'm glad. Hurt like hell, but now I'm glad. Me? Don't know a thing. Didn't know, don't know, won't know." He fell back in his chair wheezing and started another Camel cigarette from the butt he was smoking.

"Why did they kill the Gospel Singer?" asked Richard.

"Why did *who* kill him?"

"Whoever it was."

The sheriff stood up. His belly swayed under his shirt. He caught it and held it in his hands. "It ain't but two people in Enigmer who couldn't know—me and MaryBell." He picked up the package of cigarettes from the desk and turned.

"Where are you going?" asked Richard.

"I'm gone take the one good lung I got and go back here and lock myself in Willalee Bookatee's cell and lay down on his cot and smoke up some Camels."

Richard and the cameraman went back out to the truck and started for the tent. A news truck from a rival network passed them headed for the courthouse. A car stopped in front of the funeral parlor. Richard recognized a syndicated newspaperman getting out of it. He sighed and spat out of the window. He could have scooped the world. He could have had a lynching on tape. But he missed everything for a bottle of whiskey and a soft bed. He stayed in Tifton the night before instead of coming back to the revival because there was no hotel in Enigma and he was tired and disgusted with the crowd and had not been about to drive all the way back in a rain storm. So he had been on top of the greatest story of his career and missed it.

Outside of town, the entire field had been roped off. Two police cars from Tifton were parked in front of the rope, and beyond them was an army helicopter from the airforce base in Albany. Several men in white shirts roamed around under the spreading limbs of the huge oak tree at the edge of the field. Richard was relieved to see that the bodies had been taken down.

A small man the color of a walnut with a brown mustache and brown teeth got out of a police car and walked toward the WWWW television truck. His name was Chester Miles and he ordinarily worked out of Atlanta. Richard had known him for years. They had talked together over innumerable mutilations, bombings and murders. The little man leaned on the door of the truck. He and Richard Hognut looked at one another with sympathetic understanding.

"It's a strange one," said Richard.

"It's a bastard, just a bastard, Rich," said Chester.

"Have you got a lead on who did it?" asked the cameraman.

"I don't even have a lead on who *didn't* do it," said Chester. "The tracks under that oak tree look like everybody in the world was there."

"Have you found Didymus?" asked Richard.

Chester Miles took out a small black notebook. "Let me just give you what I've got, Rich. One male, white, approximately six feet tall, one hundred seventy pounds, abrasions and contusions about the head and shoulders, dead by strangulation. One male, Negro, approximately six feet tall, one hundred seventy pounds, abrasions and contusions about the head and shoulders and genital area, dead by strangulation. One Woody Pea, evangelist, suffering from shock, incoherent. One Didymus— obviously an alias—nothing known, missing, presumed dead. One Gerd, brother of dead white male, missing, may be dead or may be with one freak fair run by one midget, Foot by name, missing from area. Mother and father of dead white male hospitalized in Tifton with abrasions and contusions, suffering shock, incoherent. One large brown tent, ruined." He closed the notebook. "That's it, Rich, and you know the strangest thing about this case?"

"What?"

"No contradictions. Anything that happens, you get forty stories and all of them different. Not this one. No contradictions. Mainly because nobody's got a story. I haven't been able to get one person to say what happened, or what they *think* happened." He took a deep breath and looked back toward the police car. "Well, that's not exactly true. I've got one story."

"Well, for God's sake, what is it?" cried Richard Hognut.

"I got the brother and sister of the dead white male over here in the car. One Mirst and Avel. They're the only ones that didn't seem to get hurt in this."

"What's the story?" Richard had been writing in his own

notebook while Chester read from his. Now he sat with his pencil poised over the page and his tongue caught between his teeth.

"I'll get them over here. They can tell you." He went back to
the car and Mirst and Avel got out of the back seat. Mirst was
wearing his guitar strung about his shoulders from a red strap.
He strummed it with his thumb as he came toward them. His
hair looked wet.

"This is Richard Hognut," said Chester Miles. "He's a
newsman. Tell him what you told me."

"We caint hardly talk about it," said Mirst. "We cried all
night."

"We sure did," said Avel. "You from the television?" She
was looking at the call letters written on the side of the truck.

"Tell me the story," said Richard.

"Sure," said Mirst. "It was a accident."

"An accident!"

"A accident," said Avel.

"But how could it have been an accident?"

"You caint tell about a accident," said Mirst. "That's how
come it's a accident, right?"

Chester Miles gave Richard a sympathetic smile. "That's the
only story we've got so far," he said. "I've got to get back to
my men." He walked away across the field.

Richard looked at Mirst and Avel. "Son," he said, "you can't
hang a man accidentally." But he was saying that for his own
benefit. It seemed to him that the whole thing was somehow an
accident.

"If you'd a been there, you'd a seen," said Mirst. "Them cripples was strainin and hollerin and the wind was blowin and everbody was steppin on one another and first news you know the
stage was full of people. Somehow the Gospel Singer ended up
on the end of that rope with the nigger."

"Whatever it was, it'll make a hole in the gospel business,"
said Avel, staring at the writing on the side of the truck.

"That's for dang sure," said Mirst, giving his guitar an angry
stroke with his rigid thumb.

Richard's nose twitched. His lips pursed. His breathing went
shallow. "Do you sing gospel?"

Mirst and Avel looked at one another. "Been singing gospel for years," said Mirst. "*He* trained us." The two of them inclined their heads together and burst into *Onward Christian Soldiers.*

Richard caught his tongue between his teeth and waited for them to finish. "Do . . . uh . . . do you have a manager?"

"Not yet," said Mirst.

"I know everybody in television," said Richard. "How would you like me to be your manager?"

"Would you?" asked Mirst, his knuckles going white where he held the neck of the guitar.

"I know a lawyer in Tifton," said Richard. "He can make the contract. Get in the back of the truck."

They ran around to the back of the truck, jerked open the doors and jumped in. Mirst immediately sat on the floor and began practicing chords. Avel hummed.

The cameraman turned to Richard and said softly: "That was the worst singing I've ever heard. I've got a dog that can sing better than that."

"Nobody'll care if they can sing. Everybody'll remember *him*. They'll remember what *he* sounded like and that those kids are kin to *him*." Richard slammed the cameraman on the back and screamed with laughter. "You get to Tifton in an hour, and I'll let you be my assistant. We'll make a million dollars next year."

"But what about the story?"

"To hell with the story! Let somebody else get it."

The cameraman slammed the truck into gear and they raced away from the ruined tent with Mirst and Avel singing at the top of their lungs.

A Childhood
The Biography of a Place

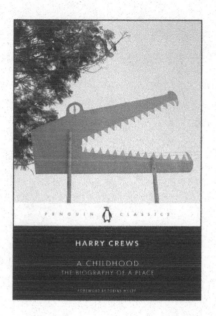

Harry Crews grew up as the son of a sharecropper in Georgia at a time when "the rest of the country was just beginning to feel the real hurt of the Great Depression." Interweaving his own memories—including his bout with polio and a fascination with the Sears, Roebuck catalog—with the tales of relatives and friends, he re-creates a childhood of tenderness and violence, comedy and tragedy.

"This memoir is for everyone. It's agile, honest, and built as if to last. Like its author, it's a resilient American original."
—Dwight Garner, *The New York Times*